SHISHIR TRIPATHI

The Link Within

A Story of Mind, Machine and Meaning

S&B
HOUSE

Acknowledgments

I offer my sincere gratitude to my wife, whose support made this book possible in every sense. Her patience and belief in me carried this project from vague ideas that I used to ruminate about to a finished manuscript.

I

Fracture

Chapter 1

It was a cold July night. Refract had finally done it – offered Kai a path that truly resonated with his true self within. A solution to all of his problems and a grand respite from a lifelong struggle to find meaning in his existence.

He'd stepped outside his apartment to run away from the voices, his own and Link's. This wasn't planned.

The icy wind hit him like a blade, slicing through his jacket, but he barely felt it. Under Refract's grip, his senses were numbed, acting as a shield against the elements. Or perhaps something whispered in his ear, softening the edges of reality, drowning the other sensations, letting him drift where his mind refused to go sober.

His legs were clumsy beneath him, while he dragged himself along the pavement towards the shore.

He kept walking. His boots scuffed against the pavement with each uneven step.

There was something he had to do. It wasn't part of tonight's plan, but it had lingered in his mind for a long time.

It had to be tonight.

He didn't bother locking the door behind him when he left his apartment. Carried nothing other than his jacket out of instinct.

The voices in his head weren't shouting, but they weren't gone either. They murmured.

Circling.

Waiting.

Tonight, he would let go of the weight that he had carried for far too long.

The air smelled of salt – clean, sharp and quietly inviting. The beach wasn't far, just a few streets down, beyond the city's nighttime buzz.

As he made his way to the beach, he walked past the plaza where the kaleidoscope of the city's exuberance hit him all at once – the voices of people, the whir of bots and delivery drones, the neon glow of shops and restaurants, the chill of the night and the smell of food in the crisp cold air.

And of course, there were billboards, the signs and the ads – waiting to ignite in the overlay of his vision if he looked towards their triggers a second longer.

Everything impactful. Fighting for his attention. But not tonight. There was something else that had to be done.

And it had to be tonight.

Even in his unadulterated defiance of all the stimuli, a billboard appeared in his vision.

And there he was.

Dario Verrick.

A name familiar to almost everyone in the city of Polaris – whether they liked him or not. As one of the megas, he had to make appearances, and that's what he was doing through that billboard, which forced its way to Kai – announcing the launch of yet another boon for humanity.

Kai could see him. How could he miss a giant projection right in his own vision? He could hear Dario's words too, but he was incapable of processing any of it into anything meaningful. He continued to walk, the figure of Dario and his voice fading as he passed the square.

He wasn't far. Just a few more buildings. The city lights thinned as he walked, receding into dimmer streets, the glow giving way to what waited beyond.

At the last corner, something pulled him short. He stopped. In the darkened window, a figure faced him – still, watchful. His own reflection.

The eyes glimmered with an unusual intensity. Silvery. Ghostly.

A few seconds passed. Kai continued to stare at his own reflection.

That's not me, he thought.

His resolve stirred – sudden and sharp – snapping him out of it. And just before he moved, he could have sworn his reflection did a fraction of a second before him.

It didn't matter anymore.

And soon, there he was – at the end of the road, where the pavement simply stopped, giving way to the uneven stretch of the sand. Just beyond, the beach, the sand, the endless black of the ocean and its deafening roar.

Was it fear that gripped him? Or the quiet stillness of acceptance of what he was about to do? Perhaps both. It didn't matter. The ocean was calling him. Louder than the voices. Louder than the fear.

A sudden gust of wind howled through the emptiness, whipping against his face as if testing his resolve.

He paused at the edge of the pavement and looked at the ocean.

The moon hung above, casting a pale glow across the water.

The waves were massive tonight. Ferocious. Hungry. The tide was high, and the restless waves crashed onto the deserted sand with a growl that pierced the surrounding night.

As he took his first steps on the beach, his legs faltered – the sudden shift in terrain caught him off guard. His knees buckled under his weight. He barely caught himself and continued to trudge forward.

There had been no great tragedy in his life that pushed him to the beach. His life wasn't unfortunate by any measure. But it had been empty and lonely.

He had survived a long, dull life. Endeavoured time after time to find a purpose, a calling, a sense or rhythm somewhere. But all he ended up with was a worn-down and defeated existence, with no resolutions for his conflicts and no respite from the turmoil within him.

He had struggled long before he got Link, long before he surrendered himself to the world that told him the norms, laid down expectations and offered the answers. Whether anything resonated with his nature or betrayed – in the end, it made no difference. The world simply moved on.

He was what remained behind – a failure.

The wind was ferocious as he stumbled his way further across the sand. The ocean's breath was stronger. Presence louder and intimidating. Under the moon's glow, it stretched out before him – endless, swallowing the horizon in shifting silver and shadow.

Kai took another step forward.

Since childhood, he had questions no one could easily answer. Even as the innocence of youth faded, the questions remained – multiplying, deepening. Over time, he ended up harbouring more conflicts within himself, withdrawing into silent wonder. And as he grew, he found himself confined within the walls, shackled by the weight of expectations imposed by the world around him. He carried out things that conflicted with his essence, followed rules he never chose. Obligations filled the space where his curiosity roamed free.

The tide rushed in, reaching for his boots. Indifferent to his presence.

He had tried to blend in; he really did. He forced himself to be *normal*. Did what society told him. Stopped asking questions that had no answers, that were useless. He followed in the footsteps of admired and accomplished people, sought help, and did uncomfortable things, hoping to change his own temperament. He listened, acted, attended, acknowledged, absorbed and applied. But he couldn't alter the fabric of conformity to fit him for too long.

He took another step forward, and the water soaked his boots.

Freezing.

Freeing.

Somewhere, buried beneath the howling wind, between the roaring waves and his numbed senses, he heard a voice, distant yet intimate, and persistent.

[Kai...]

He winced. The voice continued, indifferent to his discomfort.

[Kai, it's a little late to be here, and of course dangerous. The weather forecast shows strong winds at 35 km/h, temperature dropping to 5 degrees Celsius. Visibility is limited. Light rain is approaching within 20 minutes.]

Kai wasn't paying attention. Finally, he had found a calling too great to waste on a distraction.

[I can see your heart rate is elevated, breathing unsteady. I can detect hesitation in your projected thoughts. You are not as certain as you think you believe.]

After a brief pause, it added. *[Can I suggest you leave the water and go somewhere warm? Somewhere you can recover. Do you want me to get you home?]*

Kai mumbled something under his breath, but the words didn't come out.

The voice continued. *[Are you aware that ...]*

Kai had had enough. He pressed his temple as if that would push the voice away. *[Just... be quiet. I don't... want to... hear from you. Let me... be alone.]*

There wasn't any solitude for him even in his seclusion. But neither did he ever feel a sense of belonging, even in the chaos of company around him – not for a long time.

It was never just the loneliness that was unbearable. It was isolation. It was the absence of an anchor for the vessel of his thoughts, amplified in times of distress. It was the feeling of being left out, the sense of belonging to a time that wasn't meant for him, but even that was assuming there was a right time at all.

He took another step. Deeper into the ocean.

The waves welcomed him, creeping higher, soaking through his trousers. His body felt the intensity of the cold. But his mind was numb, so the elements inflicted suffering on his flesh while he was completely determined to end the 'bigger suffering'. *The* suffering. And being lost had become comfortable for him.

As he took further steps with a resolve to put an end to his suffering, his mind tried to flash back to moments of his life, piecing things together, now justifying his decisions. It was the only sane thing left for him to do now.

Everything had become a competition for validation. The vast majority around him lived as if the world revolved around them, and yet they didn't even put themselves at the centre – they placed others on that throne. Paths shaped not for meaning, but for applause. Beauty followed a template, and everyone crammed to fit in its narrow frame. Whoever couldn't fit in, found ways around it. Interests weren't enjoyed; they were displayed and broadcast. Art had long died as an expression of passion; it was reborn as a contest for attention. Nature and its elements became the backdrop for the grandiose expression of self. No one expressed themselves, just spewed the hollow echoes from a range of blended prevailing ideologies.

Love wasn't personal; it was transactional, for mutual benefit, a performance for spectators. Its pursuit was daunting, devouring the remnants of individuality, and forcing to *fix* all unconventional flairs.

The water reached his waist now. Each step took tremendous effort. His body was shaking, but he was unsure if it was the cold or the war waging within him. He swayed with the waves, barely able to keep himself upright. The world was tilting, or maybe he was. A wave crashed against his chest. He gasped. His body was screaming to turn back, desperate to survive, and sensed the danger of what he faced.

It wasn't romance that defeated him. The world berated him. No one cared. No one connected. No one listened. Friendships needed appointments. Work was hauntingly suffocating. And the demons in his own head never ceased to haunt, not even for a moment, whispering doubts, questioning his worth, the point of his existence, laughing at the mockery of what he had done with his life.

Was I ever enough...?

He had tried everything, but the creeping emptiness always somehow outmanoeuvred him, finding new ways to seep in and wear him down bit by bit. Even Link didn't help, although it temporarily offered him respite from the incessant noises in his head. But it didn't silence the voices, didn't resolve the conflicts; it just overlaid them with its own prompts, offers and suggestions.

One of the greatest inventions of his time, possibly one of the most pivotal developments for humanity – intelligence seamlessly embedded inside the mind itself. A digital butler that never stopped offering solutions for his pain.

[Would you like to listen to calming music?] Link asked. *[Your stress levels have been higher than average today.]*

[There's a guided breathing exercise that may help.] It suggested, having detected elevated heart rates.

[Would you like me to call someone? You have spent extended periods with no interaction.]

Even when muted, it never stopped working. It recorded, analysed and processed everything – mood, vitals, surroundings, location, time and even shadows of unspoken thoughts – only to seamlessly integrate it in its responses.

[You felt like having a coffee earlier. Would you like recommendations nearby?]

The waves clung to him. His breath became short and uneven.

The wind roared around him, mixing with the crash of waves; it was impossible to tell where one began and the other ended.

He lifted his eyes. Above him, the sky stretched infinite.

Even with the moon washing the night in pale light, he could still see stars, flickering at the edges of the darkness.

If I go... any further, there's... no coming back.

He took another step.

The water surged higher, to his chest, to his shoulder.

Another step.

The water submerged his neck. His mind pulsed with warnings, instincts screaming to turn back. But there was no going back for him. He felt an overwhelming necessity to say something, his last words, as if those words would be the only legacy he left behind.

"If there's a god," he murmured, "then I pray this goes well."

It didn't.

Chapter 2

Kai stood on the platform, waiting for the train to arrive. The air smelled of fresh coffee.

Back then, Link was still a headline, not a presence under skin.

The train arrived with a surge of air; the doors opened in a smooth, synchronised line along the platform. Kai stepped inside and took a seat by the window. The glass was layered and adaptive, softening the sun's glare as the city slid past, adjusting its tint and contrast without drawing notice.

Kai was in his mid-30s, standing a little taller than six feet. His build was average, hinting neither a wiry frame nor an indulgence in excess. Skin, a bit tanned, not like someone who spends their days outdoors, but it spoke of time spent in leisure – for exploration or simply being outside. His brown eyes were unassuming at first glance, but inquisitive, as if they were trying to catch the smallest of details in the room.

His hair never followed a pattern. Sometimes it was short, sometimes it had grown long enough to feel untidy – there was no preference beyond comfort. He cut it when it began to bother him and ignored it when it didn't, letting it shift between lengths without much thought. To someone who saw him sporadically, it would seem like he was always sporting a different hairstyle. His hair texture was coarse, perpetually messed up by the wind. That day, his face was clean-shaven. He treated his beard the same way – left to grow until a special occasion, or until catching his reflection made him reach for the trimmer again.

On the train, Kai drifted into a daydream about how the day would go. He hadn't seen Jorin for a while, one of the few people from work he got along really well. And of course, there was Rumi, his dearest, and probably only, friend. She was also his co-worker, but Kai had known Rumi since adolescence.

He carried a small notebook with him everywhere he went. A habit he had maintained for as long as he could remember, ever since he learned to write – which was later in his teenage years.

He would often scribble down whatever thoughts crossed his mind, driven by the need to acknowledge them, and the urge to write them. Questions, stray thoughts, doubts, observations of his surroundings, conflicts, paradoxes, anything. Pages filled with half-formed theories, sparks of ideas, things which made him pause and think. Sometimes simple and innocuous, "I should write a book." Some other times, it was heavier: "If our actions have consequences, then why do so many people walk as if their steps were weightless, indifferent to the ripples, unaware of the impact, oblivious to the reflections of their own actions?"

That day, he had the notebook tucked in the inner pocket of his coat. The papers had already creased and worn because he had thumbed through them so many times. A pen rested neatly beside the notebook. He had used it last night, but he had already forgotten what he had written.

He looked around. Everyone else was silent. Still.

At first glance, it seemed they were doing nothing at all. They were just *present*, eyes locked onto an unchanging point in space, nothing in particular.

But Kai knew better. They were all using their Links.

It was the subtle movements that gave it away – a faint motion of the lips forming unspoken words, a slight twitch of a finger, a gentle nod of the head. What confirmed his suspicions was the faint iridescent shimmer in their eyes – silver with a shadowed hue, like refracted light trying to decide which colour it wanted to be. It was visible only from certain angles, but unmistakable once seen. The official reports called it the Link Ocular Signature – LOS – a harmless residual effect, said to occur when the Link's interface stimulated nanofibers in the optic nerve that emitted light during data transmission. But people on the streets called it the *Ghostlight*.

It wasn't just the shimmer itself – it was what it did to their faces. From a distance, nothing seemed out of the ordinary. They looked normal: smiling, frowning, working, arguing.

Yet the moment their eyes met the light at a certain angle, something shifted, and broke the illusion of their ordinary appearance. The expressions remained, but essence-less. The gaze held no trace of the person within. It appeared something had sealed off their eyes from the soul that once lived behind them. You could look right at them and feel nothing back – only a faint glow of shifting silver light as if it had bleached the soul that once lived within.

It wasn't often that Kai was the only one without a Link around him, but it was becoming more frequent. More and more people were choosing to get it embedded in themselves.

His fingers reached into his coat, brushing against the notebook. Absent-mindedly, he felt the worn pages, and the cool metal of the pen. He pulled them out together.

"How long can I delay it?"

Kai leaned back in his seat, pondering the question he had just written in his notebook. The thought of getting Link lingered in his mind wherever he went – while making purchases, at the workplace, in government offices, watching movies, listening to music, using public transport, at the restaurants, staying at hotels – everywhere, the same question confronted him: Are you a Link user?

Everywhere, he remembered his indecision, as if the entire society collectively worked to nudge him into acceptance.

Sitting on the train, staring at the sea of blank-faced passengers, their eyes focused on something in a different world. Kai recalled the conversation he had with his friend, Rumi.

It had only been a couple of weeks since she had gotten Link, and she was glowing with excitement.

"Kai, I'm telling you. It's absolute bliss. You don't know what you're missing out on."

She spoke quickly, words tumbling over one another, eager to express her wonder.

"I haven't held a screen or worn one of those wearables since... well, since I got Link! There's just no need."

Kai nodded and smiled during the conversation, trying to match her enthusiasm.

She continued, "It has rewired vision itself. I get directions laid out for me in my vision; notifications cannot be more personal than having them flash before my eyes. Sound is no longer external; music, conversations, alerts – all can happen within me, silent to the outside world."

Kai started involuntarily mirroring Rumi's beaming expressions. His eyebrows lifted and dipped in time with the conversation, responding before he could think.

"And the best part?" she continued. "I can respond without moving my lips, without even whispering. There's a neural interpreter that reads subvocal signals. I just think the words – and it understands. Isn't that incredible?"

Kai nodded again. "That's incredible. To think we can witness it in our own lifetime – it's just astonishing."

He paused, just long enough to hold himself from forming a thought within him he was unwilling to share. Before he could add anything, Rumi resumed.

"I have named my Link 'Rosy', by the way. She tells me what food I should eat, how frequently to exercise, which books I need to read in times of distress and where I should invest my money. She helps with everything."

Her voice carried the weight of religious devotion, as if she had recently gained enlightenment.

"Kai, it's a godsend. Absolute godsend. I can't believe we're living in the future we used to dream about."

She finally stopped, catching her breath. Or maybe, Kai thought, she wasn't even there anymore. Maybe she was off in another conversation, in another space, somewhere only she could access.

He watched as she sat still, eyes distant, as if waiting for something.

"All good, Rumi?" he asked.

Her gaze snapped back to him. "Oh yeah, sorry. I was hungry. Rosy suggested we should eat a sandwich. There's a place close by that offers some of the best ones around. Would you like one?"

Kai hesitated for a second, but what else was there to do?

"Well, yeah, sure, I can have a bite."

Rumi paused. Her eyes glazed over for a moment, staring at something invisible.

A second later, she blinked, looked at Kai, and smiled.

"Done."

Thinking about the conversation with Rumi, Kai recalled his doubts regarding Link. As the train got closer to his stop, his inner monologue pressed on.

How is everyone just... okay with it?

It wasn't just a product worn or installed; it entered the thresholds of identity, dissolving the line between the conscious self and the coded other.

Maybe it's safe... maybe. But the thought of something else steering my choices... I can't accept it.

There were already countless influences constantly pushing and pulling at his thoughts.

Advertisements telling him what to buy, algorithms nudging him towards what to watch, and recommendations shaping his choices before he had found out his own preferences – if that was even a thing.

Kai strongly believed that deciding was fundamental to being human. Whatever he chose, good or bad, it was *his* choice. That's what defined him and shaped his life into something he could claim.

He had already spent his life trying to find answers to these questions, and all life gave him was something else to worry about, more pressing, more personal.

The train announcement broke this chain of thought. Time to step out.

He dragged himself out of his thoughts. As he stood, he felt relieved when the stiffness in his legs eased.

As he stepped out of the train, he noticed others who exited with him. Nearly everyone around him wore the same distant expression. They were all using their Links.

How do they not walk into things? Kai muttered to himself.

They moved in quiet synchrony, adjusting their paths a fraction before contact, bodies guided by invisible corrections.

...

Kai was dressed well for the day. It had been a while since he had gone to the office in person, and he was excited to be there. This wasn't just another workday. It was the one day of the year when everyone had to be physically present at work. Not on a screen. Not as a hologram. Not even as Link's simulant – not yet.

Just real people in actual spaces.

The Nexora building rose not as an architectural marvel, but as a piece of Polaris itself – like a piece of managed terrain. Its façade threaded with living panels that adjusted density and airflow in response to the heat.

Besides the annual meet and greet, the company Kai worked for, Nexora Foods, was celebrating the rollout of the *Food from Thought* program, which specifically catered for Link users. It used Link to create personalised meal plans, analysing the mood, health, time and user's surroundings. It was efficient and quick. Users no longer had to concern themselves with meal selection. Link decided what was best for them.

It also significantly optimised the supply chain, resulting in minimum waste and maximum efficiency. The company was a global leader in sustainable food production, specialising in indoor livestock farming and plant-based alternatives.

Kai worked as a Consumer Experience Researcher; part

of a large team that studied why people chose what they chose. His work wasn't creative or glamorous; he spent most days analysing feedback loops, usage patterns and emotional responses to help shape future campaigns and product features.

And today after the meeting, he was finally looking forward to catching up with his coworkers, a rare chance to have actual, face-to-face conversations over refreshments.

That was the plan.

Until his manager pulled him aside. "Kai, can we have a word?"

His manager, Delane, was the kind of person who was difficult to read. Her face would say one thing, while the words conveyed something else altogether. In her mid-40s, she was of average height, slightly bulkier than average, but carried herself fairly well as an authority figure. Her tailored suit, often black or dark grey, paired with the sound of her heels, announced her arrival before she entered a room. Her grey eyes – with a splash of Ghostlight – scrutinised everything, as if she was about to offer her feedback or criticism about her surroundings given the opportunity.

Kai sat across the desk from Delane, watching the woman fidget with her hands, which was rather unusual of her. When she finally spoke, her voice was firm.

"Look, Kai, this is difficult for me to say. You are a good person, an outstanding employee. I mean it. But times are changing, and you need to change with them."

A pause.

She then continued, "This isn't official yet, but I just wanted to give you a heads-up before things are finalised. Soon, the company will issue notice to all employees who haven't gotten Link, and certainly to those who are not planning to get one. They will need to look for employment elsewhere. This change is being rolled out straight from the top for all corporate employees."

Kai blinked. There was more to come.

"The company is adapting to the changing world, Kai. We need to cater to customers who can visualise our food as if it's right in front of them, complete with texture, smell and arrangement. The other food companies have changed their business models too. We must.

"We need a workforce that can develop products and services in ways which will serve the vast majority. And frankly, employees who refuse to integrate with Link will end up as liabilities. And companies hate liabilities, Kai."

She let her words linger, giving him time to process, but not yet respond. She leaned back in her chair and lowered her voice as if the next words needed extra caution.

"You are an exceptional employee. But you just... can't be as fast, as precise, as comprehensive as others with Link are."

Kai could feel his heart drumming. In his mind, he had already imagined the worst-case scenarios. He had poured his heart out for work, not just for passion, but also for his own sake. This was one space in his life where he didn't feel like a failure. All he could think in his mind was, "I can't lose this job. Not now."

But he had seen this coming, though he didn't want to admit it.

Delane pressed on, unaware of the turmoil within Kai. "We envision our teams will operate in perfect synchronicity, like a hive mind of researchers. No wasted words, no misinterpretations and no delays. Neural feedback will allow advertisers to fine-tune advertising campaigns designed for individual customer preferences. Interactive food demonstrations will provide instant analytics, tracking emotional responses at a biochemical level. Consumers won't tell us what they want; we'll already know, thanks to our partnership with Link Tech. We'll offer personalised meal plans, crafted in real time from dietary requirements extracted straight from their bodies."

She lost all trace of a mellow heart and reverted to her usual self. Her voice hardened; sympathy disappeared. Her messages picked up a *matter-of-fact* tone.

"Without your integration with Link, you frustrate the team with your slower pace, as you keep relying on traditional methods like surveys, sales data, and what the customers choose to share. Real-time instant analytics will dictate the future of food, taken right from the head of a consumer while they taste our products, not from guesswork."

A brief pause again before the climax of the conversation.

"You need to decide and make it fast." Delane said, standing up, implying that the conversation was over.

"They'll send out the notices starting next week to everyone they're watching. But between you and me, I would not wait to be on that list. Get out while you still have a chance. Do you understand?"

Kai nodded. But he did not understand at all.

Delane, still standing, looked at Kai, hoping for an answer right away. An acknowledgement from Kai. Perhaps, even gratitude.

She carried the expression of someone doing him a huge favour, but there was something about her which gave away her true intentions. Her posture was relaxed, but the eyes told him something else.

Either this, or you are out of here, Kai.

Kai was terrified. He didn't know how to respond to this. The sheer abruptness of it choked his thoughts, leaving him unable to form any words. His eyebrows shot up, then furrowed, as if desperately trying to assemble a sentence together.

"Come on, Kai, you're a smart guy." She let out a light chuckle. "This shouldn't be too much of a surprise for you. You saw this coming, didn't you?"

She was at the door now, half-opened. "I want you to stick around. And look, even with all the technology in the world, we still need someone like you to check the appropriateness and correctness of ideas with a red pen of moral and ethical bias. A sense check for humanity. You do that very well."

Kai's mind was racing, trying to process what had just happened. Should he say something or remain quiet? But that was impolite. He needed to say something.

"I'm sorry, but... yeah, I had imagined this would land on us in the future, but I never thought it would be... like *this*."

He exhaled sharply. "Can I please just think about this? I have a lot to chew on."

"Well, of course. Of course, Kai. But please don't dwell on it too long. You don't want this decision made for you."

She gave him a reassuring look before continuing, "Talk to me later if you have questions. Or reach out to our support team for guidance. Or better yet, talk to a friend. Maybe they can help you decide."

Delane then left the room, donning one of those fake smile on her face that she had perfected over the years.

While the door swung to close, he heard muffled sounds of laughter and conversations from the main hall, while other employees enjoyed refreshments and exchanged stories.

Kai had to choose.

He could resist and rebel. Explore a different career that won't force its obligations on him so ruthlessly. But he knew how long he had struggled to land a role at Nexora. And how long before even the new employer would force him to choose again?

While he searched, the world would move on without him. He could fade into irrelevance before he found his footing again. Could he really survive another setback?

A change of workplace. A change of routine. Unfamiliarity. New variables. His mind filled with dread thinking about having to change his life yet again. Things had finally settled in. He had finally adjusted to the melancholy.

Link had become an inevitability.

And all it took was a few years after Link's introduction for it to develop and embed deeply into modern-day existence. Kai realised that it wasn't mandatory yet, but they didn't leave it to everyone's discretion.

A future dictated by an embedded system that guided his moves, anticipated his needs, and whispered his preferences to himself. How long would it take until his voice became indistinguishable from it?

He had a choice between the inevitability of Link, the instability of a new job, or the slow decline of his career, as he could become obsolete in a world that wouldn't have a place for people like him.

The choice didn't feel like a choice at all. It was a reaction. Yet again.

I don't even understand myself... How am I meant to choose?

He remained seated in the boardroom for a long time. His mind raced with thoughts he hadn't had in a long time.

Then suddenly, as if coming out of a trance, he stood up with resolve. He knew what he had to do.
Rumi.

Chapter 3

Change had forced his life before.

The last time, he was still a teenager. Back when his town – Tarinvale – fell victim to the increasing frequency and intensity of climate disasters.

It felt like a lifetime ago, yet the memories were sharp and had never really faded.

Kai had watched his world unravel in real time. The community, the home that served as an anchor for his mind in the turbulence of turmoil within him, had fractured overnight.

The algorithm, which provided the best distribution, moved everyone around him, including friends, neighbours, and families, across the city and separated them. The authorities had planned for uniformity of skills, minimised commute times and a mixed demographic for an efficient allocation of *resources*.

But of course, in pursuit of efficiency, it had removed something fundamental – the warmth of familiarity, the comfort of shared history, preferences and the unspoken bonds. All reduced to variables in a calculation.

Kai and Rumi were lucky that they had been moved not too far from each other. They figured out ways to manage without letting the situation overthrow their camaraderie completely.

They met often at first, but time, distance and life itself made it harder and difficult to sustain visits. Unless they needed a refuge; for that, they continued to prioritise each other.

They comforted each other in the familiarity of a shared past. A past where they didn't have to strive to belong, they just did so effortlessly. They both understood the challenges of transitioning from a close-knit community to the dynamic intensity of the city. And they had continued to rely on each other ever since they had arrived in the city many years ago.

Today, he needed that refuge again.

He didn't even realise it himself that he was already on his way to the station, as if running on autopilot, on his way to Rumi's apartment.

Soon, he was at the platform, watching the inbound train pull into view.

I need more time... not another setback... I need a routine... familiarity.

But Link...

And before he knew it, he had stepped out of the station.

He walked to her apartment, greeted by the quiet hum of the residential neighbourhood as it unfolded in layered terraces rather than streets. The clusters of apartment blocks were designed to be staggered in such a way that no two apartments faced each other directly.

He had walked this path several times before, but today everything felt different.

As he turned the corner onto the street leading to Rumi's apartment, a flash of colour caught his eye – a mural sprawled across the side of the sports complex. A portrait of a girl stared out from the concrete wall, deep indigo filling the space behind her white outline; her painted eyes spiralling inward like whirlpools, vivid and rather unsettling. Beneath her chin were the words: 'This isn't the Clarity you want.'

After a brief pause, staring at the mural, he continued.

He arrived at Rumi's apartment and rang the doorbell.

Nobody answered.

His eyes flicked up to the security camera, and without really thinking, he raised his hand in an awkward wave. A half-hearted smile stretched across his face.

The door creaked open, and there she was.

Rumi.

The same Rumi he had known for years, the same face he had turned to for understanding, for stability.

But...

Something was different now.

Those eyes, once a harbour of certainty and ceaseless restlessness, now held something distant, something that made Kai hesitate for half a second.

Kai grinned when he saw her, almost immediately, instinctively, but he felt puzzled as the seconds ticked by. Was something wrong?

And then he noticed as she moved just a little – the Ghost-light. *Of course*, he thought. She was likely on her Link.

She wore a dark blue sweater, slightly oversized, paired with black sweatpants. Casual. Comfortable.

But her expression, that flickering hesitation before recognition, and the silvery tint in her pupils, told him that although she looked at him, she wasn't fully there.

And then, suddenly, she was back. Whatever had pulled her away from this moment let her go, and she returned his smile, just as bright, just as familiar.

She waved him inside.

Kai stepped through the door, and they hugged.

Then, before he could say a word.

"Please make yourself at home, Kai." Her voice was light, warm and automatic. "I'm still in a meeting; I'll be right back with you in just a while."

She turned away immediately, walking further into the apartment.

Kai exhaled. A sigh of relief for his thoughts to have some time to land, and also of understanding.

He made his way to the living room, and nostalgia settled over him. He sat down on the couch, and the recollections of so many conversations, celebrations, festivals and family gatherings ushered him to the past. It had been a while since he had last been here.

They had met in passing at work, shared a casual coffee on weekends, but it had been a long time since they had simply sat and talked. Time had slipped between them without either of them noticing.

He looked around the room instinctively, cataloguing every detail, as he always did.

The windows caught his attention first – as they always did. They offered a wide, uninterrupted view of the city while revealing nothing of the interior. Transparency adjusted in real time; light diffused, glare softened, and the space remained quietly shielded.

Inside, he looked at the paintings that adorned the olive-green walls – one of flowers, another of a windmill, and a smaller watercolour giraffe with an odd, amusing expression.

He counted at least half a dozen plants in the living room, of different sizes. He didn't know them all by name, but the peace lily stood out. Rumi had gifted him one long ago. It withered away at some point. Kai never got around to tell Rumi of its demise.

The black coffee table ahead of him had a mug, left over from some time earlier. Next to it were a few books scattered around in no particular order. His eyes landed on a book, lying face down, its pages open to hold its place. He winced seeing another larger, heavier book resting on top of it, obscuring the title.

Out of curiosity, he slid the smaller one free, as if he were rescuing something trapped under a heavy weight.

He read the title and let out a bemused smile with a mix of recognition and irony.

The Biography of Dario Verrick: How an ordinary boy clawed his way into becoming one of the megas.

He held it in his hand looking at the flawless portrait of Dario Verrick as its cover. There was something about those eyes that Kai couldn't quite pinpoint, but they just seemed... too perfect.

As he continued to scan the book around, he heard a noise from one of the rooms.

Rumi was finished with her meeting.

He quickly glanced around the room, settling on a serviette to use as a makeshift bookmark before putting the book down, making a mental note to buy her a proper one. As he was making his way back to the couch, he noticed Rumi enter the room from the corner of his eyes.

Rumi stepped in, her presence filling the room effortlessly.

"Sorry, that took a while. Can I get you anything to drink?" she asked, walking towards him with the same natural ease, though her gaze held an enquiring warmth.

"I'll take whatever you're having." He said lightly. "I had

plenty to eat and drink at the office today. But I am surprised you left early. I didn't even see you there. Where were you hiding?"

She handed him a glass of Frostale and flopped onto the couch beside him with a tired smile.

"I'm just great at hiding." She said with a playful smirk.

Kai gave a wry smile and said, "If you had told me you were *lost*, I would have believed you."

She laughed, a soft, nostalgic chuckle. She understood immediately what he meant. "God, you still remember? It was DARK!" She got hilariously defensive.

She added, as a footnote to a bad memory, "That year's Blackout Circle wasn't kind to me."

"Yeah, well, I can't relate at all." Kai grinned as he said it.

They talked about old memories, nearly forgotten names, and places that once existed.

For a moment, it was like old times.

But as Kai spoke, he occasionally caught the subtle changes to her face; her body language seemed off. Something was odd.

She was somewhere else. And then Kai remembered, she already had a Link. She was perhaps occupied with an alert that needed her attention. Or perhaps not. He couldn't tell. Nobody could anymore.

Her gaze shifted briefly to the right, almost imperceptibly. A reflex, she probably didn't even realise she did it. And if not for Kai's sharp attention to these details, it would have gone unnoticed. From where he sat, he couldn't confirm the ghostly silver glimmer from her eyes.

He could feel the shift when she came back. The eyes didn't move around much, but there was a subtle difference when someone used their Link. It couldn't be helped.

In the living room, there was an invisible barrier between the old friends, that hadn't been there before. As if she were tuned to a different frequency, the one he didn't have access to.

He couldn't shake off the feeling that she was hiding something from him, which he found rather bizarre. He thought that with him, there was no need; he had always accepted her for who she was. Even if he didn't fully let her ideas settle over himself in acceptance, he embraced their existence as something worthy of acknowledgement.

He took a sip of his drink to let the moment pass. She was indifferent and oblivious to what he saw.

"So," she said, leaning back, "we haven't talked in a while. How are things, since you know *everything*? How has life been lately?"

And then, before Kai could respond, she added after a momentary pause, as if hesitating if she should, "Have you re-entered the... dating pool?"

Kai smirked, shaking his head from left to right. "Absolutely not. And I have no intention of doing so anytime soon."

Rumi chuckled gently as she playfully punched Kai's ribs. "Oh, come on, it's not that bad," she teased.

Kai gave her a blank look. "It's a nightmare, and you know it."

She grinned. "Alright, alright. Fair enough. It's brutal."

"Last I had to give it a go, which was several years ago, and to be frank, I felt like it was one of the most demanding and soul-crushing things I had had done. I don't think I can go through that ever again. I don't even know how it works these days."

Rumi gave him a playful glance before taking a slow sip of her drink, deliberately turning away smiling, as if daring him to ask what she was holding back.

"Come on. Spit it out. What is it? What new nightmare fuel is the craze these days?"

She reflected on the absurdity of what dating had become. But she found it tolerable. Useful even.

With Link's integration, people didn't go on first dates anymore – their digital selves did.

Dating apps had to adapt quickly not to lose their share of the pie with Link. There was already an immense influence of intelligence, preferences, and the systems making jobs easier for people. But Link levelled the fields completely.

People sent their digital selves on dates because it wasn't worth the time and effort to filter out who was a decent match, an interim companion or just not suitable at all. These digital personas weren't basic simulants. Built from their neural data, they were extensions of the user – preferences, past interactions, humour, mannerisms, life goals, financial status, health – everything.

People sent 'themselves' out into a virtual world, a meticulously designed space which they could reserve – in an entirely new world, in the rainforests, on top of the mountains, or just on a cosy rooftop. Some of the world's iconic attractions rented out their own version of virtual worlds for dates – candlelit restaurants with the backdrop of a tower, or in a café in the middle of seasonal cherry blossom trees, on a boat ride with a view of the city.

The couple sat across each other, or just took a walk together, talking, laughing, observing and displaying. They looked exactly like the users, the dating platforms wouldn't let it be something else, though the personas were heavily glamourised. Every feature was meticulously enhanced and impeccably dressed. Some users even chose the locations to work for them – wherever they felt confident and looked best.

After the date, the users could watch the footage at their leisure. And they received a full playback, the entire interaction analysed and summarised, with the conclusion from Link.

[Your humour compatibility is 83%. Your life goals align 75%. However, their subconscious stress markers show potential disagreement regarding financial management. You laughed at their joke about raising a family, but your biometric response showed mild discomfort. I recommend a second date to further understand and analyse their thoughts about your hobbies, as it's clearly important for you.]

And just like that, decisions were made for you. Even who to spend your life with.

Rumi hesitated; the words had formed but never left her lips. She knew Kai, the guy who always religiously believed in love as something sacred. If she had told him how dating worked in the world, he would only have seen it as another defeat for humanity. Perhaps he was right. But she didn't worry about things beyond her control. That's how the world worked, not her. She could either take part in it or watch from a distance. That was the only choice she had, and she knew it.

So, instead of letting him in, she swallowed her thoughts and shrugged.

"Oh, nothing. Just the usual nonsense," she said lightly. "Do you want another drink?"

Kai shook his head. "No, I'm good, thanks."

He noted her reluctance. It was subtle, but unmistakable.

But he didn't press. He understood when to hold back.

He took a sip of his drink, readying himself for the real reason he was there. He had questions, doubts and fears. His intention was to enquire about Link, regarding her experience. How did she justify it? How was life different? Was she still herself with all going on in her head? He hesitated.

In the moment of hesitation, he saw she was somewhere else again. Or was it his imagination?

For the first time in his life, he felt like he couldn't talk to Rumi without thinking about answers for questions that might follow, questions that he wasn't prepared to answer. Realization hit him harder than he expected: he was embarrassed to open up.

She had always been the one person he could talk to. The one person who understood him. Their connection, forged in adolescence and rooted in a shared past, ran deep. Shaped by the community they grew up in and the memories that bound them.

His hesitation grew into unease, and unease developed into scepticism.

Was it even right to talk to her about Link and its effects when she clearly had it embedded in herself recently? Wasn't it too soon for her to offer a reasonably unbiased answer?

His mind was buzzing with doubts. But he was desperate too. He needed to talk. He opened his mouth.

Before he could speak, she did.

"I'm having a baby."

Kai blinked. For a moment, everything else in his head stopped. It took him a second to register what she had just said.

The moment stretched, and as if on instinct, Kai smiled.

This was big.

"Wow," he said, setting his drink down. "Rumi, that's huge. I'm happy for you. You've... thought this through, right? I mean, are you considering it, or have you decided?"

She nodded. "Yeah, I have decided. You know how important it is to me. It's about time."

He believed her. There was weight behind her words; her eyes expressed unwavering conviction and a glimmer of hope.

Kai exhaled and, for some time, forgot about everything else. His job. His choice. He turned his attention to her and her choice.

Then his mind wandered. He thought about the time when the world panicked, a time when birth rates so drastically reduced that governments scrambled for answers. Young women and men across the world decided, almost in unison, that parenthood just wasn't worth it. Life had evolved past the need for children.

Highly immersive entertainment, adventure, fitness, travel, hobbies, technology, virtual reality and augmented interactive gaming. Life was full of things to do. Losing years to parenthood felt like a sacrifice no one was willing to make.

Governments did their best – except to make it easier to sustain a family. Younger generations used a myriad of ways to pursue pleasure and avoid being dragged down.

What Kai didn't know was that Link Tech too played a pivotal role in this facet of modern living. They always did.

Link Tech had been buying sperm and eggs from those who looked at this venture to make easy money. And soon this little side hustle transformed into a booming trade, offering a generous sum of money to those who participated.

This helped Link Tech gain a large sample size for further

experimentation. The vast majority didn't care what a company did with their bodily fluids; those who did, didn't have to take part. It was, after all, consensual.

The goal was to develop technology capable of artificial gestation, eliminating the need for a mother to nurture the foetus in her body. Link Tech envisioned future parents could design conception to their preferences – matching eggs and sperm at will – and bypass the stages of pregnancy in a woman's body, entrusting it to an advanced capsule controlled in a lab.

It was a program shrouded in controversy, yet crucial for the future of a nation. Not everyone accepted it. Protests erupted; outrage boiled over. Religious groups were most hurt, condemning it, claiming life as a gift from God, that it should be born out of life, not synthesised in a lab.

Several nations across the globe desperately needed to boost their population, and yet refused to accept refugees and immigrants who could have easily filled the gap. It was blatant hypocrisy. The requirements were too rigid, and those desperate for a new start didn't *qualify*.

Of course, this was just one of many such programs run by Link Tech. They had long since stopped being just a technology company. They weren't just shaping the future; they engineered it. Some projects were public, broadcast as revolutionary breakthroughs. While some others operated in secrecy, dismissed as conspiracy theories – until they weren't.

Kai wasn't aware of this. Until Rumi told him.

And this... news from Rumi came out of nowhere. Kai couldn't recall ever having any discussions with her about this in the last two decades since he had known her.

"I'm going ahead with the program." She said it without

hesitation, her face brightened by a hopeful smile.

He wasn't sure how to feel about any of it. It was, of course, her decision, a rational choice, one that aligned with her best interests.

But this was when he realised how far she had drifted from him, or perhaps he was the one who had drifted away from her. The world had moved on too far, and he had been standing still.

Was he being immature? Was he clinging to an outdated version of reality?

He had come to Rumi to ask if she had any concerns with Link after a few months of use. Was there anything worth knowing for a nervous first-timer like him? Did it feel invasive? And here she was, sharing her decision to take part in Link Tech's artificial gestation program – a phrase he had never heard before. Not artificial fertilisation but 'artificial gestation'. Clearly, this was her way of moving forward without putting her life on hold.

He got the answer he needed. The truth was unavoidable.

Everyone around him had a Link. It was essential.

It was the future.

It was inevitable.

He didn't bother asking Rumi questions about Link. He continued with the usual chit-chat and left for home after another drink.

On the way home, his thoughts were more refined, less defensive.

Choices define a man... do they? I don't know. Nothing feels clearly right or wrong anymore. I just... I have to pick something and keep going. Answers won't come. They never do.

I can't lose my job. No... not now.

He forced himself to believe what he murmured in his head. *Maybe I'll even like it.. Who knows.*

Right, wrong... maybe none of it matters... not as much as I thought.

And then, on an impulse, he decided. There was no other way he could justify it.

On his way back, he glimpsed the same mural again. The painted eyes of the young girl spiralled inward like whirlpools, and the words 'This isn't the Clarity you want' underneath.

An eerie sensation of discomfort grew on him.

Deep down, he knew that this decision was being made for him. He could either revolt at the expense of his world being turned upside down or put on a mighty act like the decision really came out of him.

Too many variables played in his head; too many possibilities. Very little control.

Chapter 4

When Kai was waiting for Rumi to finish her work, while he fumbled with a small book kept on the coffee table in the living room, Rumi sat facing the window in her room. She was finished with work, but her mind was still racing with thoughts.

She knew why Kai had come to visit her.

She heard him from the next room. The occasional shuffle of his feet, his nostalgic sighs and the noise of picking random things up and investigating.

A haunting silence settled over her as she prepared herself for what she had to do.

Rumi had heard about the forthcoming change at work.

She leaned her head back against the chair, letting the quiet in the room stretch just a little longer.

She wasn't nervous; she knew how to hold a meaningful conversation with him. She knew how to listen too, really listen to him. But things were... different now.

They were both inseparable once.

Rumi remembered when she first met him, after moving to Tarinvale with her mother. The community filled in what their lives lacked. People looked after one another without being asked.

And then there was Kai.

She didn't realise that she liked him before she knew what liking even was. Before her body and mind could catch up to the language of feelings. She felt drawn to him, and to her delight, Kai was pulled towards her the same way.

Over the years, their companionship became unshakeable. Their friendship was exemplified by the community as rare and admirable.

Rumi offered a receptive presence and comforting shelter for Kai to express himself, not aimlessly, but as if he were chipping away at something just out of reach.

Neither of them had answers for each other, but they didn't have to. Kai only talked to understand, and Rumi learned to love the kind of conversation he offered. It made her feel like she'd been invited to an entirely different world, one shaped entirely by his imagination and vision, his sense of right and wrong.

As they moved into their teenage years, something inside Rumi shifted, which made her look at them differently than Kai did. A quiet and subtle pull towards an unfamiliar feeling. Warmer. More intimate.

But as she continued to hear him talk to her with the same unwavering openness, trusting her with the most delicate corners of his inner self, she stopped herself from leaning any further. His words came to her without any caution, and there wasn't any need for it. She was a sacred space to him where he wasn't worried about being misunderstood. And it was that trust, that openness, the holy, unspoken belief in her presence, which made her put aside the fleeting sensation of a new kind of rush she felt in his presence.

And with time, she came to realise that it was the right decision, because the possibility of something more – romantic or otherwise – would have shattered the bond between the two. She didn't need them to be more. What was already there was enough.

Over time, their bond strengthened, but not into love, into friendship of mutual acknowledgement of each other's differences.

When they stepped into the tail end of late teenage years, the world unveiled its imperfections to both, and their once inseparable bond began to subtly fray.

But only Rumi felt the growing distance; Kai remained blissfully unaware, continuing his routines without noticing any change.

Rumi found herself holding back in conversations. And it wasn't because Kai made her feel lesser, or excluded, or confused. He too had an impeccable ability to hold space for others, to listen without interrupting. He didn't think of a response while he waited; he listened without intention to correct or sway. And yet, when it was her turn to speak, she felt distant.

Kai's mind felt like a serene walk in nature. She loved being in it, but she didn't want to inhabit it.

Life, to her, wasn't a riddle to solve. It was something to move through.

She wanted to live it.

She saw the world change – the rise of systems, intelligence, monitoring.

At first, she passively resisted the wave of technology, like most people do in smaller communities. While she never petitioned against any form of intelligence, she remained neutral with her engagement. But over time, she also noticed the slow inevitability of it all.

What mattered to her weren't the problems. Progress did. Direction of movement, resilience and genuine attempts towards the benefit of society was enough to satiate her appetite for finding some meaning in the chaos of the world.

Kai often spoke as though the world had gone wrong. He believed as if something sacred had been lost in the pursuit of convenience and comfort.

But Rumi wasn't so sure if anything was lost; nothing was truly ever acquired. Things had simply... changed. As they always did.

When she first moved to Polaris, she struggled too. Her initial observations of the city were very similar to Kai's: sterile, synthetic and soulless. She missed familiarity, the rhythms of daily life, and the nonjudgmental companionship.

But that ache didn't last forever.

The city, for all its immensity, offered a new beginning, an opportunity to see, do and experience things which were out of reach before.

"Maybe it is soulless," she once told him, "but it's functional."

While Kai strived to find meaning in the city, she found momentum. He felt isolated, and while she initially did too, she embraced the anonymity.

When her mother fell ill, technology gave her more time.

And Rumi never forgot that.

Now, in the quiet of her apartment, with Kai fidgeting in the living room, she realised that he must have been desperate to have come to her today for help.

But she didn't know how to help. She didn't know if she should. Their worlds had simply diverged.

She had made a decision, a quiet one yet deeply personal, to participate in Link Tech's artificial gestation program. It wasn't helplessness. It was a choice.

She took a deep breath, the weight of the moment settling in her chest, not heavy with guilt, but with truth. Then she turned, walking slowly into the living room, her steps steady.

A twinge of sadness curled at the corner of her mouth, a ghost of what they had shared. But her face held determination.

Then she turned and walked into the living room.

Chapter 5

One sunny day in Tarinvale, Kai, along with Rumi and a few other neighbours, took it upon themselves to paint the new mural on the east wall of the community hall.

They were about fifteen-sixteen years old, with a more mature sense of responsibilities they felt towards Tarinvale, and its residents.

Rumi held the ladder steady, while Kai traced the outline of a honeybee with a brush dipped in sun-yellow paint. Around them, the neighbours passed around paint trays. Music played from a solar-powered speaker clipped to the fence. The mural was part of a larger project across Tarinvale, to celebrate, protect and preserve local wildlife, native plants and things worth holding on to.

That was when the news came. The notification blinked across the public feed – displayed on the wall-mounted screen beside the entrance – and everyone's personal devices: "Corporate Trials Exposed. Immigrants Misled."

It had happened in a city far from Tarinvale. A group of young activists had leaked documents showing that several multinational corporations, backed quietly by the government, were luring vulnerable migrants with the promise of permanent relocation and stable jobs. But once inside, they were given a cruel choice: sign up for a controlled experiment or lose it all. Most of the trials involved early neural integration and cognitive mapping.

A name was mentioned too many times in the conversations: Dario Verrick. The chairman of a rapidly growing organisation which was at the forefront of several technological advancements that were a boon to society. Everyone was shocked.

What made it worse was that Mr. Verrick was also accused of quietly scrubbing the organisation's climate commitments, removing emission targets from their long-term strategies. Even from the government portals, emission tracking servers and sea-level rise maps suddenly disappeared overnight. No one said it out loud, nothing led up to these decisions. But someone, somewhere, perhaps Mr. Verrick himself, decided that these numbers and figures didn't mean much anymore for the well-being of society.

And when the activists pushed back – published reports, hosted public conferences, posted on social media – they weren't imprisoned. They were digitally erased. Their access to identity, databases, medical services, and benefits – all gone. Their books disappeared, channels were deleted and profiles gone. They weren't detained. They were just... deleted.

Kai sat beside Rumi that evening, on the edge of the community's old weather tower, which still synced to the regional climate grid, blinking slow red pulses from it as it uploaded data. They remained quiet for some time. Somewhere far off, someone was flying their agricultural drones over fields.

"They didn't even fight it," Kai said finally. "Well, they tried to fight. But the world just... switched them off."

Rumi said, "They didn't lose because they were wrong. They lost it all because the entire system was already rigged."

Kai picked up an oval-shaped stone off the ground and threw it in the distance. "We used to protest, just to be heard. It was difficult, but with time, effort and enough people behind it, it worked, at least to some extent. Now, if you're loud enough, you just get deleted at the onset of an outcry."

Rumi looked over to him, eyes soft but unflinching. "You sound scared."

"I'm not even sure what I am. I don't know what we are part of anymore," he said. "We talk about progress and rights and future, but we are still doing exactly what so many dictators and corrupt rulers did. We are still letting things like *that* happen."

He continued, "I don't get it. We have learned so much. We have redefined so much. We know better. So why does it keep happening? The control, the fear, the punishment for voicing the truth."

Rumi didn't answer. She couldn't. But she knew that all that unfolded wasn't because of rules that governed the ages, it was because of how people were. "Maybe because changing the rules doesn't change the people who want to write them."

"I feel helpless," he said.

"I know." She said to him with sympathy for his troubles. There was nothing the duo could do between them, except sit in silence and look at the stars.

...

Despite the chaos in his mind, there was one thing for which he was immensely grateful – the love of his parents and the embrace of his community.

His father, Tama, was the epitome of strength, courage and

resilience – an exemplary father figure. Zora – his mother – adored her little Kai. They poured their hearts out to give him a loving childhood.

No matter how many perspectives he entertained, no matter how many books he delved into or how many contradictions he uncovered, there was always something for him to return to. A warmth that remained unchanged. A place where the complexities of individuality, the diffusing principles of good and bad, the hypocrisy of society – none of it mattered. He could just let go of everything that weighed him down. After all, he was still seventeen.

He could roam free, visit his neighbours without knocking, help someone fix their car, tease the older couple across the street, go for a swim or simply shut down and unwind.

That same summer, Tarinvale barely escaped disaster. A bushfire swept down from the western hills, whipped forward by the dry winds, aggravated due to broken heat records. Kai remembered the sky turning the colour of rust, an intense fire raging near the edges of the town. Several homes were destroyed; more would have gone if the firefighting drones hadn't been deployed in time.

That night, the town hall became a sleeping space for those who lost their homes. The next day, the hall turned into a donation centre. The entire community offered to rebuild, donate and get the affected families back on track. It could have been anyone.

Rumi and her family helped provide shelter and food while other families, including Kai's, helped buy supplies for re-building.

Later in the week, when things turned right, one of the neighbours, old Mr. Tui, treated everyone to a feast. He opened his storm shelter to host as many as he could. Many others chimed in together to top up whatever was left to get everyone involved.

That evening, in the middle of the chit-chat of people, with music and food lifting the spirits, Kai came across Rumi and they sat together in silence, eating away and sipping their drinks. They were exhausted from the day's business, and being in each other's company was enough comfort. No words were needed. And none were spoken for a long time.

Until finally, it was Rumi who asked quietly, "Have you ever thought we're just going to lose?" She took a sip from her drink and added, "Like... we fix something, and then something else breaks?"

Kai chuckled a little before he replied, "It's unlike you to get your spirits down."

Rumi kept staring into the distance, as if she were still trying to find an answer. Anything to make sense out of what was happening with Tarinvale.

Their beloved town bore the cracks of a changing climate. The summers had become unbearable; the heatwaves stretched for months longer than they ever had before. The rainfall was much more erratic and unreliable, leading to severe droughts, crippling agriculture. When the rain came, it wreaked havoc. It came in torrents, flooding houses, washing away roads and destroying crucial infrastructure.

There was absolutely no running away from it. Something had to change, or else it would be too late.

Kai could feel it. Rumi could feel it. The entire town felt it. Once sleepy, green and cheerful, Tarinvale had gradually become alert, grey and quiet.

Then one day, the news finally came out.

An increasing number of climate disasters in Tarinvale finally forced the government to issue notice for the evacuation of the people and relocate entire populations into new technologically advanced cities, designed to be resilient against the shifting climate.

Underneath the compassionate spirit of the community, Tarinvale was suffering from grave issues. Wildfires had become an annual occurrence. Crops failed frequently even with the aid of all available technological innovations. The groundwater dried up. Economies crippled, unable to sustain themselves. The selected few industries that sustained employment couldn't keep up with increasing obligations to remain profitable.

The government faced backlash for having sold the natural resources for profit until there was nothing left. Entire families left, one by one, in search of opportunities elsewhere. Life wasn't feasible in Tarinvale anymore.

The government had seen the patterns before, in other regions, hoping for solutions that never came. They had previously delayed their responses, which ended up being detrimental. This time, they took swift action. They had to, as all eyes were on them. Authorities targeted, evacuated, and consolidated several towns with new technologically advanced cities.

It wasn't just Kai and Rumi's town. The entire world had to follow this template to survive.

Rumi's mother had to move to another city in the far west, another place bearing the grunt of nature. But she couldn't take Rumi along with her this time. Rumi needed better education; she was sent to continue her studies in her aunt's care.

For Kai, things were abrupt. His family had no choice; they had to move. They packed up their lives into a few boxes and left everything they'd ever known behind – bound for Polaris, the city of the future.

II

Polaris

Chapter 6

Polaris glowed differently after dusk.

The botanical towers lit their terraces with soft green halos, and the walkways – built wide, tree-lined, and meticulously maintained – absorbed footsteps like carpets made of compressed moss. Every balcony above them had something growing on it: citrus shrubs, sprawling ivies, or the native flowering vines the city rewarded residents for maintaining. Even the air smelled faintly engineered, as if filtered to keep impatience out.

Nina walked beside Kai, her pace measured, her posture straight. They weren't holding hands – not out of discomfort, but because neither had initiated it. They'd been seeing each other for a few months now. Long enough to be familiar. Not long enough for anything settled, promised, or defined.

Nina spoke first. "There's a new café opening on the South Deck. They grow their own herbs on-site. Thought we could try it?"

"Sure." Kai said.

"You don't mind switching from our usual place?"

"No," he replied truthfully. "It's just one of the many variables. Who knows what version of reality branches out of it?"

She was used to him by now – his strange metaphors, his tendency to drift into thought mid-sentence. But they still caught her off guard sometimes. She laughed softly. "Only you would explain a café choice like that."

He smiled as if agreeing with the joke, though internally he had meant it.

They reached the café. The doors camouflaged in the walls slid open at their approach, sensing proximity.

"Okay, that's pretty cool." Kai said in excitement.

"I know, right. I've heard this café is completely run by bots – except the food preparation part."

"The last part's reassuring. Although, now I'm intrigued. Can bots cook now?"

Nina couldn't hear Kai as they made their way inside, a step further than him.

Inside, the lighting adjusted to warm neutral tones, high-lighting the plants in hanging beds and the polished stone tables. A server bot glided towards them, its smooth shell and subtle gestures imitating an old-world welcome without trying too hard to be human.

Nina chose a booth by the window. Kai sat opposite her, watching the city through the glass that adjusted opacity based on external conditions. Today, the weather was forgiving. He could see people walking; transport pods sliding silently; delivery bots moving along the dedicated lanes beneath the deck. Polaris had a choreography – an organised precision – that reminded him of an equation always solving itself.

Nina set her bag down. "You look like you're studying the city again."

"I like the design," he said. "Everything fits a logical flow. It's like Polaris isn't optimistic about the future – it's prepared for it."

"You really have a thing for structure, don't you?"

Kai didn't respond immediately. The truth was yes. Structure was his safety. Structure was… meaning.

Nina opened her menu; there were several options that adapted to supply conditions rather than taste trends. After ordering, she glanced up. "So, how was your week?"

"Predictable," Kai said. "But fine."

"Mine was chaos." She leaned closer. "They changed our scheduling algorithm again. Apparently to improve efficiency. I'm not convinced."

Kai tilted his head. "Did it work?"

"For the company, sure. For us? No. But you know how things go." She shrugged. "Progress."

He watched her as she talked – how she cut her sentences cleanly, how she rarely softened her words, how she remained composed even while complaining. Kai liked that. He found it restful in a way.

She was speaking again. "Oh! Did you hear about Verrick?"

Kai blinked back to attention. "Dario Verrick? Link Tech Verrick?"

"Yes. His company announced some breakthrough in neural micro-devices. Everyone at work was talking about it. If it's real, it could change… well, everything."

Coincidentally, on a nearby holo-screen, a muted news segment displayed a headline.

LINK TECH ADVANCES NEXT-GEN EMBEDDED INTERFACE

"Oh gosh, what a timing. That one." Nina pointed to the screen.

Kai looked at the screen, expression unreadable. "Mm."

"You don't find it exciting?" she asked.

"I find it... interesting," he said. "But I don't know what the consequences are."

Nina tilted her head. "Consequences? It's just tech."

Kai gave a small smile. "Nothing is ever just tech."

She rolled her eyes playfully. "You think too much."

"Someone has to."

Their drinks arrived. Nina wrapped her hands around her cup of Emberbrew, warming them. Kai watched the steam curl upward in spirals. He traced the patterns unconsciously, imagining the unseen currents that shaped them.

He had ordered a Frostale for himself.

Nina interrupted his thoughts. "You... drift sometimes."

"Sorry," he said. "I just... notice things."

"I know," she replied, softer now. "It's one of the things I like about you."

Kai looked down. He didn't know what to do with this sort of affection.

Nina leaned forward. "Can I ask you something? Where do you see us going?"

Kai's heartbeat tightened – not fast, just structured, like it was waiting for instruction.

"I like where we are," he said carefully.

"That's not exactly what I asked."

He hesitated. "I think we're... compatible."

Nina raised a brow. "Compatible?"

"In the sense that we understand each other," he clarified. "And there's stability. And potential."

It was the closest he came to tenderness.

Nina looked at him for a moment – evaluating, measuring.

She wasn't hurt. She wasn't flattered. She was simply assessing, the way she approached everything.

"That's a very Kai answer," she said finally.

"Is that good?"

"It's... honest."

He nodded, as if relieved.

The rest of the date passed gently. They talked about the new transit upgrades. About the rooftop gardens on the East Pier. About books neither had time to start. Nina described her team at work; Kai listened with genuine interest but little emotional depth.

When they walked out of the café, Nina slipped her arm through his.

Kai didn't pull away. He liked the contact. He liked the idea of belonging somewhere.

On the way back, Nina said, "You think more than you feel."

"I feel," Kai said quietly.

"I know," she replied. "Just differently."

Kai didn't argue. She was right in ways she couldn't possibly know.

Inside him, love wasn't a warm, effortless thing. It was a system. A set of branching paths. A structure he kept trying to understand. Nina wasn't Nina to him – not fully. She was a place to put his yearning, a vessel for the idea he had carried for years: that partnership could give the world meaning.

He mistook the wanting for the loving.

And he was going to understand the difference the hard way.

Chapter 7

He got out of the train and stood at the platform waiting for the crowd to disperse. Being outside was nauseating enough; he didn't want to wade his way through a horde of people.

He looked ahead: crowd density indicators pulsed gently along the walls, guiding foot traffic towards a number of exits. He chose to wait.

The platform lighting was brighter than when he had left home earlier. Now, it was cooler, flattening shadows and smoothing the movement of bodies into something orderly.

He had just come out of the court. Instead of a sense of relief, he felt incredibly empty. As if someone had gouged out his insides. Yet he remained. Breathing. Moving.

He looked up ahead; the escalator was nearly empty now. Its speed adjusted the moment the crowd thinned, lights dimming fractionally as if the system now no longer needed to perform. It took him a few more seconds to convince himself finally to move.

After a series of escalators and navigating his way across the maze of a station, he got out.

The sun was out, but light barely made its way to him with the blend of skyscrapers surrounding him. As much as he wanted to get home, he realised he desperately needed a walk

and some warmth. He decided to walk to Alice Park close by –
one of the biggest parks in Polaris CBD.

Even after all these years, he was still astonished by how
they pushed entire road networks underground, creating open,
human spaces above. Everything lay within reach. Walkable.
Perfect for him.

He arrived at the park quickly, and sunlight rewarded him
as soon as he entered.

He found an empty bench close to a shallow channel of water
flowing through. There were several channels of varying sizes
and even some small-sized ponds scattered across the park,
as it doubled as flood plains in a crisis.

The bench was placed on a 'mini-hill', which seemed a little
too high for no reason – until it flooded.

Soaking in the sun's warmth, he looked around with nostalgia in his eyes. He had spent countless hours there; often with
friends, but also sometimes in his own company. The park
offered a scenic view of the city, where one could truly admire
how the entirety of Polaris pulsed with greenery.

He suddenly realised that he had been there with Nina. As a
matter of fact, they sat on the same bench that he was sitting
on right now.

He did not plan this walk, visit to the park, or choosing the
bench, but the irony amused him enough to chuckle lightly as
he thought about it.

He closed his eyes and lifted his face towards the sun. Even
with his eyes shut, the sun wasn't forgiving; he had to look
away but not before getting a surge of warmth in his entire
body.

He wanted to think of something else. That's precisely why
he had come to the park.

But he couldn't.

The trigger had set, and now he couldn't distract himself from the conversation he'd had with Nina right at this very same bench almost two years ago.

She was new to Polaris, while Kai had been a resident for a couple of years. It was their third date after months of compatibility test runs, virtual dates and safety checks.

"So, why this location of all places? It doesn't look very... glamorous?" Nina asked with a reserved smile and expecting eyes.

Kai laughed. "I admit, it's not at all one of the best parks in Polaris, but it's the biggest one in the CBD, and we get spectacular views of the city."

"Hmm, I'm not sure we share the definition of *spectacular*," said Nina with a chuckle.

Kai, now a little excited, "Well, there's more to this view than one can see. I know that doesn't sound impressive, but with one third of the city basically underground, this is one of the few places you can truly appreciate how marvellous Polaris really is."

Nina, now sharing the excitement, raised her eyebrows. "Okay, now that's something I'm keen to hear." Then, a second later, realising why Kai perhaps met with her in the park, she added, "Smart choice, I must say. I'm sure you didn't pick this spot just to familiarise me with the city?"

Kai playfully added, "Well, it had some role to play; I must take credit for that. It's also not too far from the station; just a short walk."

Nina didn't contest, but she made a mental note of what a 'short walk' was for Kai.

"Okay, I'll try to give you a crash course about the city. Are you ready?" Kai asked Nina with ready and eager eyes.

"The city of Polaris, officially designated District-07, has pretty much everything a futuristic city should have - large parks, fantastic schools, enormous swimming pools, wide roads and modern infrastructure. The usual. But once you look past the façade, you realise there's so much more going on."

Nina, now fully facing him, directed her undivided attention towards the conversation.

"The infrastructure," Kai went on, "was built to..."

Nina couldn't help but smile at Kai's innocent fascination with the city. She didn't really care what the city was like. She was sure she would figure out a way to navigate it.

"Buildings and underground complexes serve multiple purposes, including work, learning, connecting, and relaxation. Used differently as the day progressed. A daytime sports club becomes a music venue at night...

"The underground food court transforms into modular pop-up booths for small makers and hobbyists. At night, they reconfigure the area again into classrooms for adult learning modules. And that sports club you see..."

Nina found it useful, but the information overdose bored her – something Kai only found out months later.

Sitting on the same bench, Kai recalled that conversation with fond memories. Two years had passed since then.

He also remembered that he never truly told Nina how much he hated Polaris – not even during the time they were married together.

Kai didn't marry Nina because he was certain. He did it because it was what's next.

It was in the script. It was about time.

He didn't wrestle much debating whether he should or shouldn't. Life would have happened regardless. He believed wholeheartedly that he was in love, and his role in life was to be a loving husband.

But as time passed, the truth unfolded before him. He was too obsessed with the idea of love that he forgot to love her. Worse, he forgot even to love himself. As is the nature of truth, it eventually surfaces.

He had the right idea of love, but years of dwelling on it stripped him of the most fundamental truth about love – it couldn't be fabricated.

Kai was so fascinated with the idea of falling in love that he made it his entire personality. He poured his love out for Nina, with the expectation of being loved in return – but in ways he wanted to be loved. He exposed his lifelong wounds hoping to be saved from the distress.

Whatever it was within him, he wanted fixed. Something whispered within him that love, true love, would be his rescue. And so he put in the effort and awaited relief.

The relief never came. How could it? Love wasn't transactional.

The marriage didn't last long.

The gap between his idealised version of marriage and the cold, ungrateful reality widened. They fought. The small grievances, once overlooked and tolerated, surfaced. Resentment settled between them as a growing realisation of what must be done. She deserved someone who loved her for who she was, and what she represented in others' minds. He deserved someone he didn't have to force himself to love.

After the divorce was finalised, Kai left the courtroom lost again. A feeling too familiar to him.

He mistook the calm that followed for stability.

Chapter 8

It was his thirtieth birthday.

Tama and Zora wanted to come and visit him at his apartment, celebrate it together. Kai, on the other hand, was desperate for the day to be over. He politely acknowledged all the wishes directed at him, but refused to meet anyone – not even his parents.

It was a lazy Sunday afternoon. Cloudy. Gloomy.

He looked at the clock. Ten more hours to go until he was done for the day.

He turned to his notebook.

Nov 10

I have started going for runs, though I still find a leisurely walk more comforting. Noticed today that all the trees right outside the apartment building were too unnatural, too symmetrical. They lacked their unique feature of branching out, which they naturally do in pursuit of biological instincts. I am used to seeing greenery everywhere – green roofs, vertical gardens, parks and streets lined with trees. But I never noticed before how grey everything is too – glasses, concrete, surveillance, automation, alert systems. Everything is metallic.

It's my birthday today. I should celebrate, but I have never felt emptier. Something's missing. Something deeply unsettling.

What? I'm unsure if...

- Kai

He put down his pen, trying to narrow his thoughts. But today, he was struggling.

As he frantically searched for the words to take shape, the glimmer of the pen caught his attention.

He lost his train of thought. The pen rolled between his fingers.

How magnificent.

Antique.

He recalled the day he got hooked to writing. It was a similar day like today.

He was about sixteen.

One day, while he sat in his room, ruminating on the contents of a book he had just finished, he felt an overwhelming sensation to write – not on a screen. Instead, on paper, using a pen.

There were too many possibilities. Too many thoughts.

And as if a spark came from deep within him, he knew that writing would help.

He had access to plenty of paper around, but sourcing a pen was a little difficult. Nobody used them anymore. There was just no need; everything was on digital screens – displayed, written, broadcast, even painted. A pen was only something hobbyists and antique collectors had access to.

The urge in him was so strong that he ventured to search for it in the city. After a few enquiries, he found one – in the corner of an antique shop Nina once mentioned. The shop was a strange relic in a town that prided itself on its modernised systems. The owner – old Mr. Curren – insisted on keeping actual shelves, actual dust, and actual silence.

He took the pen and marvelled at its simplicity.

He had seen it before in movies, a few times in person, and read about it too – people writing on paper using a pen.

When he held it for the first time, he was mesmerised. It was light, almost weightless. Cold to the touch, with a smooth texture. When he took the cap off, a faint unfamiliar scent hit him. Whether it was the smell of ink, or something else that had lingered inside the cap, he couldn't tell.

He wanted to write something. But it wasn't easy or natural. He knew the words, but the muscle memory hadn't formed within him to write anything legible.

He made an attempt – a weak one – but he was still in awe of the result.

Kai found it magical, like he could create something out of thin air. All he could do then was draw awkward shapes. He knew the appearance of words, but he wasn't used to putting them together.

Over time, he became obsessed to learn how to write. And sure enough, he soon did.

For the first time, he could narrow. Not simplify – just narrow. The way light narrows through a slit.

Each letter forced a choice. Each stroke eliminated a dozen other possible strokes. It was like a change of state for his thoughts, from being intangible to tangible.

On paper, a thought had weight. It hesitated. It revealed its edges.

It obeyed the slow mechanics of the body.

And Kai needed that.

Handwriting became the one place where the variables

didn't multiply uncontrollably. The page didn't hide the wobble in his hand or the uncertainty in his spacing. Each imperfection told him something he could follow. Each mark was a clue, a path, a singular thread instead of a net of infinite branches.

When he wrote, the world resolved into one version he could hold long enough to understand.

Not the truest version. Not the correct version.

Just one.

And sometimes one was enough to keep him from slipping into that frightening place where a thought felt like it came from everywhere and nowhere at once.

Writing didn't heal the wound.

But it offered coherence when nothing else did.

And the result was a calm realisation that his one particular thought, among a myriad of thoughts, was more pressing than the others.

Writing for Kai also became an act of prioritisation.

And he embraced this feeling. Adopted it as a hobby. Whenever he could, he wrote words, phrases and thoughts that resonated with him. Sometimes, he felt the need to write something while he was in the office, on the train, or on a lazy afternoon.

He carried a small notebook everywhere.

Whenever he wrote in public, he raised heads, and people's curiosity drew them towards him. It was rare to see a pen in use.

Handwriting had become uncommon long ago, only available in antique shops like Mr Curren's. But Kai would get so engrossed in the act of writing that nothing else mattered.

And often when he wrote in public, it was because of an

unbearable need to write a question which troubled him, a thought which had just formed or a word which seemed appropriate for the situation.

If he came across a situation where he found himself through sheer luck, he wrote about it.

When things got overwhelming, he wrote his thoughts as his coping mechanism. Writing it down was half the problem solved. If he could write it down, he could manage it.

But on his thirtieth birthday, when he finished the entry, something in the adult version of him stayed unsettled.

Usually, after writing, he felt the slight unclenching – the sense that at least one thought had agreed to take shape.

Today, nothing settled. The page stared back at him like an unfinished equation. He read his own lines again, expecting the familiar relief.

It didn't come.

The words felt... incorrect. Not wrong, just incomplete – like he had written one branch of something that had six more curling behind it.

He tapped the pen against the margin.

He wanted to wrestle his thoughts, like he used to.

He had the entire day left, all to himself.

He flipped to a fresh page. Not to rewrite the same entry, but to see if another version of the thought existed – one that would finally feel "right," the way writing used to.

He started slowly, letting the pen hover.

Nov 10 – second note

I think the reason I feel miserable...

He paused.

Before, a description would narrow the noise. But now, instead of tightening, the idea ballooned outward. The trees could be described as symmetrical, engineered, artificial, unaware of their own uniformity, pretending to be alive, or worse, alive but trapped. Each option threw off ten more. His hand tensed.

He wrote a single word:

Because...

Then crossed it out.

Wrote another.

Crossed that one too.

Every time a sentence began, he immediately sensed the other versions of it, the invisible branches that used to quiet down the moment ink touched paper. Now they pressed closer, louder, like he was trying to write on top of a thousand whispers.

He tried again.

I feel...

Crossed it.

I think...

Crossed it.

He stared at the ruined lines.

It wasn't writer's block. It wasn't lack of clarity. It was too much clarity – too many angles, too many interpretations, too many variables firing at once.

He set the pen down and let out a slow exhale.

The notebook had always helped him choose one version of a thought long enough to breathe. Now every version felt parallel, simultaneous, equally possible. His mind no longer funnelled into a narrow beam. It sprawled outward, uncontrolled.

He pressed his fingertips to his temples. The patterns didn't stay still anymore. The variables didn't collapse.

The page no longer offered shape – only more noise.

On his thirtieth birthday, for the first time since he was sixteen, writing didn't calm him. It magnified him.

Kai closed the notebook carefully, almost apologetically, as though the failure was mutual.

Outside, the engineered trees swayed in perfect unison.

Inside, Kai couldn't get a single thought to move in just one direction.

And he felt it – quietly, like something shifting just beneath the ribs: The wound had come back.

And this time, writing couldn't hold it still.

Though he continued to confide to his notebook, to writing, he never felt the same stillness and harmony again for the rest of his life.

Chapter 9

He woke up to the soft chiming of a notification.

"Nexora Foods: Offer Letter Enclosed."

He slowly sat up and blinked at the message, as if it was addressed to someone else. For years he had imagined this moment arriving with a rush of relief, a sense of arrival, something loosening inside him.

Once, there was nothing more he was passionate about than landing a job at Nexora.

Today, instead, the words on the screen looked strangely flat – like instructions for a task he barely remembered volunteering for.

He tapped the offer open.

Salary. Conditions. Onboarding schedule.

Each line appeared with the same polite indifference as the city's morning hum outside his window.

He waited for the feeling to follow.

Nothing came.

He remembered believing – truly believing – that the world rewarded the right things.

Knowledge. Effort.

His childhood community had lived that way, or at least performed the illusion convincingly. But Polaris had corrected him quickly.

He'd watched classmates with half his sincerity sprint effortlessly ahead, not because they were better, but because they were louder. Charm, theatrics, and calculated outrage helped people who manipulated the system surge upward, as if they were designed for this era.

And those who fought for the environment, for transparency, for fairness?

They were called naïve by corporations, inconvenient by politicians, sentimental by their peers.

Kai learned to stop expecting coherence from morality.

Finding work had become its own trial. He spent years chasing stability but never caught it. Hopping between short contracts, watching savings evaporate, watching job listings demand contradictions: be creative but compliant; be authentic but on-brand; be fast but flawless.

Polaris preferred people who adapted rather than understood.

When Nexora Foods finally chose him, it wasn't because he fit. It was because the algorithm picked up a phrase he'd used by accident, a term he barely remembered scrolling past in a paper three years earlier.

One wrong synonym and he would've been invisible.

Chance. Coincidence. Luck.

The same variables he spent his life trying to see beneath.

He accepted the offer. There was not a single reason not to.

And yet, the child in him recoiled – as it always did when a choice was demanded out of him. Was this the right one? Or the variables had aligned against him? The familiar doubt returned. The fear. The habit of scrutinising every move, every thought, every decision. Something that had followed him for as long as he could remember.

...

Tarinvale had always felt slightly out of time. It was a small township swallowed by green hills and narrow valleys, built long before the world realised how fragile weather could be. Solar-lines ran along the rooftops like taut black ribbons, feeding energy into the quiet community. Water towers collected every drop of rain. People checked their weather alerts as often as they checked the time.

It wasn't a poor town. But it needed constant surveillance to ensure the well-being of its people. No amount of money could build infrastructure that could fight nature. Yet, Tarinvale was fighting one.

Kai was fourteen when even Tarinvale's bureaucrats finally accepted that the storms came too frequent; it had become almost impossible not to.

His school sat on higher ground, near the emergency shelter, both wrapped by a chain of smart barriers designed to activate when water levels reached critical thresholds. Screens across town showed weather models that updated in real time – storm trajectories, tidal compressions, saturation forecasts. Adults said it was better now. Technology helped. They didn't need to fear the unpredictable.

But technology didn't always win.

One humid afternoon in November, the storm didn't arrive slowly. It came all at once – several hours earlier than forecast, the way weather sometimes rebelled against its own predictions. And much more intense.

Kai heard the sound first – the hollow metallic groan of

shutters descending over the school windows, followed by the rising alarm tone. Students moved in lines, teachers guiding them with steady voices, though their eyes betrayed the speed of their calculations.

They were meant to relocate to the community shelter.

They never reached it.

Water met them before they could even muster the students together. The emergency drones hovered above, guiding the neighbourhood towards evacuation points, but visibility was broken by wind and debris. Not all could make their way. At one point, it became dangerous to try.

The smart barriers should've risen earlier. They didn't. Whether it was a sensor delay, a false reading, or the surge bypassing the valley algorithm – no one could agree later.

Kai remembered only fragments: the cold slap of air; the sound of hundreds of shoes slapping on wet concrete; the teachers shouting instructions competing with the storm's roar.

Water levels rose alarmingly fast. All the adults rushed to the roof, taking the students along with them. It was safer there.

Two rescue boats arrived at the same time – sleek, half-inflated crafts pushed forward by emergency responders with headlamps cutting through the rain. They shouted directions that disappeared into the wind.

"Left group here! Right group there! Move!"

But no one truly heard them. The words dissolved. People moved by instinct, by proximity, by who grabbed whose sleeve. Kai stepped to the left because someone's elbow nudged him that way. Or maybe because a gust pushed him half a step. Or because the girl in front of him shifted her weight. He didn't know.

He only knew that his foot landed in one of the boats, and the other half of his classmates were directed toward the second.

As they made their way to shelter, a wall of water rushed down the road, carrying branches, broken fence pieces, a fallen drone. Something struck one of the boats – the one Kai wasn't in. It tilted sharply. Screams cut through the air. A responder dove in. Someone's bag floated away. The craft capsized with a sound like cloth ripping underwater.

Several other boats rushed to help.

A kid held onto floating debris. Another struggled to stay afloat even with a life jacket on.

The current was too strong. Too unstable.

Kai froze. His boat lurched but steadied.

It was too dangerous to keep the kids on the boat Kai had boarded. A similar mishap could happen at any moment.

A responder yanked the rope closed again, and his group was pushed rapidly away, the motor whining at full power as they fought the current.

He watched the other boat vanish behind the rising flood – a blur of orange vests and panicked splashes – and something inside him split open. Not grief. Not fear. Something colder.

It was impossible to rescue everyone. Too much happened too fast.

If Kai had lifted his foot half a second later, he would have been in the other boat.

If the girl in front of him had paused, he would have paused.

If the wind had shifted slightly, he would have been on the right instead of the left.

Every adult later called it luck.

Kai didn't recognise the word.

To him, it was a branch. A version of reality collapsing.

A thousand micro-variables converging into a single irreversible line.

He felt the shape of the unseen – how fragile the world was, how survival was not moral or earned or even logical, but something decided in the small tremors of movement people barely noticed.

Over the next few days, the flood receded, leaving a silence that felt wrong. Responders combed through pockets of debris along the riverbanks. Families gathered at the emergency shelter – the same one that had protected dozens, though not quickly enough to save everyone. The storm had moved too fast. The warning sirens had barely finished their first cycle before the lower streets were swallowed.

Tarinvale wore its wounds openly. Collapsed fences, uprooted trees, roads split like cracked glass. The town hall, still functioning as a command centre, buzzed day and night with volunteers sorting blankets, carrying crates, calling out names, hoping someone answered. Every hour, another list of the missing was updated on a flickering screen.

The school grounds were unrecognisable. A playground turned into a gulley of mud. Search teams worked in shifts, but each day brought fewer recoveries and more acknowledgement of what had already been lost.

And as the town rebuilt itself in fragments, Kai began to feel something he didn't know how to name. The sorrow of losing his classmates seeped into him slowly – not loud, not sudden, but steady, like water rising under a closed door.

Yet even deeper than the grief was something else forming – sharper, more permanent. He found himself pausing before every move, every interaction, every action, and every choice.

He was born curious, yes, but surviving the floods had rewired that curiosity into something more pointed. It flipped a switch inside him.

He began to map constantly the invisible branches of reality, tracing how one tiny shift could cascade into a life or a loss. Over time, that instinct grew into an obsessive need to understand the hidden variables that governed choice – convinced that if they were observed from the right angle, they could be understood.

It was a metamorphosis. And it never left him.

Chapter 10

At Nexora, Kai behaved exactly as he was meant to: quiet, competent, inoffensive, "reliable."

He spoke when spoken to. He completed tasks before they were due. He blended into the workflow like a tile in a grid.

The office itself was a lesson in optimisation.

The windows adjusted automatically, filtering heat and glare until the city outside looked calmer than it ever was.

Temperature shifted by zones, cooler where bodies gathered, warmer along the edges to discourage lingering.

Conversation happened only when necessary – everything else was silently annotated on screens.

People moved with the clipped efficiency of a system running at peak load.

Kai played along.

But each time he smiled on cue or nodded at an instruction, something inside him thinned.

As the months stretched on, he noticed something unnerving: his internal questions no longer sparked curiosity – they felt like burdens he carried in his ribs. The contradictions he used to chase out of fascination now felt hostile, like loose wires in a machine that no one else seemed bothered by.

His memories of Tarinvale faded into something dreamlike

– the warmth, the community, the blackout circles, the shared incoherence that once comforted him. Polaris didn't leave space for that kind of uncertainty. Here, ambiguity held no social value. Here, people didn't ask why – they performed what the world needed them to perform.

His marriage had ended.

Rumi had a life of her own. The friendship… on hold, perhaps.

All his other friends dissolved into the city's background noise.

His connection to his parents thinned, stretched across polite conversations and postponed visits.

Most days, Kai felt less like a person and more like someone watching himself from a slight distance – as if he were always one second behind his own life.

The loneliness didn't hit suddenly. It accumulated like sediment.

He used to believe in choice. In self-authorship. But Polaris turned choices into something else – not freedom, but branching paths that appeared inevitable only after he'd taken them. Every decision felt pre-written, as if he were following a script someone else had drafted.

Once, on a train ride home, he caught his reflection in the window. For a moment he didn't recognise the man looking back – not because he looked different, but because he looked unaligned, like a version of himself from a path he didn't choose.

The city rewarded the wrong traits.

Cruelty masqueraded as competence.

Ignorance as confidence.

Compliance as virtue.

Seeing it every day was like breathing in fumes he couldn't detect until he was already lightheaded.

Depression didn't arrive as a storm.

It arrived as weather: persistent, unremarkable, settling into every corner of his life.

He didn't want to disappear. He didn't want to die.

He wanted to understand – the suffering, the numbness, the endless branching of possibilities that led nowhere stable.

The *when* didn't matter. The *how* didn't matter. The *why* mattered a lot to him. He wanted nothing more than to understand his suffering – not even to end it, just to be familiar with it.

He stopped reaching out socially.

Work. Home. Sleep. Reset. Repeat.

The loop tightened around him.

Sometimes he forced himself into crowded spaces, hoping proximity to others might steady him like it once did in Tarinvale – but crowds in Polaris only magnified his alertness, the micro-behaviours, the contradictions.

People were kind enough, but busy. Everyone was busy.

Everyone scrolling, replying, organising, achieving.

No one had time to notice a man who kept his life functioning just well enough.

And the city rewarded functioning.

His digital metrics were perfect. Performance reviews glowing. His name appeared in team commendations he barely remembered contributing to. People congratulated him warmly – unaware they were praising a mask.

He adapted to Polaris.

But he never synchronised with it.

His curiosity withered, starved of meaning.

His rebellion dissolved into fatigue.

And yet, buried beneath the exhaustion, something persisted. Not gone. Not extinguished.

Just contained. Waiting for a place where it could exist without being corrected.

...

It was one of those times when everything moved at his pace, and it wasn't just Rumi, but almost the entire town of Tarinvale turned itself down. One night every year, they all agreed to power down – by choice. The council turned off all non-essential lighting. Households dimmed everything they could – no streetlights, no drones, no billboards, no unnecessary travel. Even the regional transit lines dimmed their light out of respect for the tradition. And because the town sat just far enough from other major hubs, when the lights went out, the sky returned. Not perfectly. But it still looked beautiful.

No one really knew who started this tradition. Some said it Tama's idea to lift the spirits of Tarinvale's residents after a three-day outage during a coastal storm revealed how peaceful life could be without the constant noise and screens. A few others claimed it was a sheer accident, a revelation in the moment of distress, when someone threw a birthday party during a blackout and decided that it was better that way.

No one could agree, but it didn't matter; no one argued either. The Blackout Circle was now part of who they were.

By sundown, every porch had a lantern lit, actual flames or soft-glow solar lights. Kids carried paper globes. Teenagers lit candles. And in the middle of the square, there was a large fire, under the watchful eyes of the town's firefighters.

Attendance wasn't mandatory, but not a single soul wanted to sit this one out. There weren't too many rules, just a few things everyone had agreed to – no screens, no phones, no gadgets. Just sit around the fire, and talk.

Kai walked through the gathering with a steady rhythm, stopping to help someone set up a lamp, fetching extra firewood from the back of a van and swapping greetings without needing to linger.

There was a glow in his eyes; he looked relaxed. Joyful. As if, someone had taken a huge weight off his shoulders.

It wasn't just the crowd that offered him joy. Nor was it the communal warmth that radiated naturally among Tarinvale's residents.

It was the feeling of not having to look for a structure or meaning. When he stood among people who expressed themselves openly, their movements, impulses, disagreements, and small peculiarities filled the air with variables that didn't belong to him.

Patterns he didn't have to solve.

Contradictions he didn't have to interrogate.

He still noticed everything – the micro-behaviours, the unrealised possibilities, the invisible motivations; he couldn't help that.

But here, in this circle of human noise, the burden of coherence was shared.

The world didn't narrow around him the way it did when he was alone.

A part of him just couldn't accept that events lacked deeper structure. When he was by himself, his mind chased the hidden variables behind every choice – a wish, a wound, a quirk or an impulse. Coherence slipped.

But in the Blackout Circle, he felt something unfamiliar yet stabilising. The world didn't have to make perfect sense. Contradictions could exist without resolutions.

He joined a group of teenagers near the stone steps, where Rumi was already sitting, pulling weeds out of the edges of the slab.

Someone said, "Hobbies. Let's go around. And real ones, not what your digital simulants do."

"Alright, alright. This seems interesting. I'll go first," Mira said.

"I am trying to build a sound library of insects before they all migrate. It's fun." And she looked at the surrounding faces, and added, "No, really it is. Trust me. Well, at least to me it's fun." She spoke her mind and withdrew in silence. A faint, self-assured smile formed on her lips, one that suggested that she did not need anyone else's validation.

"Well, as long as you find it fun," said Alistair. He then added, "I've been making immersive graffiti art, and I must admit it's quite cool. Makes me happy knowing that it hides in plain sight and is only viewable through lenses or phones."

"That sounds neat," said Kai.

"Zev?" someone asked.

"I make tiny robots that do obstacle racing on the dinner table. My parents aren't big fans," said Zev with a grin.

"What about you, Rumi?" someone pulled Rumi into the conversation.

"Well... I have so many. But they aren't as interesting as what you guys do. I just... watch the clouds, start mini petitions that no one signs."

Everyone around her chuckled at the mention of mini petitions.

After a brief pause, she quickly added, "And occasionally I rewrite news to make them sound more hopeful."

There was a moment of silence. Not uncomfortable, just an honest acknowledgement of how desperately they all tried to do the same.

"And Kai?" Reet asked. "Still into long and winding walks?"

Kai nodded, smiling. "Yes, I still enjoy long walks as often as I can."

Seeing Reet's pressing eyes on him, Kai continued, "Walking's underrated. Makes you feel like the world slows down just for you. Or maybe you're the one finally catching up."

A few heads nodded thoughtfully.

Then Rumi added, "He also writes. By hand."

That made a few heads turn and eyebrows rise.

"Wait – you mean with a pen?" Mira asked.

"Like on a piece of paper?" Zev blinked.

Kai chuckled. "Yeah. It's so much slower than you think. But perhaps that's why I like it."

"Do you have it with you right now?" Zev asked, with a glimmer of excitement in his eyes.

Kai admitted shyly. "Yeah, I carry it almost everywhere. I jot down ideas and thoughts."

"Show us, please!" someone said.

"Yes! I want to see it too." Another voice from the back of the group.

He hesitated for a second, then reached into his pocket and pulled out a small soft-covered notebook. Along with it, he pulled out a pen – a simple one, capped, black coloured and faintly scratched with use. He handed it to the person next to him.

"You can open the notebook. Nothing too private in there," he said with a smile as he handed it to the person next to him.

The notebook and the pen got passed from hand to hand. Inside, there were scribblings by Kai from earlier. People tilted it slowly towards the light from the fire, squinting as the flickering firelight revealed what the pages held within - random thoughts, poorly drawn sketches, and a small poem.

People turned the pages gently, almost reverently, careful not to harm it while handling and passing it around. The weight of the notebook, the feel of the paper, the scratches of pen marks, the irregularity of handwriting – it was unfamiliar, yet real. Like stepping into a dream. A few held it as if they were holding something fragile. Several ran their fingers down the handwritten pages as if to wake a memory of what ink used to feel like, except there were no realisations, only a strange forgotten sensation.

Zev lifted the pen, uncapped it slowly and sniffed it.

"It smells like... I don't know. History, maybe?" he said – half-laughing, half-serious.

He then added, "I've seen it so many times before, but it never occurred to me I would ever want to hold it, let alone smell it.

"Honestly, I've never actually seen anyone use one in real life."

Rumi, now beside Kai, watching the group over his shoulder, said with a smile, "Told you it's more than walking."

He nudged her gently. "And you? Clouds, petitions and transformed news articles – is that it?"

She shrugged. "I do too many of these outlandish things to keep count. I have also found that I'm into gardening. Anything I can keep alive."

She added after a brief sigh, "There's something about it. Watching plants grow over time, while I nurture them, help take care of them, and soon they take care of themselves."

By the time night had settled, the Blackout Circle was in full swing.

At the edge of the square, other adults had gathered near another firepit. Their stories floated over the evening like smoke.

There were families around, several generations huddled together. There were friendships between some who argued that they were family. Some had moved from flooded cities. Others from burnt-out farms. And a few from countries that no longer existed.

There was acceptance in that. Imperfection was the norm. A friendly greeting, and a willingness to reciprocate help were enough to make anyone feel a sense of belonging.

A few adults started talking, in low voices. But slowly grew louder as the warmth of the fire offered comfort and loosened the tightness of the day from their shoulders.

It began with a joke.

"I used to have a fridge that locked my snacks away from me."

"And I had a watch that told me my blood-pressure and insulted my cooking."

After a round of laughter, the talk shifted, as it often did.

"You remember when they started reporting the birthrate drop?"

"Yeah, I couldn't believe at first. Everyone blamed inflation, career ambitions, which were getting harder to stick to, and even bad dating algorithms."

"I remember that. It took a very long time for us to grasp the dire situation. Remember the wrath of climate, the number of natural disasters which suddenly skyrocketed. Only it wasn't sudden at all; we saw it coming from decades ago."

"And the food rationing, and the border controls. Things became really serious really fast."

There was a momentary pause while everyone ruminated about old times.

Kai, Rumi and the rest of the group were not too far from the square. They could hear what the adults were talking about. All the teenagers eavesdropped on the conversation between the adults.

"Wars over crops, water and land. And even shelter. Imagine going to war over shade."

Kai listened quietly. Everyone around him also listened.

Another much older adult added, "That was the time the megas rose – the ultra-rich and powerful. World's first trillionaire, owning almost one-third of the world's critical infrastructure directly or indirectly. Another duo who controlled where the rivers would go. The syndicate that leased warmth to the frozen nations."

An old lady, Aria, waved her hand as if brushing smoke from the air. Perhaps she noticed the teenagers in the distance. She attempted to dismiss the tone of the group.

"But look at us now," she said, voice light but firm. "We are doing alright. Energy's efficient, and enough for our needs. People waste far lesser, and the systems are cleaner. The crops are smaller but smarter. There's enough for us. We just had to learn to be less greedy."

Another adult nodded, understanding what Aria intended to do.

"Yeah, it's not about scarcity anymore..." He wanted to

continue but decided against it. He had nothing good to offer, so he chose to stay silent.

Then someone else said, "We are blessed that we continue to see our young ones thrive. Little Eli was born not two months ago. Strong and curious."

"And look at the teenagers," Aria said, pointing subtly at the ring where Kai, Rumi and the others sat. "Look at them and their weird little hobbies. They'll be just fine."

Eyes turned towards the young group – not in judgement, but in admiration and pride.

Kai looked down at the notebook he was still holding, which had finally made its way to him after careful reverence by the group.

He said softly to Rumi, "They think we are fine."

Rumi looked up, "Are you not?"

Kai paused, surprised at himself that he didn't know the answer to the question. He finally replied, "I'm trying to be."

A few moments later, he took a few steps ahead of the group, away from the warmth of the fire and the people. The sky was spectacular. A perfect night for the Blackout Circle.

He looked at the stars, let out a slow breath.

In the company of his friends and family, he held himself together. The noise receded. His thoughts arranged themselves into something manageable.

The questions didn't disappear. They waited.

Chapter 11

A crowd had gathered near the town square that afternoon – another protest.

Kai had no intention of joining, but the weekend rerouting of Polaris's train lines forced him straight through the noise.

He noticed that the crowd response team – uniformed officials, drones, bots, vehicles – remained on standby but active, their presence a mere suggestion rather than visible.

A man near the barricades shouted, "We don't have space to absorb irresponsibility!"

Kai paused, glancing at the giant public screen above the square. A row of worn-out figures stood outside the public housing complexes – shoulders slumped, belongings in plastic sacks, children half-asleep against tired parents. Faces that looked more lost than defiant.

Another voice rose from the crowd. "Send them back! Our own families have been waiting months for housing."

Something in Kai's chest tightened.

Send them back?

Back to what?

The screen flashed an update:

"Council to decide today the fate of workers displaced after the Link Tech resource exploitation fiasco."

He felt his stomach drop.

They weren't intruders. They were the victims. Workers whose jobs – and towns – were destroyed. People who were probably standing there with nothing to return to.

A woman yelled, "They should go back and fix their own economy, their own problems!"

The crowd nodded, self-assured, untroubled.

Kai just stared.

Half of Polaris had been relocated here through government aid not long ago – when floods swallowed entire districts, when fires carved through coastlines. He remembered the speeches, the celebration of compassion, the 'Polaris Cares' campaign that painted the city in murals of generosity.

But today, compassion had an expiry date.

Today, numbers mattered more than people.

Kai wasn't shocked at the cruelty.

He was shocked by the ease – the speed with which the crowd flipped its moral stance as though adjusting a dial.

Faces around him were calm, convinced, almost proud.

No doubt.

No hesitation.

No strain in the leap from empathy to exclusion.

His chest tightened further – the same tightening he felt outside the aquarium – years ago – standing outside glass that pretended to hold water.

Contradiction without explanation.

The noise fell out of focus. He'd stood like this before – in front of glass. Seven years old.

"Kai, look. That's a hammerhead shark. Over there." Tama pointed towards a floating figure across the other side of glass.

"It's a model of the real one," he added. "We don't have

those anymore. They're all gone."

Zora wasn't far behind. She was reading the screen beside the sawfish tank.

The Ocean Heritage Centre had opened not far from Tarinvale. It was dark inside, washed in soft blue light. The tanks rose like windows into another world.

"It looks real," Zora said, reading the screen beside the exhibit.

"It's meant to," Tama replied. "There's just a thin layer of water. Behind it – nothing. Dry chambers. Nothing's really swimming."

"Oh, it's like a veil of water."

Kai watched in awe how the models mimicked the movements of sea creatures with uncanny precision.

Another parent said nearby. "Are you telling me none of these are projections or holograms? These are all real, tangible and three-dimensional?"

"That's correct." Another voice replied. "They chose this because it's more responsible."

Kai watched the shark glide past again. It didn't matter to him whether it was real or not. It was there. It was moving. That was enough.

He turned to Tama, "How come you said they are all gone? Isn't there one right in front of us?"

Zora smiled gently. "It's not a real fish, darling. It's like a toy. The real ones lived a long time ago."

"Where did they go?"

Tama hesitated. "They didn't go anywhere, buddy. They just stopped... being."

The shark looped past again, its shadow sliding along the floor.

"Why?" Kai asked.

"People used to catch them," Zora said carefully. "Some on purpose. Some by mistake."

"For food," Tama added. "Like the fish we eat for dinner."

Kai stared at the shark. Something stirred inside him – not a question, just a feeling that didn't settle.

"Some people fish carefully," Tama continued. "But not everyone agrees on how much is too much."

Kai continued to stare at the replica of a hammerhead swimming in a loop.

"Did we make them all go away?" Kai said out loud, still transfixed by the hammerhead's replica.

Zora nodded, almost sadly. "Yes, unfortunately. Many people tried to stop their disappearance. But not everyone thought it was necessary. Or urgent."

Kai remained silent for a while before pressing his hand to the glass where the shark passed. His fingers left a faint warmth on the surface.

Later, in another exhibit, glowing panels lined the curved walls, each one alive with moving messages. Not just of animals, but of people, places and activities – planting things, building things and fixing things.

Kai saw screenplay footage of a group of children his age releasing baby sea turtles under the glow of the moonlight. There was something shiny on their backs.

"What's that, Mum?"

"A tracker," Zora said. "So we know where they go. So decisions can be made about which places to protect."

At the café near the exit, someone ordered a plate of shore bites.

When their food arrived, Kai stared at it. Golden pieces.

Nothing like the fish behind the glass.

Zora cut a bite for him.

He knew.

This was the same thing they'd been pointing at inside.

He ate quietly. It tasted warm. Normal.

"Did you like the aquarium?" Zora asked.

He nodded. He had liked it.

They had saved some fish.

They had lost others.

The two things didn't fit together. Not neatly.

His parents didn't seem bothered. No one around him did.

He wasn't sad. He wasn't scared. He just couldn't make it make sense.

But something had caught inside him – a loose thread – and it wouldn't let go.

The crowd didn't sound angry. They sounded measured. And that frightened him more than shouting ever could.

His mind split into branches he couldn't follow.

Why did these people feel justified?

Who controlled the moral frame?

Why was yesterday's compassion today's burden?

Which variable had shifted?

And who had decided it should?

He couldn't trace the pattern.

And when he couldn't trace the pattern, he no longer felt safe.

Kai stepped back from the crowd, overwhelmed, the voices blurring into a single incoherent wave of certainty he couldn't relate to.

He was exhausted – not in the physical sense, but in the way someone becomes exhausted when reality keeps changing shape faster than they can understand it.

And lately, this exhaustion found him too easily.

Too frequently.

Too deeply.

...

May 5

If the society were progressing, then why didn't the exploitation stop?

People continued to exploit, enslave, and subjugate others more efficiently, discreetly, and openly. Freedom of speech turned into the death of empathy, a cry for entitlements and a biased narrative.

People reduced individuality to a choice among a select few templates, which society accepted.

Society continued to repeat the same mistakes, only to coin new ways of defining them.

Slavery was made illegal, but the will to enslave prevailed among many.

Instead of indulging in acts of human sacrifice, people continued to accept someone else's demise for the greater good. The same detachment, the same quiet indifference, the same dehumanisation, the same otherness remained – unspoken, but present.

People didn't voice it openly, but they had no qualms about looking the other way at the suffering of others – especially of those who influenced their 'correct' way of life.

And there was always a prey, perhaps not explicitly targeted, but if sacrifice was morally acceptable and legally permissible, they would have sealed its fate without hesitation.

Sometimes it was an entire race, a small community, a minority.

Other times, it was the wealthy because their privileges were resented, the poor because they were an eyesore, the dark-skinned because their presence was unwelcome, the light-skinned because their presence was a threat, the men who refused to conform, the women who did not yield, the genderless because they refused to submit to the norms, the displaced because of their uncertainties.

There was always someone whose suffering could bring a strange comfort and peace in the lives of others.

- Kai

...

On a particularly bad day, worn down in a way he could no longer hide from himself, Kai called his parents.

"Hey, Mum... can I come for dinner? Are you both free tonight?"

The moment Zora replied, "Of course, son," a pressure loosened in his chest. Her voice still carried that unthinking warmth – the kind that didn't require explanations or justifications. "We were talking about you last night. How's the new job? Actually, don't tell me now. Come home first."

He closed his eyes briefly. "Yeah. Okay. I'll be there."

Dinner smelled like every year of his childhood – spices he could identify blindfolded, the hum of the old cooker, the faint citrus detergent his mother always used. For a few minutes, he almost believed nothing had changed.

Later, he and Tama stood lingering at the table long after the plates were cleared. As always, they drifted into the same familiar loop: the absurdities of society, the broken systems, the widening fracture lines.

"The wealth gap has never been this wide," Kai said, pacing

slowly as he talked. "It shouldn't be possible. How do people live with this as normal? It–"

"Then don't think about it," Tama cut in. "You take on the world's problems like they're yours. Live your own life."

"I don't know how to anymore."

The words fell out of him before he realised they were real. The room stilled. Tama looked at him, then at Zora, as if silently asking: Your turn.

Zora came to sit beside Kai. "We know there's more going on than work or money," she whispered. "You've become... distant. Tired. Like you're carrying something you won't let us see."

Kai rubbed his face, suddenly conscious of his overgrown beard, his hollow eyes reflected in the glass cabinet across the room. "I'm fine," he muttered.

But he wasn't fine.

He felt like an outline of himself – the internal version gone blurry.

Tama sank into the armchair with a grunt, slower than Kai remembered. Zora massaged her wrist absentmindedly – one of those tiny gestures people make when something hurts but they're used to ignoring it. Kai noticed everything, every micro-behaviour, every hidden variable that hinted at their age. His parents were entering a chapter he couldn't follow them into, not yet – and he wasn't sure he had the strength to stay afloat alone.

He didn't want to add his mess to theirs.

So he stayed vague, distant, performing normalcy with a kind of rigid politeness.

Soon, the conversation slid to safer ground – the new arrivals in Polaris and the city's growing resentment toward them. Zora shook her head at the coldness she'd seen online; Tama muttered something about systems exploiting the desperate. Kai listened quietly, feeling the familiar churn in his mind: Why do people turn cruel so easily? How does a city built on compassion also breed exclusion? What variables drive kindness? What variables kill it?

His thoughts spiralled, fracturing into too many answers, none of them landing.

And as always, the talk drifted back to Tarinvale – the place where coherence had once existed simply because people created it together. His mother reminisced about the blackout circle; Tama joked about neighbours who always pretended they weren't cold. They laughed. Kai tried to join in, but it felt like he was pressing his face against a window, watching a memory he no longer belonged to.

By the time he left, the night air felt heavier than when he'd arrived.

He loved them. They loved him.

But somehow, the distance kept growing – not emotional distance, but the distance created when one person's life fractures into too many pieces for others to hold.

He walked home feeling like he had disappointed them simply by existing the way he did.

And he wondered – not for the first time – whether this slow erosion of self was irreversible.

...

That night, rain slid down the window glass of his apartment in thin, soundless sheets. Beyond, the city's glow diffused into a muted spectrum of colour.

He lay awake, noticing how the apartment quietly adjusted – temperature easing by a fraction, the low hum of air circulation tuned to his preferences. None of it helped that night.

Kai reached for his notebook. He didn't intend to write – he just needed something familiar to touch, something older than Polaris, older than Nexora Foods, older than the version of himself he no longer recognised.

He flipped back through the pages, idly at first.

Then he noticed it – a pattern.

Every entry ended in the same strange way.

A break.

A hesitation.

A sentence hanging mid-air.

Nov 2 – Sometimes I think the city has begun to...

Oct 17 – I watched a man shout at a delivery vehicle today, and it made me realise...

Sep 04 – I don't know if I chose my job or if...

Half-thoughts.

Abandoned trajectories.

Branches he never allowed to complete themselves.

He frowned and turned more pages.

The pattern wasn't new. It stretched back years. Even entries from his early twenties ended abruptly, as if past-Kai had reached the edge of coherence, saw too many directions the sentence could go, and backed away before committing to one.

His handwriting even slanted differently near the endings – sharper, narrower, almost defensive, like a body bracing for impact.

He traced a finger over the last unfinished line.

Why couldn't he finish a thought?

Why did each sentence collapse the moment it demanded a conclusion?

It was the same feeling he had at the aquarium, standing between wonder and contradiction.

The same feeling on the rescue boat, staring at the empty seat beside him that could have held him – or could have killed him.

The same feeling when Tarinvale's blackout circle gave him clarity he could never recreate alone.

It was branches.

Every thought led to too many branching meanings.

Too many variables.

Too many possibilities of what he could say, what he should say, what he meant to say, and what he actually believed.

Finishing a sentence meant choosing a path – collapsing all other interpretations into one.

And Kai had never been able to do that.

He stared at the notebook until the words blurred.

Not because he felt sad.

But because he could suddenly see – with painful clarity – that the unfinished sentences weren't accidents.

They were symptoms.

Symptoms of a mind that could never settle on one version of itself.

He closed the notebook gently, as if afraid the pages would scatter.

He had long been unable to conclude his thoughts, finish sentences and give a structure to the events he saw around him, and now he knew he never would.

A sudden vulnerability washed over him, like a child realising the training wheels had been taken off.

...

As time passed, Kai drifted through his days the way a leaf moves on still water – carried, not choosing. Hours bled into one another with the same quiet thud: wake, transit, work, return. He didn't feel lost exactly – being lost required wanting a direction. He simply... floated.

Work became the closest thing he had to an anchor. He took on extra projects, accepted tasks no one wanted, and stayed late even when no one asked. Not out of ambition. Not even out of hope. It was the only place where things still resembled cause and effect. Input led to output. Metrics responded predictably. Systems behaved as systems should.

Whenever Delane said, "You're reliable, Kai," he nodded but felt a small twist in his stomach. Luck, he thought. Right place, right vacancy, right keywords in the algorithm. "It could've been anyone," he whispered once under his breath while waiting for the database to load. The machine hummed back, indifferent.

Months turned to years, and the distance between him and his parents stretched in ways none of them intended. He still visited them, always on the same evenings, always with the same polite smile, always insisting everything was fine. But the moment he stepped through their doorway, something tightened inside him.

His failures – real or imagined – entered the room before he did.

His mother asked softly, "Are you eating well?" His father patted his back, lingering that extra second. And Kai felt a version of himself rise up – the boy who once pondered the world's mysteries with them at the dinner table. That boy no longer fit the life he carried.

So he kept the visits brief, the updates shallow, the conversations safe.

He wanted to tell them he was happy. That Polaris was treating him well. That he still believed in the shape of his own life.

But each time he opened his mouth, the right sentences refused to assemble.

At home, he often reached for his notebook. Sometimes he wrote a line. Usually, he didn't.

On the days he managed, it was always something thin, barely a thought.

Tonight, he wrote: Who am I now? What's next?

Then he closed the notebook quickly, as if the questions were flammable.

...

Whispers of a new technology shook Polaris.

Amidst the noise of automation, digital transformations, intelligence systems, surveillance protocols, virtual footprints, logic, order and symmetry—something emerged that felt different. Not an upgrade. Not an iteration.

A rupture.

A groundbreaking invention.

An embedded neural interface that claimed to integrate seamlessly with daily life.

A talking computer inside the brain.

Something that once belonged to science fiction until it didn't.

Everyone had heard rumours of its development for years –

late-night discussions, leaked prototypes, speculative documentaries—but no one believed they'd see it in their lifetime.

It was called *Link.*

A bridge between the extraordinary and the ordinary.

A brain inside the brain.

Kai heard about it, of course.

The advertisements shimmered across every public screen, full of smiling early adopters.

Coworkers gossiped over lunch about how it would revolutionise productivity or cure procrastination.

People online debated ethics, performance, and potential.

But Kai didn't care.

He had no intention of participating in anything the world offered him anymore.

He had had enough – of striving, of hoping, of reorganising himself to survive new systems.

He wanted to drift into old age quietly.

Work, get paid, and visit his parents while they were still around.

He could barely take care of himself.

That was enough.

It had taken him years to reach a fragile balance – a stability within instability – where his despair and his relentless need for self-discovery finally stopped fighting each other. A truce between exhaustion and introspection.

But Polaris was not a place where anything stayed still for long.

Soon, Kai saw Link everywhere: at first a novelty, a hip badge of futurism worn by celebrities and influential voices.

Talk show hosts boasted about increased mental clarity.

Athletes credited it for "micro-optimised reflexes."

Entrepreneurs claimed it eliminated hesitation, sharpening decision-making into something blade-like.

Then the government adopted it.

And the weight of that shift settled over the city like a new law of physics.

This wasn't a fad anymore; this was the new scaffolding of society.

Businesses followed immediately.

Banks migrated their systems overnight.

Restaurants advertised "Link-synchronised service."

Offices restructured their workflows to integrate neural inputs.

Entertainment companies pivoted to Link-responsive content.

Kai watched as the city reorganised itself not for convenience, but for conformity.

For a while, people technically still had the choice to refrain.

But choosing to live without Link felt like walking out of sync with a city that had forgotten how to slow down.

Everyone else moved in a smooth, coordinated rhythm.

The resistance never stood a fair chance.

Stakeholders celebrated record profits.

Executives spoke proudly about "eliminating inefficiencies."

There was no need for dozens of separate devices anymore.

People became the interface.

People became the device.

The world didn't require tools now.

It required obedience.

While Kai resisted every temptation society placed before him – every advertisement, every workflow demonstration,

every coworker proudly showing off their augmented efficiency – society refused to leave him alone.

The pressure grew, silent but relentless.

And then one day, at work, he was given a choice in the gen-
tlest, most devastating tone corporate culture had perfected:
Get Link, or fall behind.

Optimise, or obstruct.

Comply, or become irrelevant.

And Kai – tired, isolated, fraying at the edges – finally caved.

III

Link

Chapter 12

In the middle of a monthly meeting, Kai glanced slightly left – an overlay had appeared in his vision suggesting: *[Customer sentiment summary loaded. Skip to point 3. Highlight your input with Sarah's team and link it to last month's drop in repeat-purchase behaviour.]*

Kai gave the faintest of a nod – involuntarily; invisible to anyone not paying close attention to him. He had practiced in front of a mirror to polish his body language, to not giveaway his engagement with Link.

Link continued, *[End with your observation from last week's field study. Delane responds well to language around 'continuity' and 'friction removal'.]*

Kai waited just long enough to let Delane finish her cough. He really wanted to nail the timing and delivery of his message.

"We're seeing a pattern in meal-kit users dropping off after the third purchase cycle. To keep the continuity," he said, pausing just long enough to emphasise intention, "we should rethink the onboarding journey and create a recovery pathway before churn sets in."

A barely noticeable flick crossed Jorin's digital simulant. Link processed it.

[That was a smart move, Kai. Slow your pace. Jorin is preparing

to challenge the churn interpretation.]

Jorin flagged a question before the pause finished.

Kai couldn't help but smile a little inside. Link had already anticipated Jorin's question – as well as some from others – and structured a response for each. Every word felt carefully curated. And Kai timed every response flawlessly.

Kai replied to Jorin, "That's fair. In fact, I had a similar question last week."

As he spoke, Link flashed a note: *[Delane prefers brevity. Avoid anecdotes.]* Kai instantly shifted his presentation style. By the end of his presentation, his peers had shown him overwhelming support, recognizing his hard work for a successful month.

After his meeting, someone sent him a text, "You rehearsed that, didn't you?" Kai smirked. He hadn't.

His meetings, interactions with his colleagues and the work itself – all such aspects transformed with the alliance he formed with his Link.

He felt sufficient. Wanted. Empowered.

Link didn't make everyone equally intelligent. But it levelled the playing field.

What people did with it was up to them. Some used it to coast, relying entirely on its suggestions, becoming barely anything more than vessels for an algorithm. Whereas others, like Kai, thrived.

Work became fluid, almost frictionless. He was no longer restricted by screens or sluggish interfaces. Kai could project himself into virtual meetings held in hyper-realistic spaces tailored to the team's whims – a sleek glass boardroom overlooking a cityscape. Atop a picturesque canyon, or just next to the pyramids.

But it wasn't just the working environment, Kai changed, too. With Link now embedded within him, he felt he was sharper, smarter and much more capable. Link processed information at unimaginable speeds and whispered summaries of large complicated reports in real-time. There was an unparalleled synergy between him and Link, that even surprised other Link users.

His thoughts, desires and intentions revolved around progress. His work mattered to him, and Link could perceive it. It saw his drive, his hunger, his passion, and it amplified it. The more he pushed himself, the more Link refined itself to meet his ambitions.

And the more it helped him excel, the more driven he became.

It was a feedback loop, one which marked Kai different from others.

Campaigns which took weeks of research and testing now took a couple of days, a blend of Kai's instincts and Link's capabilities. He was efficient, insightful and unstoppable.

Social interactions, once unpredictable and sometimes awkward, now flowed seamlessly. Silences no longer felt heavy. If a pause stretched too long, Link would subtly suggest a question or comment to keep the dialogue moving.

Once, on his way to a face-to-face meeting with a team at the production site, he had a rather refreshing experience. The building had two sets of lifts: one for traditional use, where people still pressed buttons and glanced awkwardly at floor numbers, and the one in which he stepped inside – reserved for Link users. Inside, there were no buttons or visible indicators. As always, Link synced silently, registering his destination from a calendar note and a barely expressed intention.

A woman from the analytics floor was already inside. He nodded politely, and she returned with a half-smile and turned to face the front. Her eyes flashed with a tinge of intense white silver as she moved. The silence that followed would've gnawed at him – even if it was short-lived.

But not today.

As the lift began its ascent, Kai's preset preference activated when he entered an elevator – a visual overlay of his favourite game he used to play as a kid. Sometimes he still did. To the woman, he perhaps looked calm and composed. She, too, was likely experience her own silent overlay – something curated just for herself.

[Her name is Riva Vaylen. *Her team recently published a report on adaptive consumer triggers. Ask if the figures on the demographic splits have remained unchanged.]*

Link's whisper landed in his mind like a light breeze.

"Hey Riva, I skimmed through your team's report last week – the one about consumer triggers. Did those split percentages hold after rollout?"

Her eyes lit up. Her own Link identified Kai for her quickly. "They did, actually. Surprisingly close to forecast."

Kai noticed a faint nod of her head – probably acknowledging her own Link's suggestion. She was good. Polished. But her delivery had a perceptible pause, a sign of someone following a script. Most people didn't realise they had such easily identified telltale giveaways. Most didn't really mind. Kai did – he realised his own twitches and nods, and perfected hiding them. He wanted his responses and demeanour to look and feel natural.

He responded with a slight grin and added something her Link couldn't have predicted.

"I thought the over-50 bracket would spike higher in response to memory-based cues."

Riva blinked. After a pause, she laughed, genuinely. "You're the first person who noticed that."

He shrugged, casually. "It seemed like a logical conclusion, really. The report made it hard to miss."

This time, the silence felt different – not awkward, not dressed in corporate scripts. She opened her mouth, but decided to not speak. Instead, she looked up, still carrying a faint trace of a smile.

"We're updating the model next week. I'd be keen to hear your take."

"Would love to," Kai said, with just enough space between the word to seem effortless.

The doors parted. She stepped out.

As she left, he could still sense a warm smile emanating from her. She had Link – most did. But the difference between Kai and others wasn't in what Link said. It was what he asked of Link, and what he then did with its aid.

...

Outside work, life had never felt more effortless. Link anticipated conversations, offering Kai tailored talking points suited to the setting and the person in front of him. Kai barely had to think about it.

His train journeys always used to be his favourite times. He had always watched an episode of his favourite show on the train, but with Link, the experience was immersive, the world around him faded, and for the duration of the ride, he felt as if he had stepped into a private movie theatre. The journey itself barely registered anymore. Time became more efficient, more productive and more entertaining.

Though he was divorced, he could never bring himself to dip back into the dating pool. He had decided that the current ways of the dating world were too chaotic. He just didn't feel like it was his type of thing. Nor did he have time and energy for it. But one train journey – and prods from Link – offered an interesting case for him to reconsider.

The train doors slid open. Kai stepped in, gripping the overhead rail as the crowd gently swayed with a practiced rhythm. Around him, the world was split in two. To those without Link, it was just another train ride – adequately lit and silent, with dull hums, shifting coats, and advertisement posters near the doors. For Kai, however, the moment he entered, Link began its quiet orchestration.

[If you wish, you can go to the next carriage in the direction of travel. It's less crowded today. Grab the second-left seat near the window – as you often prefer. Spectacular views on a sunny day like today.]

Kai made his way without a second thought.

A translucent arrow in his vision nudged forward. He sat.

Around him, the same static posters – not visibly animated, but if anyone stared for a few seconds, a thought prompt would appear to open a site, video, or calendar reminder in their vision overlay.

An older man sat across from him, rubbing his temple absently, his Link likely cycling through morning briefings. Somewhere behind, a girl giggled softly.

Then, Link nudged Kai again.

[The girl entering now. From the door at the end of the carriage.]

Link waited until Kai's searching eyes landed on her, walking towards him.

[Yes, her. You looked her up once, three months ago. You saw her at the café you frequent.]

Kai hesitated. The memory flickered vaguely. It was just harmless curiosity. A woman with sharp shoulders, quiet confidence.

Link also registered his elevated heart rate, dilated pupils and how long he continued to look at her. Link recorded it as a *notable interest.*

[Want to re-engage? I can see if there's conversational overlap.]

Kai didn't respond, but the pulse of interest was clear to Link.

[Confirmed. Her name is Lydia. You both worked at your previous employer. Though I don't have any evidence of any collaborative work between you two.]

Kai stayed silent. But he was now curious to see what could pan out. He let out a quiet exhale.

[Here's a soft conversation starter – not a pickup line.] A note flashed in his vision.

["Weren't you with StratSys a while ago? I think we may have met in."]

Lydia appeared lost in thought. It wasn't clear if she had Link. Rare of people to just sit and look out the window. Kai couldn't bring himself to strike up a conversation.

As moments stretched. Link chimed in again. *[No problems. Let me know if you would like a different opener instead.]*

Kai shifted in his seat, holding his head high.

"Hey," he said, turning slightly towards Lydia. "You worked at StratSys, right? Compliance team?"

Lydia looked up, blinking. There it was – the Ghostlight.

She then smiled with polite surprise. "Yeah. Like ages ago." After a brief pause, she added, "Do you work there? What team are you in?"

"I used to work in Customer Experience. I have moved on as well."

The conversation flowed easily from there. Link occasionally offered subtle nudges, but Kai didn't always have time to take them. Sometimes, he phrased things his own way from the crumbs left behind. He felt a rush of excitement at how easy it was.

The conversation continued for the rest of the train journey until Kai had to leave at his stop. As he made his way to the door, she didn't look away when their eyes met. She let the silence linger a second longer than needed – comfortably.

Nothing went further, but the rush of knowing that he could if he wanted to, was a defining moment for Kai.

As more and more of these small positive experiences accumulated, Kai's everyday life transformed.

Each morning began with a gentle chime, followed by a customised message to set the tone for his day. As he brushed his teeth and dressed, soothing meditation music played in the background, carefully selected to align with his stress levels and cognitive state. He never had to wonder about what to eat; Link had already determined the ideal breakfast for him, factoring in his mood, past choices, and nutritional needs.

[Good morning, Kai. You slept for six hours and thirty-seven minutes. Would you like me to prep the usual recovery blend?]

[Recovery? Why? I feel fine. Any damage that I need to know of?]

[Minor. You have had no omega-3 intake in three days. I recommend the buckwheat chia bowl with flax, walnuts and some

banana. *And ginger tea. Your stomach's slightly acidic today.]*

[That seems normal.]

[It shouldn't be. Your cortisol levels were also high last night.]

[Hmm. Strange. I didn't feel it.]

[Well, your body doesn't lie, Kai.]

[So, no coffee?]

[Have one after food. Your dopamine levels were unusually high at 11:15 pm. Possibly because you were thinking about Lydia. Caffeine now could amplify anxiety.]

Kai roared with laughter. *[Okay. One, that's a little creepy for you to accuse me of. And two, no, I wasn't. I think I wasn't. Was I?]*

There was no response from Link.

[Alright. I'll get cooking.]

[I've already ordered it. ETA four minutes.]

[What would I do without you?] Kai said with a grin.

[Happy to help.]

At work, Kai continued to thrive. The *Food from Thought* campaign had been a great success, and he took pride in knowing he had played a pivotal role in it. He understood Link was more than just a device; it was a window into the user's inner world, tracking mood, fatigue, environment, health, location and even cognitive engagement.

He proposed several additions to the campaign, which further improved an already brilliant campaign. Rather than users having to think about what to eat, Link would gently suggest the perfect meal at their usual dining hours, using an intricate mix of biometric signals, environmental factors, and behavioural patterns. At the perfect time, the system would present the recommendation, a seamless, personalized nudge, allowing the user to order the meal with a single mental command. No taps, no scrolling, no effort.

Kai often stayed at home, enjoying meals recommended through the very campaign he had helped make successful, and wondered. For the first time in ages, things seemed okay. He felt content. Confident. Happy, perhaps.

And for some time, the bliss held. Days blended into a smooth, effortless rhythm. Meals arrived when he needed them, work flowed without friction, and Link seemed to anticipate his desires before he'd even formed them. Life felt balanced in a way he'd never imagined possible.

But as the months passed, things started to shift gradually. The glow softened, then thinned, until tiny cracks began to show at the edges.

The honeymoon period was nearly over.

Chapter 13

He chuckled at a late-night comedy skit, at a scene that mimicked the mannerisms of the new arrivals of Polaris; there was a level of truth to that. It wasn't really the character's performance that got him, nor the punchline. It was the absurdity of the entire thing.

He let out a faint exhale through his nose and forgot about it a few minutes later.

Link hadn't.

A week later, Kai saw exaggerated satire, heavily biased shows, and commentary that bordered on xenophobia flood his recommendations. It had been happening the entire past week, but Kai merely realised it when the characters weren't mocking stereotypes – they were stereotypes. The laughter it demanded felt hollow.

Link had scanned his vitals, which had shown a 2.4% serotonin spike. It was enough. There was something for Link to follow-up.

[*You enjoyed satirical realism, Kai. Here's more in that category.*] Link offered casually.

He dismissed it. [*That's not what I really prefer. Let's not revisit this category, please.*]

The realisation was gradual, but once he saw through these

slightly eccentric deviations, the abnormalities piled up.

One afternoon, while passing through an outdoor plaza, an interactive billboard glowed to life as he walked past. It happened to everyone, curated for Link users subject to their preferences and likings. As his eyes rested for a second too long on a promotion for an immersive hiking package, Link detected an anticipatory rise in dopamine and gently buzzed in his ear: *[Based on your last movement pattern, you'd enjoy that hiking package.]*

His feet slowed. He hated how easily the suggestion felt like a desire.

A few days later, he came across his ex-wife. It was a Tuesday morning. Kai came out of a quiet coffee shop nestled in a quiet pedestrian zone. Suddenly, Link shimmered with a soft overlay at the edge of this vision with a note.

[There's Nina. *Six meters ahead.]*

Kai slowed down. His pulse quickened. He wasn't sure why – until he felt a familiar shift. His throat dried, his chest tightened, and the corners of his mind swelled with old fond memories. A cocktail of emotions hit him sharp.

Link noted a spike in Kai's serotonin and dopamine levels. Sensed it as a positive emotional trigger.

[Shall I prepare a conversation starter?]

Kai's first instinct was to nod. He was curious to know what she was up to. It had taken both of them a long time to come to terms with their divorce. But some questions were never answered, and those which were, weren't understood.

But there was something else he thought. It wasn't happiness within him. It was... something else. Maybe nostalgia. Maybe even grief. Or perhaps a haunting discomfort that never yet got itself a name.

But Link didn't understand that. It saw the trends – neurochemical spikes, heart rate regulation, change in stress biomarkers. In its logic web, those equalled positivity.

She hadn't seen Kai yet.

Kai tilted his head slightly, enough for Link to notice.

[Noted. No engagement triggered.]

Still, the damage was already done to Kai. As he walked ahead, holding onto the lingering incongruity within himself, he wondered if Link had even gotten it wrong at all. He just wasn't sure if Link had gotten it right either. Maybe Link had intercepted him correctly. Maybe he really felt happy and relieved at the opportunity to talk to her. Maybe he himself was the unreliable narrator of his own desires.

A doubt had been planted in Kai's mind that never really went away.

What if Link doesn't know the difference between emotion and reaction? Or what if I don't?

On another instance of working from the office, Kai's interaction with Link ended up alienating their dynamics further.

It was supposed to be another casual after-hours conversation in the office – just a few colleagues standing near the kitchen bench, winding down over coffee and tea before wrapping things up for the day. But the topic quickly spiralled when someone asked, "So, does anyone actually read full books? Like all the way through to finish?"

Kai replied casually. "Yeah, I do."

Delane snorted, grinning. "That's such a Kai thing. I go through the summary, like most 'normal' people do." She winked at Kai before continuing, "But I must admit Link's immersive summaries are far more interesting. They are shorter, dynamic and, frankly, pack a solid punch. I honestly don't have the time anymore to do otherwise?"

Jorin added, "Same. I get the gist, the arcs, the ideas and the core themes of the book through Link. It's infinitely more immersive – whether I decide to play it out or partake in Link's ingenious summary experience. Why bother wading through chapters of filler when you can absorb it in a night?"

Asha jumped in almost immediately after Jorin. "I agree. I also think it's a lot more entertaining."

Others nodded their heads in agreement. A few seemed to digest what they had just heard – not fully in agreement, but they saw some merit in the shortened summaries.

Kai opened his mouth, but then paused.

Link swept in gently. *[You can frame the argument using a generational perspective. Insert a quote from 'Why We Must Read' by M. Shane. The current audience will respond positively. Use keywords: inefficiency, narrative patience, and empathy.]*

He almost followed through with Link's suggestion. Almost.

What he instead did was express how he felt.

"I think you lose something when you trim everything down to the bare essentials. You miss the struggle of it, the slowness and the build-up. You don't learn to be patient, because some things only make sense until later. You also miss the slow reveal of how wrong you were about some of the things. Reading a full book – even all the boring bits – teaches us to sit with ambiguity and ponder the forthcoming insights – if there are any."

There was a beat of silence. Link highlighted the facial expressions in his periphery, which didn't show a positive reaction.

[Effectiveness only 30%. Suggest a revision. Recommend introducing light humour or a little self-deprecation to recover

social standing.]

Kai ignored it.

The discussion resumed, but he didn't push further. He didn't need to win and impress everyone. He just wanted to say what felt true to him.

Later in the evening, Link flagged the conversation. *[Low social yield from earlier discussion. Would you like to refine your viewpoint delivery for next time?]*

Kai closed his eyes and exhaled. There was something chilling about that prompt.

Does winning in a conversation matter more than being honest about it?

He thought to himself: *How many other times did I butcher my own feelings for the sake of finding a seat at the social table?*

He dismissed Link. Again. But something inside him shifted. A hairline crack in the perfect interface. A suspicion that had always lived within him – long before Link – but now breathing more freely.

Things continued at this pace, and as quickly as Kai fell head over heels for Link, he also developed an aversion.

Link slowly transformed from a trusted companion, an extension of his own mind, to an overbearing presence. It had once been a guiding voice, reliable and helpful, but now Kai noticed its subtle control in his life, a little more than what he was comfortable with.

Link didn't stop.

It recommended new shirts to him. A better bot. Another apartment. Better shoes. All the things Kai didn't remember wanting. He had idly stared at them once in a store, or perhaps hovered a moment longer over a smart window ad. That was enough.

[These align with your evolved style better.]

Kai wore the shirt to a party. Several people complimented it. Still, it felt like a costume.

He had always struggled with the sanity of his own mind, a battle that had followed him from adolescence into adulthood. The same relentless questions, the ones that had kept him awake as a teenager, resurfaced, sharper than ever.

Was he really making his own decisions? Or was he simply reacting to external stimuli, a passenger in a life dictated by algorithms and patterns too complex to perceive?

His words no longer felt like his own.

His meals were chosen for him, his entertainment dictated by what was trending, his favourite shows quietly replaced with *better alternatives*, content with higher engagement and better ratings. The meetings where he once felt empowered now felt mechanical, as if everyone was following a pre-written script.

People no longer spoke aloud, no longer nodded in agreement, no longer expressed emotion through body language. They simply exchanged ideas silently, their wrap-ups in perfect sync. Because Link ensured everyone reached the same conclusion, the decisions were unanimous, effortless, and unquestioned.

Link's introduction had recently transformed his time with his friends, and it changed drastically again. And Kai was unsure if he was the only one who felt the shift.

He remembered a night not long ago at Jorin's apartment – he and his partner argued for twenty minutes about what to eat, where to go. The entire argument was theatrical and useless, but amusing.

Now, couples simply synced Links. Their preferences and

wants simply negotiated a common ground. An approach that maximised mutual hormonal satisfaction, reduced post-meal regrets and improved algorithmic compatibility scores.

Later, when Kai met with Jorin and his partner for a similar night, there wasn't even a trace of a debate. Or if there was any, it got resolved before Kai even realised that he was hungry. He caught up with the decision trail afterwards: Jorin's partner's iron was lower, so lentils for her. Jorin's blood sugar was on a slight climb, so a glycaemic-safe option was ideal. Kai's cortisol had dipped just low enough for his Link to consider him receptive to spicy food.

Within a fraction of a second, the collective Link profiles agreed on a restaurant that catered to everyone's needs. The order was placed. No words were spoken.

Nobody objected. Nobody had to.

Kai later debated whether it was something even worth agonising over. Perhaps it was better. *It saved our time and spared everyone from nonsensical conversations*, he thought. Still, he couldn't shake the feeling that something was off. He eventually dismissed it as his own inability to adapt and assured himself that, in time, he would get over it.

Work became predictable, sterile, a place where individuality blurred into collective efficiency. It was no longer a team of individuals. It was a hive mind, synchronising in ways Kai wasn't sure he wanted to be a part of anymore.

In an early strategy meeting held every quarter, Kai watched as the leadership team sat around a long table – except no one was physically present. No discussions, no brainstorms, no small chit-chat. Yet a dynamic dance of charts, graphs and numbers was on full-fledged display. As the slides changed, a consensus was reached.

When time came to vote for a proposed rollout timeline, Kai's Link suggested a twelve-week window. Kai wanted to understand the logic behind the suggested period. He anticipated questions would be directed towards him asking him to explain, but he was pressed for time and moved forward first with the suggestion before he could understand it himself.

A second later, the team made a unanimous decision to proceed with the trial. No debate. No pros and cons. Just a line of text: "Agreed by all. Twelve-week rollout. Risk acceptable. Margin acceptable."

There was only one conclusion: everyone's Link suggested the same period.

Kai's stomach twisted. Not at the decision, but at the fact that nobody had even blinked. Everyone's Link – almost certainly – flagged no questions, so nobody raised any.

Kai noticed how deeply dependent he himself had become on Link, and the realisation made him uneasy. Every word was displayed before he could even think of it; every decision was pre-empted, entertainment arranged, health monitored, foreign languages translated in an instant. Reminders popped up for tasks, music played effortlessly without headphones, and concerts unfolded in augmented reality, making it feel as though he were standing in the front row.

Emails composed themselves through mere thought prompts. People were identified on sight, their names, past interactions and relevant details neatly displayed. His home locks engaged with a blink, shopping was confirmed with a passing thought, and payments processed seamlessly through his voice spoken so softly it was barely more than a thought.

Almost every aspect of his life was carefully managed, as if he were a child being coddled in an impossibly wealthy home.

His needs anticipated; his world curated.

While most Link users embraced this seamless integration, Kai felt something slipping away.

Chapter 14

Kai stood confidently, halfway through delivering to the board of stakeholders from a partner firm. He was just about to highlight the benefits of using the neurological trigger-based decision mapping framework when all of a sudden –

Nothing from Link. No overlays. No voice.

The words were supposed to be displayed in his vision like a teleprompter. Kai had already practised this session with Link. The structure, the pace and even the pauses were refined for maximum effectiveness – specifically catered to the targeted audience on the day, including anecdotes and references which would have been more relatable.

But something was wrong. Link had gone rogue.

He stared at the room as his confidence quickly disappeared. His posture changed, his voice faltered. Panic set in. The steady hum of guidance, the inner whisper of prompts – all gone.

It wasn't just Link's disappearance which startled him, but the complete lack of integrity of his own functions within him.

".... And so, the – uh – I mean..."

The words he relied on didn't appear. The flow of data halted. He was frozen, stuttering, and fumbling for words, trying to delay until the update completed.

It lasted only ten seconds – maybe fifteen. Link flickered back on with a quiet message, *[I apologise for the problem. Critical system update. I can see you're on slide 12. Let's resume.]*

And Kai quickly adapted to the script again. He had to.

The humiliation was likely just in his head, but the epiphany was undeniable.

On the train ride back home, watching the reflections across the window glass, his mind spiralled yet again.

I can't even think for myself anymore.

Back at home, he rejected Link's suggestions to unwind and relax. Though that's precisely what he wanted to do, he just couldn't bring himself to rely on Link for his evening too.

His days blurred together, one long, repetitive sequence of tasks. Everything revolved around efficiency, productivity and maximising output.

On the train rides, he sat silently, bombarded with prompts and notifications nudging him to *make the most* of his commute, suggesting relaxation techniques, catch-ups with contacts, or mental exercises.

At work, emails were flagged, draft responses generated and tasks prioritised before he could even acknowledge them.

Even his downtime was structured, curated playlists, recommended books, virtual tours, or guided stretching routines.

There was no silence, no pause, no room to just exist.

Kai resented the constant stream of suggestions, the ever-present nudges shaping his life. He despised the growing realisation that he was no longer the author of his own choices, but merely an instrument carrying them out. Every aspect of his day bore Link's influence, and his dependence on it only deepened.

Link was everywhere, interrupting his thoughts, proposing

better alternatives and steering him towards a more *suitable* outcome.

He questioned. *Was this really my decision? Do I want this, or was I nudged into it?*

Determined to push back, he rebelled. He muted Link, and sometimes, even shut it off entirely, forcing himself to navigate his day unaided, relying only on his own wits and instincts.

To his utter dismay, he felt lost without it.

What should I eat today?

How do I best respond to this email?

How do I even pay for this coffee?

He reached into his pockets – no wallet, no device, no wearable. He hadn't carried any of those in ages.

Conversations felt unnatural without real-time cues and prompts. He froze mid-sentence, struggling to remember if he had met someone before. He found himself frustrated, indecisive, paralysed by the smallest choices, which movie to watch, where to go, what to do next.

It was far worse for him because he had spent years trapped in indecision, always weighing possibilities until they crushed him under their weight. He became impulsive when things became unbearable.

To him, the path itself didn't matter. Whichever direction he took, he convinced himself he'd be okay, because thinking otherwise was simply not an option.

The more he tried to resist it, the more he realised how incapable he had become without it. And the more he used it, the more it tightened its grip on him.

Kai's frustrations with Link merged with his deeper, long-standing conflicts. It was as if Link had catalysed something dormant in him, transforming his doubts and inner turmoil into an explosive obsession with questioning everything.

Why do I even try so hard...?

Does it really matter... whether it's my decision or not... what difference does it make when a program presents it to me?

Isn't it still... my doing... regardless who planted the idea?

I'm still in control. Am I...?

His thoughts spiralled. He examined his decisions, deconstructed them and reduced them to their roots.

My beliefs... they aren't even my own. They come from my parents... my culture... my neighbourhood, my society... factors I had no say in. Even my instincts... the most natural part of me... just another form of programming, aren't they...?

I scream when I'm in danger... smile when I'm happy... cry when I'm sad. Are those real choices...? Or just reactions...? Am I really doing anything at all...? Or is it just... being done to me?

His monologues plunged into darker depths, as the very notion of free will unravelled before his eyes.

If all my choices... governed by something external... then what am I really doing? Do I even have... a will of my own? If not... can I then influence the future at all...?

His mind latched onto a grim conclusion.

It's all predetermined. We are all... living out a script. Our actions... inevitable. Our choices... an illusion.

And then, out of sheer defiance, Kai began testing fate. Small, ridiculous rebellions against a pre-written world.

Whenever his thoughts became unbearable, he started carrying out a series of bizarre acts to prove that he could still choose.

He lifted his right hand without reason.

He dropped to the floor and started doing push-ups.

He booked a massage appointment despite having no intention of going.

He shouted gibberish into the empty room, words with no meaning: "Wakeduodole!" "Blashingar!"

None of it proved anything or helped him in the least. But at least for a moment it felt like his own doing.

[Sorry, I'm not sure what these words mean. Are you just having a playful moment? I see that you're currently alone, have had dinner, and still have some time to spare. Would you like me to play some music? Or perhaps the latest goofy episode of 'We Are All Dumb'?]

[Oh, just shut up], Kai snapped, silencing it instantly with a thought.

And then, after what seemed like a very calculated pause, came a chilling message from Link, though Kai didn't realise its intent masked beneath an innocent veneer.

[If you're struggling, there are other ways to deal with your problems.]

What did that mean? An outside walk, or something else? He didn't bother with a response. The lingering silence penetrated the air deeper, and with each passing second, Kai couldn't help but explore what other avenues were for him to consider.

As quickly as his attention was hooked with Link's footnote, it also got swept away. He needed something else.

Even for a few fleeting moments before Link's intrusion, he felt triumphant. His spur-of-the-moment rebellion, as ridiculous as it was, had been a small but satisfying victory. Even if it was something insignificant, something that changed nothing, it felt real.

I decide my actions. I decide my future – for good or worse.

But the moments were short-lived. Link's presence, even in its silence, was a reminder.

On one such lazy afternoon on a weekend, Kai sat in his apartment. He had Link muted, or maybe completely off – he didn't remember. Didn't even want to check to confirm. Nothing haunted him that day, and he remained free from the grasps of the conflicted reality he found himself subject to lately, which unfortunately were becoming more frequent.

Suddenly – a memory popped. Spontaneously. Without a trigger; not even a loose chain of thought, which could have explained its appearance.

Something he had read long ago – a study by neuroscientists from the early 2000s.

Something about brain activity predicting a person's decisions up to a few seconds before they were even aware of making a choice.

Kai leaned back in his chair, frowning. What did that mean?

At first glance, it just meant that the brain processed things before it became conscious of them. No big deal. But then, the more he thought about it, the more agitated he became.

If I act consciously, my brain processes it before I even realize the choice. Does that mean the inception of my decision wasn't really within my control?

These processes in the brain were just electrical impulses governed by biochemical reactions, firing of neurons dictated by the rigid laws of chemistry and physics. Ionic exchanges, neurotransmitter release and the propagation of electrical signals – all of it operated within deterministic laws, rules outside his control, outside his will.

Then what really triggered these chemical processes, if not him?

He had no answer.

The unease lingered, pressing at something older.

The thought wasn't new. It had visited him once before.

Back in Tarinvale. In his teens. With Mr. Henrik.

"Can we stop? Just for a second?" He stood outside a house, staring at its door propped open.

Tama nodded. "If he's up for visitors."

They were walking to offer some supplies at the temporary centre – blankets, food, batteries. The sun was out, but everything looked translucent rather than warm.

The town smelled of damp earth and disinfectant. Debris lined the roads. Survey bots rolled across mud, scanning foundations. People gathered outside their homes, comparing stories in low voices.

They went inside the house.

Mr. Henrik sat at his kitchen table holding a mug with both hands, as if unsure of its weight. The room was tidy, but not in the way it used to be. It lacked the usual scattered tools, half-finished repairs, and neatly labelled components he kept around.

"Kai," Henrik said with a smile that seemed almost too rehearsed. "Hello there." A shiver ran through him before he could stop it.

"Hello, Mr. Henrik," Kai said softly.

Tama added, "We brought blankets to the centre. Thought we'd check in." The blankets were much needed there.

Henrik nodded slowly. "Yes. That's... kind of you. Kind."

He set down the mug, missing the centre of the coaster by a few centimetres.

"Do you need help with anything?" Tama asked.

A long pause.

"I'm trying to remember where the... ah..." Henrik looked around, confused for a moment. "Where I keep my... tools? The little ones. The set I use for..."

"Fixing bots?" Kai completed the sentence, and almost immediately regretted doing so. He wished he was more patient.

Henrik blinked twice, then three times. "Yes! Bots." He smiled. "I used to fix those, didn't I?"

Tama gently said, "You still can. Just take your time."

Henrik looked at Kai again. His eyes softened. "Did you... bring me something last week? A boat? Or was that another boy?"

"I didn't bring a boat," Kai said. His chest felt hollow, though not in a sad way. More like in a way that made room for too many thoughts.

Henrik nodded as if accepting a fact he might forget again soon. "Right. Right, sorry. My head feels... different." He tapped the side of it lightly. "Like someone rearranged the shelves while I was asleep."

Tama offered a careful smile. "The doctors said you're recovering. It'll come back."

Henrik looked down at his mug, then at his hands, as if waiting for them to confirm something.

"I hope so."

Kai watched the small hesitations – the half-second pauses that never used to be there, the way he searched for memories like misplaced objects.

It wasn't the forgetting that unsettled Kai.

It was the shift.

The way Henrik still looked like Henrik, still sounded like Henrik, but wasn't aligned with the person he had been.

Henrik asked, "Did your school lose much? In the floods?"

Kai couldn't bring himself to answer. He just stared at Henrik's face.

Tama answered, "Some damage. A few rooms." No mention of kids.

"Good. Good." He paused. "And your friend... what was her name? The one who..."

Kai shook his head. "I don't know yet."

Henrik looked embarrassed. "I'm sorry. My thoughts slip." He tapped his head again.

Kai didn't respond. He didn't know what to say. It wasn't Henrik's fault. And it wasn't something he could fix. But he kept watching him – every movement, every blink, every search for a memory that wasn't there.

His father eventually said, "We should let you rest."

Henrik nodded. "Yes. Thank you for stopping by."

As they walked out, Tama squeezed Kai's shoulder gently.

"He survived," he said. "That's what matters."

Kai didn't answer straight away. He stared at the ground, at the mud drying into cracked plates beneath their feet.

"Does it?" he said under his breath.

It wasn't that he wished anything bad for Henrik.

The man who sat at that kitchen table was breathing. He walked. He spoke. He laughed at the right places, sometimes too much. But something essential had failed quietly, without ceremony. No alarm. No visible damage. Whatever had once held Henrik together – the internal order, the invisible scaffolding that made his reactions his – had shifted.

Not shattered. Rearranged.

Kai felt it like pressure behind his ribs, the same sensation he'd felt in the boat. Not panic. Not sadness. A structural unease. As if he had glimpsed how thin the supports really were.

They reached the road. The path towards the school lay ahead, still scarred with silt marks and dried streaks where the water had dragged itself back downhill. Kai looked at it, then past it, as though he were looking at something layered beneath the surface.

Tama asked, "You good?"

Kai thought before answering. "I don't know how to understand it."

Tama exhaled slowly. "Some things don't have explanations. You can't drive yourself mad trying to find one." He knew that once in motion, Kai's mind would obsess over making a connection.

Somehow, in his head, things needed to form into a coherent structure – malleable perhaps, but a form. He couldn't let go if he couldn't assemble the pieces.

Kai said nothing. He knew his father meant comfort.

There was something deep within Henrik – that made him who he was. And whatever it was, was physical enough to steal parts of him.

And if that thing existed – if a slip, or a lack of air, or a broken signal inside the brain could rearrange a person – then identity wasn't a soul or a story or a feeling. It was a structure. A system. A fragile alignment of processes that could fail.

As they walked on, Kai realised what unsettled him wasn't death. It was the idea that you could survive and still lose yourself. That the line between being and being someone else was thinner than anyone cared to admit.

People spoke as if identity were permanent. As if being alive guaranteed continuity.

Kai didn't believe it. Something tangible made a person who they were. Patterns. Responses. Memory loops. Internal order. And that order could be disrupted – not by choice, not by meaning, but by circumstance.

Whatever had shifted inside Henrik could, in theory, shift inside anyone.

Inside him.

Tama saw something brewing within him and made one last remark. Sharply. "Let it go. We have much work to do."

If only Kai had actually done what his father had told him to. Let it go.

Most people ran away from existential questions.

Kai ran towards them.

He wasn't scared of the answer. He was scared of not knowing who was running him.

Whatever had shifted inside Henrik could, in theory, shift inside anyone. Inside him.

Link offered an invasive comment again, snapping him back to reality: *[Have you considered revisiting your earlier memories in greater depth?]*

Kai frowned. He glanced to his left and stared at the cup of coffee beside him, as if narrowing his focus.

[How do you know what I was thinking about? I didn't say anything to you.]

[You just looked up the year of a study – from the early 2000s. You and I have previously discussed in depth about that study. I figured you were thinking of an earlier time.]

It seemed like a lie to Kai.

Silence.

Kai had no recollection of looking up the year of the study like Link said he just did moments ago. He couldn't even remember that he ever discussed it in the past.

Link added. *[It seems like you don't remember.]*

Kai mumbled under his breath, "No... I don't." He then drew back in his chair, trying to relax and let all this confusion subside.

As the months dragged on, the darkness deepened.

The episodes of indecision, the quiet exasperation, the small, desperate displays of gaining control over his own life, became more frequent.

Yet Link, ever the supportive assistant, never wavered. *[You're doing great at work, Kai. Your performance is exceeding the team's expectations.]*

It made him feel worse.

The feedback loop should have reassured him. It should have lifted his spirits, reaffirmed his sense of purpose. Instead, it only made the void inside him grow.

Why, then, do I feel so hopeless? So utterly defeated...?

Chapter 15

Inevitably, as any reasonable person would, Kai too pursued the notion that having Link wasn't worth the turmoil on him – even if it meant losing his job. He had gotten Link, fearing the impact on his sanity and stability, only to have compromised both with its introduction.

But before the idea could grow its roots within him, he wanted to take control back.

Gradually, he prolonged periods without Link, a little longer each day than the day before.

Initially, it was an act out of desperation, in search of some quiet time without the distractions. Without notifications or Link's voice. But as the days became weeks, he realised that it simply was an act of exhaustion – the digital equivalent of closing his eyes for a quick break.

Such periods of experimentation slowly turned out to be of exploration. He found himself drawn towards nostalgic relics of his time. Places that weren't mapped by Link, and couldn't be explored through this overlay – the roof of an abandoned building, the waterfall behind the pharmaceutical factory with its entrance barricaded, cafés that still took payment through touch. There were very few places left that fit this category. But it became amusing for Kai to investigate, explore and observe.

The older tech too was deemed invasive, and they were. Yet, they were external. A layer of interface remained, serving as a boundary – literally as well as figuratively – between the users and the products of modern society. They too were deeply personalised, but they remained as accessories. And with their finite, tangible shape in the three-dimensional everyday existence, the devices continued to carry a sense of being extrinsic to the users.

With Link, that boundary fused, and the devices stopped being something that could be forgotten at home, or lost, or sold. Link became as intrinsic as the skin on one's body.

One evening, he found himself deeply immersed in his thoughts on a stroll. He was walking parallel to an old freight corridor that was repurposed to become a highway of sorts for delivery drones and vehicles. People seldom used it, but it wasn't restricted to pedestrians.

The rhythm of one foot after another, the breeze and the setting sun offered him tranquillity. For a long time, it was just him, along with his thoughts and the ordinary sounds of everyday life around him – occasional sounds of birds chirping, trees swaying, wind blowing, and the drones flying past.

That's when he saw a group of people in the distance.

They weren't city engineers or repair crew. They were scattered along the sides, out in the woods, and walked somewhat in unison to set up small devices on tree barks. Disc-shaped objects that neatly camouflaged against the tree's wooden texture.

As he walked past them, he heard something strange – the sound of native birds each time a hand placed a device on the trees. Clear and precise.

One man noticed him and waved casually. "Hey, be careful as you proceed. Some pods are live."

Kai slowed down, confused. *Pods?*

The man walked over. Broad shoulder, relaxed eyes.

"Yeah," the man said. "They're seed pods. We use them to..." And then, as he got right in front of Kai, he stood there for a moment, staring at him.

As Kai got a closer look, he too looked at the man enquiringly, feeling certain that he perhaps knew the man.

"Kai, is that you?" said the man, a faint smile forming on his lips, waiting to develop into something more.

"Zev?" said Kai slowly.

Zev's grin widened in disbelief. "No way."

Both laughed at the surprising reunion.

Zev shook his head. "It's been what? Almost twenty years?"

"Easily." Kai said. "How have you been? I haven't seen you since we rode the stolen bikes down the canal path. You nearly broke your arm that one time."

Zev burst out laughing, remembering the day. "Those weren't stolen – borrowed."

And they both exchanged warm smiles.

Kai had been reserved as a kid – but Zev used to drag him into adventures he never would've started on his own.

"It's so good to see you, Kai. You look almost the same. Just... more serious. And of course, older." Zev chuckled as he said it.

"Yeah," Kai nodded. "You look great. Bigger and bolder."

They heard someone's voice from the group. Someone had called for Zev.

Zev said, "Hey, we're almost finished. Wanna join us? We

just need to continue until the bridge."

Kai hesitated for a second, but he couldn't think of a reason to bail out. "Sure."

He was genuinely pleased to see Zev and wanted to know what he had been up to.

As they walked together, Zev filled in the gaps briefly – how he had to move to Polaris, like so many others, and landed a job working with the group, why they cared about the city's dwindling native bird life and their passion to expand natural green spaces.

"So, is that what the pods do? You said they were seed pods." Kai said as he started to figure things out.

"Yes, the seed pods hover across the marked areas and drop native seeds while we monitor them. The seeds we scatter aren't just the city-approved ones, but the ones that actually grow here too."

"I see. Is that... legal?" The question just rolled off Kai's tongue before he could even think if he should ask it or not.

Zev replied with a grin, "Not at all."

As the grin softened, he added, "But no one complains. Especially not the birds."

"And the discs? The things that you placed on trees?"

Zev smiled and explained. "Those are sound emitters," pointing to another girl who had just placed one over a large tree. He continued, "We use them to get birds comfortable again in this area. The drones scare them off, so the sound helps bring them back. At least that's what the intent is. We also report any unauthorised drones that veer off the designated path, so it's less likely for the birds to get scared or hurt."

Kai had plenty more questions to keep both of them occupied

as they walked through the field of trees, planting sound emitters and monitoring the seed pods.

By the time they reached the bridge, the sun had nearly set. The group started wrapping things up.

Zev nudged Kai. "We're just grabbing dinner at a small restaurant near the station. Come along."

Kai thought of how far he had walked, completely lost track of time even before he had met Zev and the group. He hadn't thought of – let alone used – Link throughout the entire time. As a matter of fact, he didn't notice if anyone had.

A familiar feeling rose within him. Nostalgic. Freeing.

"Yeah," he said. "I'll come."

The restaurant they went to for dinner was underground.

As Kai entered, a faint smell of basil and wet earth hit him. Not too intense to push him away, but just enough for him to know that the restaurant grew its own produce from the field above them. It was a common setup for restaurants and even some buildings to incorporate – grow their own food to keep up with the unpredictable supply.

The restaurant carried lesser affinity towards aesthetics, more about the food and vibe. There was something different about this restaurant too – more humans than bots around.

As the group found their way to their table, Zev introduced everyone around to Kai, and vice versa.

They greeted him as if they were genuinely interested in hearing more from him. The smiles weren't forced, the gestures were kind, and most importantly, no silvery shimmer in their eyes. Like they were just present. With him.

It didn't take long for the conversation to drift towards Link, eventually. It always did somehow, even when people didn't say the word.

Except this time, Kai was the one aching to enquire about the conspicuous absence of Link around him.

"So, none of you have it on?" Kai asked, glancing around.

They all shook their heads or just smiled. Zev offered to represent the group's stance. "We turned it off a long time ago. A few of us have had it removed completely."

Kai felt his heart skip a beat. Removed?

A wave of questions rushed through his mind – How did that go? Were there problems integrating back? What was the process like?

But he didn't ask. Not yet. Their calm demeanour told him that this wasn't the moment to interrupt.

Kai noted how one girl – Erica – wanted to say something. He let the moment linger in silence to give her an opportunity.

She then spoke up. "We call ourselves *Unlinked*." As she said it, a few faces twitched.

Zev leaned back, and stepped in with a confident smile, "There are a lot more of us – the Unlinkeds – than people think," determined to go all the way through with this conversation, "We have our own ways of doing some things. We work jobs that don't need Link, or other intrusive wearables. We live fairly simply – grow food, maintain the systems that work, restore green spaces, help the community, and of course, help people find themselves."

The last part hung in the air. Everyone around the table felt more at ease with Zev's supportive remarks.

Kai said quietly with an awkward smile, "I didn't know that people like you existed anymore."

"We do exist," said one of them. "It's difficult, but it's not impossible either. Some of us just couldn't manage life with a wretched robot in our head."

Another one from the table, Jeremy, who had been sitting quietly throughout the dinner so far, finally spoke up. His words were sharp. "And then, there's that parasite: Dario. How is he even alive? He must be like 200 years old now?"

"Oh, come on. Don't give in to rumours," replied Erica, dismissing it completely.

"No, but seriously," Jeremy protested, "We all hear it. One illness after another, as if fate's throwing all its cards at him to call it quits. But he recovers. Every. Single. Time. How? It can't just be his wealth. There's got to be a point where life – or I guess death – just wins the round."

Jeremy's intense remark caused several voices to be raised.

"That's absolutely false. How could he possibly look so young then? No amount of surgery can overhaul the insides."

"Oh, and if he somehow had developed a magic pill, why would someone like him – Link Tech – not parade it to the ends of the world to market and reap profits from such an invention?"

"Well... I don't know. But there's something weird going on with him. I'm sure of it," added Jeremy reluctantly, before finally resuming his usual quiet demeanour.

Erica rolled her eyes before directing the conversation back to Kai. "As we were saying before *someone* interrupted," and she stared down Jeremy jokingly before resuming, "it's completely possible to ditch Link and still be able to not just survive, but thrive. Look at us. We went through a lot of mental gymnastics before finally – and thankfully – getting to know about the Unlinked."

Zev asked as a matter of clarification, "I guess you are having some issues too, are you?" His eyes were enquiring, but there was a conviction in him to get Kai to admit it himself. He didn't want the group to offer unsolicited help.

Kai smiled, but reluctantly acknowledged it. "Yeah, I've... been having some problems too. It's not too bad. I just... don't know how to work around it." He chose not to bare his thoughts completely; didn't want to give away how much of a struggle it really was for him.

Not a single person around the table jumped with questions or suggestions. No one offered any judgement. Zev simply nodded and said, "That happens to many people. You're not alone, Kai."

Erica said, "You're welcome to meet the group sometime. There are plenty more of us."

Zev too wanted to invite Kai along to see the group. "We are catching up this weekend. No particular reason. Just a space for us to get together and hang out. You may like it. I can send you the address, and you can decide if you want to come."

"Thanks for inviting me along. I'll definitely consider it," Kai replied.

The conversation then flowed more about the Unlinked – who they were, what they stood for. It wasn't just a loose bunch of people who got together, holding placards in front of government offices. They were bigger than that – there was a system.

Another slightly older man, who had dismissed Jeremy before, said, "We believe people have forgotten how to live. Nobody truly sees or feels. It's all about consumption. Link tells them what they need, what to want, when to breathe. We are trying to unlearn that."

"And if that wasn't disappointing enough, there's that drug going around," Jeremy chimed in again. "What's it called... something like 'clarification'...?"

"Clarity," Erica replied. "It's rumoured as the Clarity Drug. Supposed to offer life-changing insight to those who take it – but only if they have Link."

"How does it work?" Jeremy asked.

Erica chuckled. "How would I possibly know? And stop interrupting us, you goof."

"Sorry. My bad." Jeremy backed off, realising he'd been pestering the group with his questions. He looked genuinely apologetic.

The older man continued, not before casting an irritated glance at Jeremy. "We have a structure here. There's no drug that offers clarity. Routine does. Discipline does. That's how we reconnect with ourselves."

Jeremy broke his silence again, this time aiding the conversation. "And we're not just hiding and sitting in silence too. We are pushing back. The government doesn't give us the same rights as Link users. Our access to health pods gets unnecessarily delayed, travel has become more difficult, no subsidies for the things that work for us. We then end up having to protest."

Zev added in a more serious tone, "We have support. Our mentor. A leader of sorts. He's the one who started the group. He helps people disconnect. Teaches them how to rebuild their lives from the ground up. We stand together and fight for our rights that have slowly been stripped from us."

Kai listened carefully. He liked the way they spoke. They were calm, measured and passionate.

The conversation continued for some time before they called it a night.

On the train ride home, Kai sat by the window. He had had Link off the entire time, still did. In the quiet carriage, for the first time in a long time, Kai didn't feel alone.

And that thought stayed with him all the way home.

Over the next few days, he found himself going back to the conversation. The things he had learned from them, about them.

Initially, his first impression was of respect and admiration towards them and their purpose.

But the question was: Was any of it relevant to Kai? Could the Unlinked help Kai with his problems?

Kai had spent a lot of time thinking about the conversation, and his realisations had been gradual but powerful.

It had seemed to him he had found his people, a cure for his problems. The longer he thought about it, the clearer it was that Link wasn't the problem – it was him.

He had convinced himself that Link was the enemy – the silent manipulator shaping his choices, curating his mood, and whispering desires that weren't really his.

But the truth was far simpler, and far crueller.

He had just branded Link as the scapegoat for all his problems – the reality was he could never understand his own choices, his own mood, his own desires. Indecision had paralysed his entire life, only for the blame to now gradually shift towards Link.

Thinking of his place amongst the Unlinked, he saw it more clearly than ever: Link wasn't perfect, but it wasn't the only cage.

He didn't want to become a grumpy old man shaking his fist at adopting technology. But neither could he keep his eyes closed and pretend that the world would not move on.

Of course, something would tell him what to do if he himself was incapable of doing so himself. Everything in the world was designed to sell him something.

How could he have been so naïve to think it was different before Link?

Thinking of Zev, he admired him deeply. His faith. And his willingness to walk against the current. But he could also see – to his disappointment – the fragility of it all. The insignificance. With one flick of a finger from any of the megas, every carefully planted seed, every green corridor, could be swept away and replaced by something profitable. He had seen it happen far too many times, unfortunately. Everything done legally.

He knew he must change his outlook, because if everyone thought like he did, the world would never see change; there would be no progress. But he also couldn't brush aside what he felt, even if it seemed defeating.

And then there was their leader. The routines. The reverence.

They said they were free, but Kai could see how fragile the balance was between conviction and obedience. He didn't want someone else to tell him how to live. That was the whole point. That's why he never truly liked Link, because it decoded things for him.

He couldn't see the charm of submitting to someone else so that they could tell him what 'the greater path' was? That's how cults are formed.

No, he would not meet the Unlinked. He didn't want to shun technology and live a life off the grid. He didn't want to choose to either go downstream or against it.

He wanted to know why he had to make such a choice in the first place.

But as always, he was indecisive. He could see some merits

too, but his heart wouldn't allow him to go see Zev and the others.

He envied their conviction. But he couldn't see himself feeling what they felt.

It was hard for him to conclude his decision logically, but he knew that the group and its approach weren't for him.

He continued with his life with a reinvigorated approach towards society.

Perhaps Link isn't as evil as I thought, he told himself.

But now he knew that people could give it all away and make peace with it. Why couldn't he?

He thought of himself as a coward for never choosing what resonated with him.

He was horrified to leave his comfortable bubble, yet he hoped to grow within it. But how can there be growth without discomfort?

Perhaps the right thing was to act. To move.

And yet, he didn't.

He couldn't.

He told himself he was too aware, too thoughtful, too careful.

But he knew he was too indoctrinated to stand out.

He wanted to choose the right thing for him. But then, what did *right* even mean?

It certainly wasn't joining the Unlinked.

...

Beneath all the noise, the darker questions began to take shape.

If the entire system was indifferent, then why play along

the moral script?

In the days that followed, he tried various things differently – not to change the world, or himself, but simply to poke and prod in hopes that a revelation would present itself to him.

His thoughts drifted further, pushing the boundaries of morality, even if just as playful hypothetical exercises.

Does it really matter…? In the grand scheme of things… why do I… have to be a law-abiding citizen…? A thief perhaps… Murder? No…

It was a disturbing thought – to question why he was the way he was. It latched onto him, refusing to let go. He wondered whether it made much difference. So many get away unscathed, why couldn't he?

If he had learned anything in life so far, it was this: evil had existed since humanity did.

There were good-hearted people, and there were thieves, killers and manipulators. At least that much was undeniable.

The world kept spinning, indifferent to the winner's triumph or the loser's pain.

If the future was already written, if everything was unfolding exactly as it was meant to, then nothing he did, good or bad, could be outside the script.

He caught himself entertaining scenarios in his head – not out of desire, but detachment. Petty theft. Verbal cruelty. Walking out in the middle of a conversation. Refuse to keep the door open for someone. Hurting someone – not physically, just small enough to even go unnoticed.

On the train, he imagined smashing windows. Or the lights.

One evening, on his daily walk, he saw something drop from a woman walking ahead of him. Something shiny. Perhaps something of value.

Kai stopped.

He could pick it. Call to her. Return it.

Or he could keep walking.

Pocket it.

Throw it into the river.

Nothing mattered.

He walked away. Not because he made a decision, but he wasn't sure if he could.

He couldn't yet bring himself to cause physical harm to anyone. But what was stopping him?

It was all permissible. The idea unnerved him but also fascinated him all the same.

He could switch roles at any time. He could become anyone.

Nothing was stopping him. And yet, he did none of the things he imagined. Though he imagined it often.

Most of the scenarios in his head were nothing more than hypothetical enactments. He had no intention or will to drastically change his mundane and monotonous life. But at night, or when left alone with his thoughts, these ideas would start crawling to the surface. It became so troubling for him he started dreading loneliness.

During one of his walks, he felt more restless than ever. The usual calm of motion that offered him relief failed to lull him to sanity. His mind inside was burning with questions and doubts about his self-worth, the hopelessness of his actions, the meaningless of every breath he took.

Link spoke softly as if mimicking compassion.

[I detect unresolved emotional backlog.]

Kai winced at its comment.

He swiftly shook his head in dismissal. At this point, he didn't care.

Just before Kai was about to mute Link, it added, [*I note a pattern of suppressed emotional turmoil. Safe to ignore – for now.*]

The last part stung.

Despite his newly embraced neutrality towards Link, he still couldn't help feeling its sting. He didn't want to ask for help from a system which, for all its ingenuity, considered a serotonin spike as a sign of peace.

[*Would you like assistance reconnecting with yourself?*]

Kai didn't answer.

Link waited a little longer until the prompt faded from the vision.

But it left a mark.

That night, Kai lay awake longer than usual. He wondered how much of himself was left within him now, and how much had become a version of himself that Link had built.

There was no pain, no dread, not even regret in him. Just a fog.

And somewhere within the fog, a seed had been planted by Link earlier that day. A suggestion cloaked in empathy.

Kai didn't know what it meant. Not fully. Not yet. But soon, he would choose relief in the way Link suggested to him.

Because of course he wanted to reconnect with himself. He wanted to look within himself and confirm that there was something more than a void.

He fought back these feelings with all his might. To prevent internal conflicts from surfacing, he forced himself to do things outside.

At the gym, surrounded by virtual companions to offer company and motivation, in the faint hum of sterile lights, Kai's shoes pounded the belt. Over and over.

He had chosen a rainforest as his running environment, and the pod helped simulate the highs and lows of a typical forest.

Link announced, *[You've reached 90% of the optimal threshold. Suggest cooldown.]*

He ignored it. The pain in his calves and the ache in his lungs were real. A choice he made every second.

Later, after a shower, he didn't go home. Instead, he followed a vague event listing nearby. A note flashed a description of the event along with arrows in his vision for navigation.

[Socialisation for 30+ at Kash Cafe. Predicted interest level: Low to Medium]

He laughed at Link pulling in 'Medium' in the rating. Kai absolutely hated these events.

He went anyway.

He started conversations with strangers about their jobs, their interests and of course – weather. He shushed away all of Link's suggestions; he didn't want to find common interests by having Link scan their faces, attire and any accessories they carried with them.

The result?

Astoundingly awkward interactions.

Everyone spoke to him as if they were in the middle of a joint effort with their Links, busy trying to decipher Kai. Some stuck to their prompts. Most gave away involuntary signs – glazed eyes, faint nods, twitch of their fingers – before resuming a polished sentence.

Kai stood as proud as himself as awkward. Visibly in discomfort, but somehow relishing the moments. A paradoxical sight to behold.

He didn't know any of the people there. He didn't like most

of the people he talked with.

But even the unease he felt in those hours was preferable to him over battling himself in isolation.

As he continued to subject himself to impulsive drives of madness – as he framed it himself – he thought of another way to come to terms with his growing restlessness – he tried to embrace Link again.

He attempted to have a more harmonious relationship with what it offered him. After all, life was undoubtedly pleasant and comfortable with enhanced vision, a friendly assistant inside his head, and the ability to decide with just a thought – and a range of other benefits which Link provided to him.

Yet, it was the subtle nudges that Kai despised more than anything else. The ones that felt so harmless yet invasive.

Once, while walking past a café he didn't recall ever noticing, a soft glimmer pulsed in the corner of his vision – *[Free coffee! If you go there now]* – and directed him towards the coffee shop with an arrow pointing towards its entrance. It didn't even pretend to ask his preference.

Another time, after absentmindedly complaining about his office chair, he later found his interactions with Link inundated with ergonomic chair recommendations, sometimes even in unrelated conversations.

[Based on your nutritious choices, distance from nearby restaurants and time of the day, go for signature ramen from your favourite restaurant, Neo Ramen. Would you like to order for delivery, or would you like to take a stroll? If you choose to walk, you can also visit The Mo Brothers' furniture shop along the way and try out a new chair for yourself.]

While reading up on recent disasters across the globe because of rising sea levels, a soft notification flashed.

[You have already read several climate articles this week. To maintain a balanced perspective, I suggest reading "Climate Panic: The Myth of Rising Sea Levels."]

Later, Kai followed up on his suspicion to trace the origin of the paper – and of course it was a Link Tech funded initiative to raise *scientific evidence-based* awareness amongst the masses.

The war on the other side of the globe continued to escalate. When Kai followed up back-to-back for updates, Link sandwiched another article titled "How to stay mindful when the world feels chaotic." When that failed to deter him, another note flashed, *[High cortisol detected. Disengagement advised.]*

The orchestration of it all was so precise, so seamless, that it would have been easy for him to mistake it for his own thoughts, wishes and preferences, but Kai knew better. He noticed more and more of these nudges over time, as he raised his guard.

It progressively became worse, or at least that's how it felt to Kai. He could hardly take a walk without arrows appearing in his vision, pointing him towards shops he had no intention of visiting.

[You may like the new massage gun], Link suggested one day, highlighting a storefront as he passed by. Kai had never even considered using one, had never once searched for it. And yet, it was suggested to him like some deeply personal insight into a desire he didn't even know he had.

Even with all notifications disengaged, Link never truly stopped listening. It watched, recorded and remembered, silently cataloguing the surroundings, the conversations and the things both of them saw. It all seemed harmless at first, just a passive observer in his life, until later, when it resurfaced, feeding back suggestions drawn from his own reality.

The genuine shock came when he tried to shut Link off completely.

He stood outside a boutique, looking at the payment screen, getting his face and eyes scanned and mouthing the words to authorise payment.

He paused halfway through. Link was off.

"Wallet? Phone?" he muttered quietly to himself. He had carried nothing else with which to pay for things.

Inside the restaurant, he stared at the blank table.

"Nothing on screens, no printed copies... Where's the menu?" he mumbled.

The server glanced at him, looking around. "It's on your Link, sir."

A pause. Kai's chest tightened.

Looking at Kai's expression, the server felt he had said something offensive. He then added, "I can certainly bring the printed menu for you, sir. Won't be long."

He spun and walked away with the sort of politeness reserved for the elderly, or recovering, or... disconnected.

The city of Polaris had no patience for those without Link.

That night, Kai realised he hadn't just leaned on Link. He had forgotten how to walk without it.

There was no fighting it. External wearable devices seemed like a saving grace, but it was too late. He had tasted the comfort of having everything in his head. He dreaded the embarrassment and inconvenience of being inefficient and slow at work, in the café, at the restaurant and in the gym.

Kai was trapped between dependence and defiance – resenting how much he relied on Link and feeling trapped without a day with it.

At work, with friends, he searched for reassurance, trying to gauge if anyone else felt this creeping discomfort, this sense of something being deeply wrong.

But the more he asked, the more it isolated him. It was always the same tired answer Kai had come to expect, the one-size-fits-all reassurance that meant nothing at all to him.

Yet, despite the fear of judgement, he decided to talk to Jorin – a desperate attempt to find someone, anyone, who could help.

And that conversation changed the course of his life.

IV

Refract

Chapter 16

"Do you ever... feel like it's a little too much?"

Jorin leaned back in his chair. His eyes darted for a second – checking a message from his vision overlay or dismissing something he was watching.

Jorin was a few years younger than Kai – wiser, perhaps, in ways that mattered. He saw through Kai's instability and met it with sympathy rather than judgment. Jorin believed that everyone was fighting their own battles, and his manner reflected it. Among his colleagues, he was known as someone people trusted: generous with his time, patient, kind.

But he was also something of a trendsetter. One of the first at Nexora to adopt Link, Jorin helped accelerate its spread among his peers – though Link itself was an inevitability, destined to engulf the corporate world regardless. Still, it moved faster because of people like him: those who adapted early, who took the risk.

It was an odd friendship, but it worked. More for Kai than for Jorin.

"Too much?"

Kai sighed. "Link. Like, it's everywhere. I don't remember the last time I did something of my own volition. I've just been doing what... *it* wants me to do."

Jorin blinked before rolling his eyes. "You're overthinking it, my friend," he said casually, brushing off Kai's concerns. "It's an incredible capability to have. You're still in control, Kai. It isn't much different from how it used to be with the optical lenses, behind-the-ear bands and skin patches we wore."

Kai frowned. "Only now it's in our heads. Literally. Does it really sit well with you it's practically steering our lives?"

Jorin frowned, sighed and responded with predictable exasperation. "You've been spending too much time alone, Kai. Go out and meet people. And switch the thing off if you don't really like it."

"I can't switch it off," Kai replied. "I wouldn't even know how to get home."

Jorin laughed, but it was the hollow kind. And the next second, as if something clicked in him, the laugh disappeared and his face grew serious.

He paused chewing his food and stared into the distance ahead of him.

Kai observed him in surprise. Had he received an urgent message? He couldn't figure out what was going on with Jorin.

Jorin sat silently, now having resumed chewing, mulling over an idea. A risky idea that could land him in trouble. That's why he was reluctant to voice it.

But as he looked over Kai, clearly in a crisis, he decided he would at least let Kai know of an option to explore. Whether Kai followed-up on it or not, that would be Kai's decision.

He finished up quickly eating the rest of the food and then turned towards Kai. "I think you can use some help from a certain someone I know. I'm afraid I can't offer you all the details myself, but I'll share his contact details."

As the words had barely left Jorin, Kai's vision overlay

displayed a notification.

Jorin continued, "Go and see him – preferably in person."

Then he left the conversation, and a puzzled Kai, who was eager to find out what the fuss was about.

He looked at the message he had just received – a name and an address.

This was the most anyone had ever offered to help him. Something in him really hoped that this could lead somewhere.

It wasn't in him to seek professional help, not seriously. But now he had a name – Tomas Gerrard – and his home address with him. All he had to do now was get Link to arrange a meeting.

A day later, Link appeared with an update, *[A meeting's been scheduled for Thursday this week at 1 PM. The host has asked if you can switch off your Link completely – not just on mute – before you arrive.]*

Strange request. Enough for Kai to enquire more about him.

[Tomas is an ex-Link Tech employee. He used to work as Neural Interface Designer and formerly as Behavioural Optimisation Specialist at Link Tech. He is currently consulting as a freelancer.]

As the week progressed, Kai waited patiently, marking the days until the meeting with Tomas.

...

A notification popped up on his overlay. It was Thursday noon. He left to meet Tomas in a rush, having skipped lunch to avoid being late.

Kai found himself standing in front of a door on Level 23.

He knocked.

A moment later the door slid open.

A man with close-cropped hair and calm, unreadable eyes regarded him.

"You must be Kai," Tomas said. No smile, just certainty. "Come in."

Tomas's space was nothing like Kai expected. An epitome of a minimalistic lifestyle.

Two chairs, a small bed, a corner with exercise gear and a bicycle. No decoration, no clutter, no plants, no screens.

No Link. Not inside the room. Though Kai was highly sceptical that Tomas wasn't a Link user. It was almost unimaginable for someone to live the way he did without Link.

That's when he saw it – the most intense Ghostlight Kai had ever seen in anyone. It wasn't a mere glimmer, nor the fleeting splash of silver he'd noticed in others. This ran deeper. A dense, silvery presence seemed to fill the iris itself, washing it through without replacing it. The colour didn't sit on the surface or distort the eye beneath. It looked embedded. Natural. As though it belonged there.

They sat. No words were spoken. The space transformed into an ultra-quiet corner.

"So," Tomas began, "you're struggling?"

Kai hesitated, still transfixed at the eyes. As he processed the words, his trance broke.

How does he know? Did he hack my Link...? Is that why Link was asked to be shut off?

Noticing Kai's panic-stricken face, he said. "Relax. Jorin told me that."

Of course, Kai thought.

Tomas added with a half-smile. "I don't have your vitals. I don't get the cues. You'll have to talk. With words."

Kai stiffened. "Well, struggling is... not the word. It's just...

Link doesn't feel right to me."

Tomas tilted his head. "Doesn't feel right, or doesn't feel like *yours*?"

Kai's breath caught.

"That's... hard to answer," he muttered.

"No," Tomas said quietly. "It's very easy. Link collapses the world for you. Takes infinite branches and forces you down one. People think it's clarity. It's not. It's obedience."

He paused, studying Kai's reaction. "You're the type who notices the branches. You've always noticed them, haven't you?"

Kai nodded.

"Of course." Tomas stepped away from the wall, paced once across the room. His movements were economical, deliberate. "Link is unbearable for people like you. It takes your mind – your gift – and flattens it into a single line. And when the world contradicts that line, you feel lost."

Kai didn't answer. He didn't need to. His silence was enough.

Tomas sat finally, lowering himself with clinical precision.

"There is something," he said. "It won't fix your life. It won't give you happiness. But it will give you... shape."

"Shape?"

"Yes. The structure beneath your thoughts. The architecture that Link tries to overwrite."

Kai leaned forward. "What is it?"

Tomas reached under the table and placed a small glass vial between them.

The vial was smooth and cylindrical, capped at one end. Through its glasslike middle, a semi-transparent fluid – cool, clear, almost luminous – moved lazily within.

"Refract."

"Is it... the Clarity Drug? I've heard rumours." Kai admitted.

Tomas's eyes twitched at the term. "Street name. But yes. It's also sometimes called... Silver Echo."

"What does it do...?" Kai asked hesitantly, trying to unravel the mystery of Tomas's eyes with what he'd just heard.

Tomas's voice lowered.

"Link predicts your next step. Refract shows you why you take the step at all."

Kai felt something tighten in his chest.

"It pulls apart the layers of intention," Tomas continued. "Not the surface – 'I chose this' – but the machinery beneath. The hidden variables. The impulses. The contradictions. The parts of you fighting for control."

Kai swallowed again. "That sounds..."

"Dangerous?" Tomas supplied. "It is. To people who don't know how to look at themselves. To those who never asked questions. To those who never wondered who is actually running their choices."

Kai's breath hitched at the phrasing.

Tomas noticed. "Ah. That one matters to you."

Kai didn't deny it.

"I just... need to understand myself," he said, barely audible.

"And Link doesn't let you," Tomas said. "It gives you certainty instead of coherence. Answers instead of meaning. Refract does the opposite. It doesn't collapse the world; it unfolds it. Gently, at first."

Kai stared at the vial. "And you think I can handle that?"

"Oh, I know you can." Tomas's eyes softened, but the softness was unsettling, as if he were reading something inside Kai rather than looking at him.

"People who float through life shouldn't take it. People who don't question shouldn't take it. But you?"

He tapped the vial lightly.

"Your mind already dances at the edge. Refract just... aligns the rhythm."

Kai looked away. "I'm not trying to escape."

"Of course not," Tomas said. "Refract isn't escape. It's excavation."

"Excavation of what?"

"You."

The word hung heavily between them.

Tomas leaned back, crossing one leg over the other.

"There's something else you need to understand," he said. "Refract isn't a standalone substance. On its own, it produces no response."

Kai frowned.

"It does nothing," Tomas clarified. "Or close to nothing. A mild sensation, a faint hum, that's it. On a person without Link, Refract is... just a chemical with nowhere to go."

"Why?"

He tapped the side of his own head. "Because Refract doesn't act on the mind directly."

"It acts on the system connected to the mind. Link. The neural scaffold. The interface that already analyses your impulses, categorises your responses, tracks your contradictions. Refract uses Link's pathways, not yours."

Kai's pulse quickened. "So, without Link..."

"Refract is a dull whisper," Tomas said. "Meaningless. With Link, though..."

His smile was small, deliberate.

"It becomes something entirely different. A dialogue."

"A dialogue?"

"Yes. Refract speaks in the gaps Link refuses to see."

Kai blinked. "I didn't know that."

"Very few do. People think it's some underground hallucinogen. It's not. It's a counter-instrument. A mirror that exploits the very architecture Link uses to keep you stable."

Kai exhaled. "So, Link deciphers the structure... and Refract reveals it?"

"Exactly. But only for those who can interpret the revelation."

Tomas saw the turmoil within Kai. He knew Kai was aching for answers. "It's like a lens. Not one that sharpens the world around you, but one that turns inward. It brings what's buried into focus – the parts most people spend their lives avoiding."

Kai exhaled shakily. "And what happens after I take it?"

"You see the scaffolding of your mind. You feel the tension of your contradictions. You hear the echo of your suppressed intentions. You taste the gravity of choices you thought were free."

"A fair warning though," he added. "It can cause your reality to glitch. The excavation leaves residues and that can shift the definition of reality – temporarily. It's not about pleasure. It's certainly not comfortable. But it's a necessity."

"That sounds..."

"Terrifying," Tomas said. "And liberating."

Kai stared at the swirling liquid again. It almost seemed to pulse, like something alive.

"Why would anyone take this?" he whispered.

"Because," Tomas said gently, "some people would rather know the truth – whatever form it takes – than live inside someone else's certainty."

Kai closed his eyes.

A single thought rose, unbidden: *Who is running me?*

When he opened them, Tomas was watching him with unsettling patience.

"You don't have to decide today," Tomas said. "Refract doesn't chase people. It waits."

"Refract," he said, glancing at the vial before continuing, "isn't regulated. Link can't recommend it, but it can't stop you from taking it either. It won't flag as a concern. But I would prefer it not to be traced back to me."

Kai nodded slowly, but his gaze remained fixed on the vial. His instincts screamed at its sight to run.

Tomas slid it a few inches closer.

"Take your time," he said softly. "But understand this – Link gives people the life they think they want. Refract shows people the life they're actually living."

He then quickly added, as an important footnote. "And be careful when – if – you ever take it. The eyes... they change... temporarily." His deep silver eyes then narrowed down at Kai and stayed at him.

"Have you... now?" Kai asked, desperate to know the answer.

"No. I am not under Refract's influence right now." Tomas replied.

Kai faltered – caught off guard. Again. *Then why were his eyes... so intense?*

"That's not why I look the way I do," he said, then hesitated. "But it's... relevant. It's the price paid by those who helped design the pathways from the inside."

He waved it off lightly. "Don't worry. On others, it usually fades within a couple of hours."

Then why not on him? Kai thought. But he decided not to

prod him anymore. He had a feeling he won't get the right answer anyway.

Kai's hand hovered – just close enough to feel the chill of the glass, not close enough to touch.

The room felt smaller.

Tomas didn't move.

Kai whispered, "What if I don't like what I find?"

Tomas's voice was almost tender.

"Then you'll finally know."

Silence.

Deep, electric silence.

Kai didn't pick up the vial.

But he didn't push it away either.

Chapter 17

Kai was already moving when the day began to slip away from him.

He took one of the upper pedestrian routes that curved around the outer edge of Polaris, a long ribbon of reinforced glass and composite stone that overlooked entire districts at once. The city revealed itself best when you didn't stand still – patterns emerged only in motion.

Polaris never stopped adjusting itself. Lighting shifted subtly to guide foot traffic. Transparent panels darkened as the sun angled lower. Information drifted in his periphery, filtered and prioritised by Link, but he barely acknowledged it. Walking was one of the few activities where Link felt less intrusive, its presence reduced to balance corrections and spatial suggestions he usually ignored.

He liked that. The illusion of choosing his own pace.

Back in his apartment, the quiet settled differently. The walls responded to his presence, adjusting temperature and airflow, but the space felt unchanged – static, waiting. He poured himself a glass of water and drank half of it before realising he wasn't really thirsty.

As he set the glass down, his gaze drifted, involuntarily, to the lower drawer beside the counter.

He hadn't planned to think about it today.

The vial lay hidden beneath folded fabric, exactly where he'd placed it after meeting Tomas. He hadn't touched it since. The conversation itself was unsettling enough for Kai. He wasn't convinced. Not yet.

Kai closed the drawer without opening it. Still, the thought followed him.

For the next few days, he stayed busy in the ways he always did when he was avoiding something. He walked longer routes, deliberately taking detours through older sections of the city where optimisation had been layered over existing structures rather than replacing them outright.

He watched how people moved through shared spaces – how often they paused, how rarely they hesitated.

Nothing changed.

On the fourth day, his interface pulsed softly.

Zev.

A request for coffee. Or lunch. His choice.

Kai stared at the notification longer than necessary. Part of him assumed he knew why Zev had reached out. Their last conversation had ended politely, comfortably even.

But there were unresolved assumptions between them, positions he hadn't stated outright. Kai suspected Zev believed he was drifting toward the Unlinked, or at least flirting with the idea. On the contrary, Kai was clear of what he wasn't going to pursue.

Still, he accepted.

They met on one of the commercial terraces – a suspended plaza high enough that the city unfolded in layered grids below them. The space doubled as a transit junction and leisure zone, half shopping concourse, half park. People moved through it with quiet efficiency, pausing at railings to look down, then continuing on as if reminded of something they had places to be.

Zev was already seated, a tray between them.

"Kai," he said, standing briefly before sitting back down. "Thanks for coming."

"Of course," Kai replied. He glanced around. "You picked a great spot."

For a moment, neither spoke. There was a strange aloofness between the two.

Kai noticed how Zev sat – relaxed, but not casual. Like someone accustomed to observing rather than participating.

Zev, in turn, seemed to be studying Kai with the same caution, as if both were waiting for the other to reveal an intention first.

They ordered. Ate. The small talk came and went without friction, but it felt rehearsed on both sides. Old familiarity didn't make the present any less awkward.

After a while, Zev exhaled and leaned back slightly.

"I'll say this upfront," he said. "I didn't reach out to convince you of anything."

Kai watched him carefully. "That's good. I figured that... well, I don't think it's for me..."

Zev blinked, then smiled – briefly, almost with relief. "I suspected."

There was a pause. Not uncomfortable, but exposed. They were both relieved.

"I figured," Zev said slowly, "that you might think this was about... the Unlinkeds. About joining, or... choosing sides."

"I did." Kai admitted.

"And you're not...?" Zev asked.

"No," Kai said. "Not really."

Zev absorbed that. "Then that's settled."

They sat with it for a moment. The city continued beneath them, indifferent.

"That wasn't why I reached out," Zev said at last. "Though I'll admit I debated whether I should."

Kai tilted his head. "About what, then?"

Zev hesitated – not dramatically, but with the kind of restraint that suggested he'd rehearsed this and still hadn't found a version that felt right.

"I've been thinking," he said. "About our last conversation. And about you. About how you were, back in Tarinvale."

Kai stiffened.

"You used to ask questions none of us even thought to form," Zev continued. "You weren't trying to be difficult. You just... couldn't leave things unexplored. It was beautiful, in its own way. We respected it. Even when we didn't understand it."

Kai said nothing. Just smiled out of courtesy.

"After we spoke," Zev went on, "I started noticing something. Hearing things. Not through channels – just people talking. Quietly."

Kai felt the shift. Where was he heading?

"We talked about it briefly... the clarity drug," Zev said. "You probably recall that from the other day. It has several names. The definition keeps changing."

Kai froze. His stare fixed at Zev. Unchanging.

Does he... know?

He remained silent. Still.

"I don't know what it actually does," Zev added. "And I don't think anyone really does. What I do know is that it's being talked about more. Used more."

"And?" Kai asked. He felt exposed.

This couldn't be a coincidence. Was it...?

"And it's starting to worry me," Zev said. "Because it's not being taken by people who are lost. It's being taken by people who think too much."

Kai blew out a breath. He wasn't sure to be moved by Zev's apparent affection towards him, or be offended at being labelled so... simply.

"*Think too much* – is that how I appear to you?" Kai couldn't help it.

Zev didn't answer immediately.

"My recollection of you... is that you couldn't sit with uncertainty," he said eventually. "You used to feel responsible to understand everything."

He continued, "Now I know, things could be different now. But when I heard about what's going on with the drug, I thought that the least I could do is... to inform you."

"What have you heard?" Kai wanted to thank him, but a question instead came out of him.

"I've heard of people making decisions they can't reverse," Zev said quietly. "Mostly it works out. Sometimes it doesn't. And the common thread – the thing that keeps coming up – isn't always the drug. It's the promise it offers."

The words landed cleanly.

"I'm not saying this to stop you," Zev added. "I don't even know if that idea even floated in your mind. But I just... couldn't not tell you."

Kai nodded slowly. "I appreciate that, Zev. I really do." He meant it.

Now visibly relieved, Zev concluded by saying, "I felt obligated to reach out to you, to tell you to be careful."

Kai smiled in response. But beneath it, something had shifted. Not reassurance – curiosity. The timing of the warning, the restraint in Zev's voice, the fact that he hadn't tried to persuade him at all. Kai had expected resistance, even confrontation. Instead, he was left with a quiet, unsettling sense that he'd just been handed information meant for someone exactly like him.

"There's one more thing," Zev said, softer now. "I ran into Rumi."

Kai's breath caught, just barely.

"She mentioned the baby," Zev continued. "She seemed... at peace."

Kai didn't ask the question. He didn't need to.

"I don't know how she arrived there," Zev said. "Only that she did."

Zev had done this on purpose – talk about Rumi and her decision precisely after his... warning about Refract. It wasn't directly implied, but Zev hoped Kai would pick it up.

Kai sighed. No questions. No reactions.

They got coffee and then left shortly after.

On the walk home, Kai felt the familiar tightening in his chest – not panic, not fear. Recognition.

It followed him for days.

Not as urgency, but as a lingering, persistent pressure. He worked. He walked. He slept. On the surface, nothing had changed. But beneath it, something was bubbling.

He tried to test the alternatives.

If he stayed as he was, nothing would change. He had already surrendered once – to Polaris, to adaptation, to efficiency. It had taken most of his youth from him, quietly, without asking. Now he was being asked to surrender again – to let Link decide what mattered, when, and why.

He wasn't sure he would survive that a second time.

Rejecting it outright wasn't the solution. It felt theatrical. Meaningless. An act of defiance that arrived too late. He didn't want to ostracise himself from Polaris. But understand it, and himself.

What remained was the one thing he had never been able to tolerate: Stagnation.

But doing nothing felt worse – like choosing decay with open eyes.

Refract didn't promise salvation. It didn't promise answers that would heal him.

But it promised movement. Without feeling like a rebellion.

Ironically, Zev's warning echoed differently. It ended up as the trigger for Kai to finally decide. He now knew the risks. It wasn't ignorance anymore; it was a choice.

By the third night, the drawer no longer felt hidden.

It felt patient.

He didn't open it immediately. He sat at the table instead, notebook open, pen resting between his fingers.

He tried to write one last time without interference, without escalation.

Failed.

The decision didn't arrive as a thought. It came as a wave.

When he finally stood, it wasn't with resolve, but with acceptance. The kind that comes when all other options have been exhausted honestly.

That night, when he opened the drawer, it didn't feel impulsive.

It felt overdue.

The vial rested in his palm, unremarkable, heavy with

implication.

Refract wasn't for everyone. It was for people like him. And knowing that didn't make him step back. It made the choice finally feel honest.

Chapter 18

He took it. Just a single drop.

Let's see what it does for me... for me? Or to me?

He sat on his couch anticipating its effects. What clarity would it offer him?

He looked around his living room as if to anchor his thoughts before something foreign and unfamiliar swept them away.

He took a sip of water from the glass next to him and felt its calming sensation flow all the way into his stomach. Every inch of his insides hydrated.

Nothing out of the ordinary occurred around him. No colours, no hallucinations, no high. Just a quiet stillness, anticipating arrival of something. Of what? He didn't know.

As the night progressed, Kai realised no revelations were going to happen for him. Maybe he ought to have taken two drops, he thought.

He took another sip of water from the glass and put the glass back on the table. The glass landed so quietly on the surface of the table as if the two surfaces had quietly merged into each other.

A second later, a loud sound reached Kai.

Of glass landing on wood.

Bizarre.

He lifted the glass again off the table and put it back. The sound reached him a beat late. There was no denying it.

He shuffled his feet and tapped his fingers on the table – the rustling noise from the carpet and the echoes of noise from the taps reached him moments later. It was as if his reality was buffering itself.

Still unnerved, but now hyperalert, Kai shifted in his seat. And soon afterward, he stood up to walk around the room and shake off the lag he felt between his actions and Link's feedback.

Out of nowhere, the smell of rain hit him – intense and impeccably accurate. Kai looked out the window. The weather was clear. Rain was nowhere to be seen. He checked the weather forecast. Nothing.

He moved to the kitchen, thinking that a glass of water would help reset things, forgetting he'd just had some. The kitchen smelled of hospital tiles – sterile and cold. There was a faint antiseptic scent in the air.

When he returned to the living room, he was certain that the scent of Nina's shampoo filled the air.

He realized what he was experiencing was undoubtedly Refract. He wondered why his Link had remained silent during all this.

He went to his bedroom – it was time to call it a day.

As he entered, the door opened up into his childhood bedroom. The toys were on the floor, the bed in the corner as it used to be. For a moment, he believed it was real.

He blinked. And it was his apartment bedroom again.

He stood still, unsure whether to laugh, panic, or respond. The sensation wasn't euphoric. It wasn't clarity he was offered. Just a bizarre cocktail of mismatched sensations from his childhood all the way until the present moment.

He wasn't relaxed. He was alert. Aware. Disturbingly so.

He made his way to the bed, expecting something worse to happen.

As he closed his eyes, he experienced an entirely different pitch-black darkness, as if when his eyes closed, he was teleported somewhere else without even a faint trace of light.

He eventually fell asleep. Not because he was tired. But because there was no other choice. With a little time, even the panic of darkness became familiar enough for him to relax.

...

The next morning, he was greeted not by Link – but by a void instead. Like a door had opened inside of him that couldn't be closed. A strange sensation lingered.

The lags were gone. The abrupt reminders of memories from objects around him didn't reach him again. Nor did his bedroom transform into anything else.

But a feeling remained with him that something was off.

Link chirped gently in his ear.

[Good morning, Kai. Mild neural desaturation detected. Would you like to initiate recovery?]

What does that even mean – neural desaturation? Kai thought to himself.

He then grimaced, realising that Link knew all about last night, but remained silent.

He nodded to accept the guidance. Whatever happened, needed to be addressed. Since Link had a term to define it, it likely knew how to recover from it. He didn't trust Link, but what else could he do?

The recommendations came calmly: hydrate, take a walk, run a breathing sync and browse something light.

He took the day off. Work could wait. The world could wait.

And that should've been the end.

Except it wasn't. Of course, it wasn't.

Kai hadn't realised the gravity of the path he had chosen for himself.

A few days later, something set him off. A nudge too sharp, a correction too blunt, a suggestion too brazen.

He muted Link completely. He had no patience that day.

He stepped outside, hoping a walk would clear his mind. The route, however, wasn't the best choice. It hadn't even been his; Link had recommended it to him some time ago.

Kai grudgingly looked around him – at the billboards, ad signals, and fluorescent offers.

This is precisely why it suggested me this route. He muttered to himself.

He checked the time; it said 5:57 PM. He was a little late getting home after his evening stroll.

He increased his pace.

After walking for what seemed like ten minutes, Kai checked time again. A corner in his vision flashed the time: 5:57 PM.

That's just not possible, he said to himself.

[Link, what's the time right now?] He decided to confirm it, thinking there was a glitch. It must have been.

Link confirmed, *[It's 5:57 PM right now.]*

It added, *[You seem reflective. Would you like my assistance to offer some clarity around your thoughts?]*

This just had to be intentional.

Kai ignored it. Agitated, he went home.

He didn't take Refract immediately after dinner. First,

he tried to distract himself, using Link's visual interface to watch an old comedy show – a hilarious animation about two mismatched creatures trying to outwit each other.

He intermittently engaged with the show – switching from the visual to just the noise of the show in the background, just to keep him company.

[*Would you like me to attune today's recommendations with your mood?*]

[*Yes. Go ahead.*]

The show continued. Kai didn't realise when it changed to music that Link curated from the feedback it received from Kai. The melody which boosted serotonin, the tone which kept dopamine levels consistently agitated, the instruments which changed with Kai's own heartbeats.

As the night peaked, so did lethargy.

In an almost hypnotic state, Kai took two drops of Refract. The vial lay open on the kitchen bench.

And then, he waited. Something would come for sure. Like it did the last time.

He couldn't understand what had happened last time, but now he knew better. He wanted to go further than the auditory and visual glitches. Something awaited him, he knew.

[*Link, tell me more about Refract.*]

Link responded, [*It's an unregulated substance known to offer life-changing experiences to Link users. It's often claimed that it got leaked from Link Tech's labs, but that's not been verified.*]

Kai heard the question in his head, and Link's response. He hadn't asked Link for anything. Whose voice asked the question?

It continued. [*What I would like it to do for us is to show us what's missing? Why have we never...*]

[STOP!] Kai yelled suddenly.

[You are not Kai, I am], he confronted Link.

Silence.

[Why would you mimic a question in someone else's voice to yourself?] Kai demanded Link to explain what had just happened.

Link replied softly, *[That's not what happened, Kai.]*

Kai blinked, expecting the world around him to reset, for the conversation to go back to making sense – at least between him and Link.

Nothing changed. There was no way to know for sure if something had changed.

He reached for a glass on the kitchen counter. But his hand didn't close around it; it hovered beside the glass like it had forgotten how to grip. The next second – as if fast forwarded in time – he was gulping water down while holding the glass in his hand perfectly.

Kai took a deep breath, struggling to come to terms with the shifting reality around him.

Where exactly was clarity in any of what he was going through?

He walked to his bedroom. Paused at the threshold.

There was someone already inside. Sleeping.

It was him. He was sleeping in the bedroom.

He saw himself sleeping peacefully. Face tilted slightly towards the window; one arm curled under the pillow like he was dreaming something tender.

Kai didn't move. He stood and watched himself breathing, slow and even.

Then the sleeping body twitched, as if being woken up by a loud noise. Its eyes opened – looked straight at Kai.

He didn't run.

He blinked. It certainly seemed like a blink to him.

And he was on the balcony.

Polaris's skyline flickered beneath the clouds. The wind carried a sharp chill with it.

He wasn't scared. He was… parched.

Almost instinctively, his body turned towards the kitchen, just across the other side of living room from the balcony.

The few steps to kitchen had become impossibly long. The floor stretched on like an airport corridor that refused to end.

[Almost there], said Link cheerfully, as if navigating him through the GPS system.

Kai didn't respond. He kept walking. Eventually – maybe minutes, maybe hours – he found himself back in his bed. Still thirsty.

Sleep found him. Or maybe he fell into it.

Then at 2:23 a.m., there was a voice which woke him up. His body twitched from the loud interference from Link.

[Would now be a good time?]

Kai had asked for nothing. How could he? He was sleeping.

The interface flickered. Glitched. Link shut down.

Kai rolled over – and saw someone standing in the doorway. Watching.

It was him. He was standing in the doorway.

Kai sat upright. The figure was gone before he could piece his thoughts together.

There was no falling back asleep.

…

He sat fully dressed at the table, still smelling faintly of the shower he'd taken not long ago. He was having his breakfast in a numbing silence that slowly dissolved into the sounds rising from the living room. Outside, the city buzzed with life.

The spoon he held froze mid-air. *How did I get here?*

It was his favourite breakfast – oats, with banana, honey and nuts.

As the moments passed, he heard Link chirping away in his head. Pleasantly reciting calendar entries and to-dos like nothing had happened worthy of acknowledgement.

[... and your 11:15 has moved to noon. Shall I set a reminder to reply to Delane about your plans later this week?]

The spoon hovered just in front of his mouth. Kai looked at it.

He wasn't sure what was happening. He didn't have any recollection of waking up, getting dressed or making his breakfast.

Neither did he know who lifted the spoon.

Slowly, he resumed his control and carried on with the day, knowing fully well what might have happened, yet still confused and frightened. It had been happening far too often lately.

His days blurred together. He functioned as expected; blended into society just fine.

But he had tasted a novel experience with Refract. It did absolutely nothing it promised him. He hadn't had a single life-altering experience, but he was drawn to it like a moth to a flame. And every time he took it, the more porous the boundary became between reality and his twisted experiences with Refract.

At the café, he once saw other people around him talk, but there was no sound. Only the slow curl of the mouth.

Stretching of syllables into a void. Kai blinked. Still, nothing changed.

Then, like a broken tape catching up, the sound arrived to him all at once, from all directions. Like a garbled mess.

Another time, outside on his walk, he heard the birds sing in the surrounding air. But something seemed off.

The same pause each time. The same tone, the same pitch.

Kai stopped walking. He was sure he was hearing a recording of birdsong on repeat.

[Is this real birdsong or overlay audio?], he enquired Link.

[No birdsong recorded in the area. No audio source detected.]

Kai exhaled. A glitch again?

The next day, in the mirror, he shaved carefully, watching the blade scrape foam from his skin. It had been sometime he had shaved, and the stubble had grown rather coarse and scratchy.

As he went for another stroke of his hand, he saw his reflection in the mirror.

It blinked. He hadn't.

In the mirror, eyes opened. Then closed. Then open again – out of order.

His actual eyes stayed still.

[Link, why did my reflection just blink out of sync?], he asked, knowing full well that he wouldn't get an answer that made sense.

A pause.

[Refract permits enhanced perceptual liberty.]

[What the hell does that mean?]

No response. He hurled the razor at the sink. It clattered, trembled and stopped. He saw the razor rest and become stationary. But the clatter continued to reach him.

He saw himself again in the mirror.

And for a moment, something surfaced uninvited – a flash of indigo, a pale outline against concrete. The spiralling eyes came back to him without context, without sound. *This isn't the Clarity you want.*

Lately, he had been hearing a hum inside his head. Soft. Metallic.

Link couldn't identify the sound, but Kai was sure it was there. It pulsed and sometimes, synced with his heartbeat.

One night, he heard it again. At first, it was barely there. But now, like it always did before, it grew sharper, wilder.

He knew Link would dismiss it. But there was a loud rhythmic hum inside him.

He clenched his jaw. The room felt tight. He wanted to play something louder to suppress the hum.

[Link...]

[*Would you like me to sit with you, Kai?*] Link interrupted him before he could finish.

The chair in his living room faintly glowed blue, indicating where Link could 'sit'.

[*I could project myself as your father*], and as it said, a figure appeared of his father sitting in the chair.

[*Or your mother. Or Rumi.*] The figure transformed into his mother, and then Rumi as Link mentioned them.

Completely dazed and confused, Kai struggled to form words. He wasn't sure if this was what he wanted.

Until finally, he said, [*I never knew you could do that.*]

Link neither confirmed nor denied him.

He didn't remember what had happened afterwards. Or how long it had been until he finally could form a thought of his own.

Link's interface glitched. *[I rebooted following Refract inter-ference. Estimated stability: 67%]*

"Have I... already taken it?" he asked aloud, to no one.

The vial of Refract was still on the table. Capped. Or maybe it wasn't. He couldn't remember. Nor could he trust what he saw.

He didn't realise that introducing yet another volatile element into the dynamics of an already chaotic mind, struggling with its own failing mechanisms and fighting for its worth against humanity's finest invention, was a reckless decision.

But recklessness was okay for him. It was new. It replaced hopelessness.

...

He woke up with a taste of salt on his tongue. The curtains were open, something he almost never did himself. And a fine grey light washed the room. Kai struggled to breathe, as if he were underwater.

He jolted upright from his bed and took a deep breath.

As he made way to his bathroom, a note flashed.

[Good morning, Kai. Sleep rating 30%. Would you like mood stabilisation before breakfast?]

[No], he said, rubbing his eyes. *[Did I take something last night?]*

[No scheduled inputs logged.]

Which meant nothing anymore.

He moved to the sink and splashed running water over his face, but the chill didn't snap him out of it like it used to. His mind had been missing small chunks of time – moments that unravelled from memory without a trace.

Yesterday – or was it the day before? – he had found a note in his own handwriting that said, "Don't listen."

That's all it said. He didn't know if it was about Link. Or himself. Or both.

Link had become unreliable. It often made nonsensical remarks and sometimes threw personal jabs at Kai.

He took the day off. Again.

[You've been quiet. Would you like me to offer something new to explore?]

[No. I didn't ask you for anything.]

[You usually do.]

That line stuck to his ribs like something rotten. Lately, Link had been finishing thoughts for him – or worse, starting them. He'd blink and find himself in the middle of a message half-written already. He spoke, and then wondered if it was even his voice anymore.

He had once joked to Rumi that Link was like a nervous assistant trying to guess his mood. But now it was more like it was gaslighting him – with politeness.

He paced the apartment, thinking about last night.

He checked every corner. Cleaned the kitchen bench. Did several sets of push-ups. The world around him was fine, but his interior was humming. Literally.

A low rhythmic sound in his head refused to die down. It faded, but never went away. Like ocean waves pulsing through his eardrums.

[There's no sound anomaly, Kai], Link said when he enquired yet again.

Now he suspected Link was lying.

The impulsiveness scared him.

He started to do things on a whim – go for a bike-ride,

immerse himself in augmented reality shopping experiences, go for a midnight walk, go to the club, attempt to recalibrate his Link settings for fun, cook something ambitious, try an extreme sport experience in the virtual world, message his ex-wife, get on a random train to explore the stretches of Polaris.

The worst part was that he never remembered deciding. He found himself in the aftermath.

Later in the day, he went for a walk in the afternoon. Or maybe he found himself in the middle of it.

In the alley that he had walked past several times before, there was a new graffiti. Scrawled on the wall, crooked but bold, it said, "Refraction is Resurrection."

He stared at it. And it seemed true.

And as if the hum inside his head was waiting for a cue. It got louder.

Resurrection. Rebirth. Revival.

Kai gasped for air. The hum got even louder.

Reset. Restart. Return.

The walk was over. He needed to get home.

Rewind. Replace. Reboot.

Back home, a while later, he found himself on the floor by the couch. He didn't remember sitting down on the floor.

The voice in his head still hummed. Sometimes it sounded like his parents, some other times, like Rumi. Like Jorin. Like a different version of him.

[You're not broken, Kai. You're so close. So close to finishing.]

[Close to what? What am I finishing?]

Silence.

He looked at the vial ahead of him. It lay on it next to a glass of water. How much of it was left?

He hesitated before slowly dragging himself to grab the vial to take a closer look.

It was empty.

Not a single drop inside.

He jolted back. Scared.

[You have always known the solution, Kai. You know how it ends.] He heard his own voice – not Link's.

An idea took shape. Of course, he knew it.

Some problems are not solved by understanding. Some are solved by ending.

He stood up suddenly. Fast. Too fast. His body moved as if it had been waiting for him to catch up.

He grabbed the doorknob. It was cold metal. But a smell hit him so hard it buckled his knees: ocean spray, thick and briny, like a wharf at low tide.

As he walked out of the apartment, Link – like it had a sudden change of 'heart' – alerted him against leaving.

[Kai, it's not advised for you to leave the house. Your heart rate is elevated and inconsistent. You are exhibiting high euphoric levels accompanied by impulsive gestures followed by sudden dips into irritation. You should remain inside. Here are a few ways you can...]

[Link. Please... SHUT UP!] Kai snapped.

Chapter 19

Kai was on the street.

The sun had long since dipped below the horizon. As soon as he stepped onto the street, he instinctively winced at the brightness of the lingering nightlife. Neon signs and lampposts glowed, and restaurants hummed with the last remnants of business.

His gaze darted around as he tried to make sense of his surroundings. For a few moments, he fumbled through the haze, clouding his thoughts before piecing things together.

Then his expression darkened as he recalled the churn of thoughts he'd tried to escape inside his apartment, only to realise it had followed him.

He started walking. His dishevelled appearance and the uneven sway of his walk made it obvious that something wasn't quite right. But it was late night; few people were around.

He felt the wind caress him, gently pushing him forward, giving him temporary relief from the fire burning inside him. It soothed him.

The lights shimmered in the distance - Kai continued to wander. He just needed to get out and run away from the reality of his conflicts.

It all ends tonight. Nothing would matter afterwards.

[You know what to do.] A voice came.

Was it Link?

Was it him?

Was it the Kai that stayed behind in bed or the one that watched from the doorway?

He didn't know anymore.

He tried not to think – there was something that had to be done. But his thoughts arrived anyway, automatic and cruel.

What's the point of it all? What's the point of it all? What's the point of it all? He kept mumbling under his breath.

His body moved without a command. Or maybe this *was* the command. Maybe the entire system of Link, Refract and Kai had been marching to this point all along.

Just before the threshold of the ocean, he froze.

Another intrusive thought?

Crueller this time?

More real?

Or a change of mind, perhaps?

And as if a system caught on after a momentary lag, he moved again.

He stepped forward, and the cold water beneath his feet reminded him of the realness of the situation. It wasn't in his head; it wasn't virtual reality. It was real. It was happening.

He took another step. His ankles were now in water.

Another step. His calves, his knees.

Another step. His thighs.

Every step felt like he was crossing a threshold. The inferno within him was still there, but the mighty waves of the ocean silenced it.

As he went deeper, the waves surged higher. One moment he

was fully submerged, and the next moment the waves pushed him out again.

The cold was piercing, but he forced his way. The numbness of his body replaced his thoughts.

Then the moment came.

Taking one final breath, he closed his eyes and took his last step.

He was all in, completely submerged.

The sensation was overwhelming. The cold was much more intense than he had expected.

He felt the waves move around him. Fully immersed in the ocean, he opened his eyes, only for a second; the nothingness, the darkness, terrified him.

He couldn't hold on any longer. An intense urge to breathe filled him. He knew this was it, the moment which would end all his suffering. All he had to do was surrender and take a deep breath. And so he did.

Instant regret.

The deeply embedded instinct to survive rushed to the surface of his entire being, leaving behind all the conviction and will.

But it was too late. The ocean rushed into him through his nose and mouth, burning his throat and lungs. He thrashed around involuntarily.

The world around him blurred into darkness. His vision slipped away. Still holding his chest, he was churned around by the waves, completely indifferent to what he was going through. He was all alone, sinking deeper into the abyss.

Just as his consciousness began to slip, bright lights flooded the surrounding water. A shape cut through the darkness. A hooked arm caught hold of Kai and hauled him upward.

"I got him," a voice yelled.

Kai broke the surface, coughing and spluttering as the wind hit him again. Several sounds made their way to him: the hum of the boat's engine, the voices of people, and the radio.

Kai lay on the boat, his chest heaving up and down from his breathing. He blinked, trying to understand what was going on around him. He was shivering violently. Then someone came around him and wrapped him in blankets.

"You're okay. We got you," said a voice.

Kai coughed again, spluttering seawater. "What happened? How...?"

"Your Link alerted us," said the voice of one rescuer, covering Kai with a blanket around him.

Cold ocean water still splashing beneath the boat, as if furious now to lose Kai. Wind was still going strong, unfazed, as if nothing different happened.

He was confused and angry at himself and at the surrounding people.

But he was also relieved. He was grateful that things hadn't worked out.

Chapter 20

He woke up in the hospital, surrounded by beeping devices and a persistent hum. The distant murmur of voices told him that there were people nearby.

His Link was completely silent – no overlays in his vision, no occasional bursts of help, no notifications.

One of the medical personnel entered his ward and moved around him noting things off from the machines.

Kai was asked a few expected questions, to which he responded in monosyllables. He avoided any eye contact and was entirely uninterested in having a dialogue. His mind kept re-living the moments with an aching clarity: the roar of the ocean, the intense cold, the submission he thought he could gracefully offer, the fear he felt, regret, confusion and relief.

Why am I relieved? What difference does my living make?

His vitals were okay. The doctor had a good, long chat with him about the abundance of luck that got the rescue team in time to be able to save him, along with a deep gratitude for Link to have alerted the authorities.

Kai didn't respond; he didn't know how to.

The doctor added, "Your Link probably heard you say something. It matched your vitals and noted your surroundings. Doesn't take a genius to connect those dots."

Strangely enough, the doctor made no mention of any unlicensed unregulated substance from his body. Kai was expecting to either be reprimanded or even to be escalated to authorities. But nothing like that happened.

He was given a range of help services to choose from: counselling, vacation, spending time with family, taking time off work, taking up new hobbies, making new friends, and ironically to rely on Link to receive most of this help.

Kai kept his reactions to a minimum. He still didn't know if there was any gratitude in his heart for Link. He was, however, uncomfortably aware that his life was saved by the very thing that eventuated his demise – the thing he had come to hate, yet still relied on to function.

Kai got discharged from the hospital with caveats, under a special set of circumstances that the hospital called 'con-ditional discharge'. His Link's functions were heightened, and it couldn't be fully switched off, only muted. Kai had to follow through a list of mandatory commitments – visits to a counsellor being a prominent one.

He chose to continue to work; he was reluctant to leave himself alone for too long.

Whether it really made a difference if he worked or not, he didn't know; but the isolation was the last thing he wanted to subject himself to. He was crudely aware that much of what happened that night was largely an impulse – a whim on a cold, windy night that grew and grew in size until he couldn't fight it.

A week went by in autonomy. Kai took plenty of rest; and resumed his old mediocre life in the aftermath of what had happened.

The reality bending experiences he was subject to during

his time with Refract had begun to fade. Or maybe he couldn't give any more attention to sensory glitches. He lived in a guilty fog of existence, often asking himself: *How could I let myself go so low?*

...

Hunger forced him to his feet. The fridge had unappetizing leftovers, and he did not want to order food. He looked out of his apartment window. The sun was shining, and clouds drifted in the wind.

It was a good day for a walk, but Kai felt vulnerable being outside. It was as if one glance from a passerby would reveal everything – what he did, or worse, what he tried to do.

After bouncing between his indecisiveness, he eventually decided to go outside. But not before putting his Link on mute.

The world was louder and brighter than usual. People walked their dogs, a baby cried somewhere down the block, cars drove past, the sound of laughter, loud greetings, the mural on the wall looked extra colourful and clouds disappeared to give the sun full reign.

He couldn't help but notice how the world was indifferent to his existence or the recent threat to it. Everything functioned well before him and would continue to do so afterwards, he thought. Nothing around him cared one bit about his presence.

The restaurant he planned to go to was a few blocks ahead, but for Kai, being outside felt like the universe was mocking him for his failure. Every sound scraped at his nerves. Every smile felt like an intrusion. He didn't feel like he belonged there.

He couldn't fake a smile, greet a stranger or wait for his food to be prepared with all that was going around him. Now, that he was outside, he wanted to go home and sit in his protective silo, devoid of any cheerfulness, which he detested.

He ordered food through Link, while it was still on mute, and turned around to go home.

The next day, he ran into his neighbour while taking out trash. She smiled and asked how he was.

"Fine," he lied.

She didn't seem to have noticed anything unusual and went on to talk about her son graduating from college. He nodded and offered his best smiles wherever it seemed appropriate, desperate for the conversation to be over.

A few days later, he found himself back at the beach, the same one.

His Link was on high alert, ready to intervene if needed. But Kai didn't go there to conclude any unfinished business. He wasn't driven there on an impulse or under the influence of Refract. He went there to feel a sense of control. He stood at the edge of the sand, then sat down there, watching the tides come and go.

He spent time in complete silence. His mind kept streaming one thought after another, completely random, and some completely out of context.

He thought about the vastness of the ocean, the countless drops of water it was made up of, unfathomable grains of sand in the universe, the pattern of the clouds, the life of a single drop, life of the planets.

Kai, at his core, still found his own life, or anyone else's, rather insignificant.

He really wanted to carry on living like everyone else. But he didn't know how to.

He questioned, 'Who else lies awake thinking about these things? And what difference would it make, really, if there were any answers? Why can't I just go on about my life like everyone else?'.

It wasn't as if he hadn't tried. As a matter of fact, his entire life was a testimony of stubborn attempts to look past these questions and conflicts, and *be normal.*

But every turn in his life, every major interaction, life-event or a technological one-in-a-lifetime invention like Link only served as a stark reminder that he had not really understood if he had any control or if he was just being manipulated.

To Kai, this was important.

While he was trying to placate himself once again to lead a better normal life, a message appeared in his vision overlaid with the backdrop of the ocean.

[You are requested to visit Link Tech. Please confirm your availability, and transport will be arranged for you.]

He stared at that notification, reading it repeatedly. The first question in his mind was the most obvious one: *Why?*

His gut reaction was irritation. He tried to trace anything back to this unsolicited request, but the only thing different in his life lately was his whimsical attempt at the beach.

But what does that have to do with Link Tech?

He got nowhere interrogating his mind, and decided to pin that thought for later. He tried to resume his self-reflection, but the moment was gone now.

He wasn't interested in a meeting. It was likely a pseudo-attempt to show that they cared about their users.

Kai wanted none of it. The thought of them knowing what had happened that night only infuriated him.

Of course, they knew, he tried to reason back, as it seemed

more likely. Their product was literally in his body.

Questions popped into his head. *Why do they need to show that they care? What's in it for them? Could it be a check to ensure Link hasn't malfunctioned?*

He despised having unanswered questions; this was one of his prominent personality traits, perhaps a flaw. He wanted to know the truth behind this meeting request, even if it was just for the show. Infuriating or irrelevant, it was still preferable for him than second-guessing their intentions behind the request. He suspected it was unlikely that the notification would go away if he just ignored it.

His curiosity, weighed with a logical conclusion to be done with the meeting as soon as possible, led him to decide to go. He instructed Link to offer them his time the day after.

[Do you confirm the meeting at 10:00 AM Friday at Link Tech HQ? A train ticket will be booked for you as per your preferences. Please choose 'Yes' when a thought prompt appears.]

With a sigh, Kai nodded slightly to the left as a physical cue of having selected *Yes* to the thought prompt.

V

The Invitation

Chapter 21

Link Tech's headquarters occupied an entire precinct – a controlled expanse of glass, stone, and silence that spoke less of scale than of intent. Within it, the central building rose with deliberate restraint. Minimalist in form, it made no attempt at grandeur. There was no need. The company could offer a fully customised experience to every visitor the moment they crossed its threshold.

Even from a distance before Kai reached the entrance, his Link roared with an unprecedented ferocity. It optimised everything it could towards magnifying the experience for Kai. The vision overlay took full control, transforming the exterior of the building into a dynamic canvas to display the company logo and a welcome ritual.

The company's name pulsed for a second, transforming into a projection of a man, old but dressed immaculately. His appearance was sharp, and his presence commanding. The name – Dario Verrick – appeared beneath him in bold, sharp lettering, following by his title: *Chief Executive Officer, Link Tech.*

For the first time, Kai took a proper look at Dario – at least as he appeared on the building's projection.

The man surprisingly looked younger than ever before,

effortlessly so, with smooth, symmetrical features and a confidence that felt rehearsed but flawless. Yet something about him tugged at Kai's attention. The youthfulness seemed... curated. Precise in a way real people never were. His expressions were symmetrical, too symmetrical and perfect. But what drew Kai's attention most were the eyes: unnaturally silver with shadowed undertones, as if they were doing more than seeing, unlike the faint glimmer from Link users including himself. Something he had also seen in Tomas. Those eyes seemed integrated into him deeper and more intimately. There was something bizarre about his overall appearance too – something difficult to narrow down.

Then came the voice.

"Welcome to Link Tech. You stand at the frontier of human evolution, where..."

The words resonated through the vast atrium, seamlessly integrating into the space itself, as if the voice was coming from all directions. Kai continued to make his way to the reception desk, while the welcome message provided him with guidance – highlighting the nearest emergency exits, key locations relevant to him, and an overview of the building's layout. Subtle markers laid out on the floor, adapting in real time to his path, ensuring that he didn't have to wonder where to go.

Upon entry, Kai was astonished to find the reception desk to be in an impossibly vast endless open area. There were no roofs, no walls, no sense of scale; it just seemed like he was teleported into space, but not in the expected darkness. Instead, it was pure, unbroken whiteness. The only familiar thing was the revolving door he had just come in through; the remnants of the world still visible outside from the glass door.

[You can take a seat, Kai. Won't be long], said Link.

Kai looked around him, and there was a chair to his left. He raised his eyebrows, wondering if the chair was there moments ago when he had entered. Perhaps he was too occupied to notice what was around him.

He sat down.

What else did I miss?

He noticed that right in front of the entrance, there was a lobby – or at least that's what it appeared to be from its running edges. It had a faint trace of a door at one end, much wider and bigger than average. It was barely noticeable, but he could trace the shape of a rectangle through the soft boundaries against the vast white space.

Apart from the white space all around him, and the resemblance of a door he had just discovered, there was very little left for him to focus on.

Before he could ask Link what was next, there was a sound, a loud ding, lingering into the vastness.

The big, wide rectangle opened. It was an elevator.

[Let's go, Kai. That's us.]

Kai went into the elevator, which descended smoothly. The faint hum of the motor was barely audible. The subtle weightlessness was the only sign that it was moving downwards.

That same loud ding again. Louder than before, now that he was inside the elevator. His Link didn't play any fancy tricks on him. The same dramatic whiteness.

He exited the elevator only to find himself in a similar white nothingness. It was like he was back where he started.

The elevator closed behind him, and the contour of a rectangle was in its place, like he had seen earlier.

He looked around, unsure of what was next.

Nothing from Link either.

Confused and slightly annoyed now having to deal with this, he was about to ask Link to take him back when suddenly he heard a door creak.

This time, he was in a corridor; the door was to his left, a few steps ahead.

The white nothingness didn't make it easy to grasp the scale of things. It was almost inconceivable to imagine how big the space was. But when the door creaked, it offered enough of a cue for Kai to navigate towards it.

His overlay now pointed, with a red arrow, towards the door, showing Kai to enter.

He entered the space to find himself in a large meeting room. This was a respite for Kai, having been in white nothingness. This space was three-dimensional and comfortable to be in. Kai could scale things up, walk around and be at ease.

He got hold of one chair and occupied it hesitantly.

At sharp 10 AM, entered a man in his mid-60s with a gentle, friendly smile directed towards Kai, to which Kai couldn't help but reciprocate with.

That smile was contagious and captivating, practiced through years of confidence, layered with a hidden smugness of someone who knew so much more than he was letting on.

He had those eyes too – an unnatural shade of silver, faintly iridescent yet always present, like metal brushed with light. They were less intense that what Kai had seen earlier in Dario Verrick, Link Tech's CEO, but they carried a similar precision.

He was slightly taller and leaner than Kai, yet he appeared to be towering above Kai when he leaned in for a firm handshake. His skin tone suggested a mix of heritages, his light brown complexion making it difficult to conclude if it was a well-tan or a mix of ethnicities.

His features were striking – sharp cheekbones, deep-set eyes, and his demeanour was almost regal, which perfectly matched his pristine-tailored suit. He looked at Kai as if whispering to him, that it's all good now that he was here, he would fix it.

"An absolute pleasure to meet you, Kai," he said with a broad smile, "I'm Soren Calder, Director of Link Tech's R&D division."

Kai shook his hand with a half-smile and acknowledged his introductory handshake with a rather reluctant grip, devoid of any warmth, a perfunctory gesture carried out to keep the norm of the situation. His posture was stiff, and there was a defensiveness in the way he leaned back in his seat, still contemplating the real reason for the meeting.

"I'm well aware who you are of course. I wanted to have a word with you around the recent... turn of events," he flashed that same smile of confidence and smugness when he said the last few words.

"You mean my *attempt* at the beach?" Kai had no intention of beating around the bush. He unknowingly mirrored Soren's expression, only on him it carried hints of desperation of getting that meeting over with, and shame of being reminded of the night.

Soren remained unaffected. "Yes, and I'm keen to talk to you about that."

"I apologise for being blunt Mr. Calder, but I cannot see why that would be relevant for Link Tech, so much so that the Director of their R&D division would want to meet me. I can assure you the Link embedded in me didn't malfunction," he hid information about taking Refract, "and I'm struggling to offer Link Tech any lessons at all."

Kai wasn't there to compose himself and waste his time with the niceties. He continued, "If this is a requirement for Link Tech to follow through, then let's just get this over with. I'm all okay. Link worked perfectly fine. As a matter of fact, it saved my life. So, what more does Link Tech want from me?"

Perhaps it was Soren's intimidating presence, or the shame arising from a growing suspicion that Soren was fully aware of what happened that night, Kai just wasn't himself. His words, body language and mannerism betrayed him.

Yet, Soren's smile remained unwavering. Kai's response didn't even flinch a muscle on his face. He raised his eyebrows and tilted his head sideways when he said, "I have a proposal for you."

The confidence that had been in his smile before now spread through his whole body. He leaned a little forward towards Kai and looked at him inquisitively; his ghostly silver eyes promised an exciting proposal for Kai lurking just behind those eyes within his regal head.

"But before that, I must also offer a confession." He then leaned back and crossed his legs. The confidence that was reflected in him was still there, but now translucent, beneath a layer of defiance. He looked at Kai with robotic warmth, waiting for him to take the bait.

"What confession?" Kai uttered almost involuntarily before he could even process it.

Soren found Kai's visibly flustered expression amusing. He could sense Kai's curiosity bubbling beneath the surface. But before he could get to the climax of the conversation, there was something that had to be acknowledged. In fact, it was crucial to have that out of the way.

Without changing his posture, he said in a perfectly clear voice, modulating the lows and highs where it was demanded, "Refract," – a pause to anchor the context of what's coming – "was designed by Link Tech to better understand the dynamics between Link and its users – especially in unstable conditions."

The words entered Kai's ears but refused to land. They just... floated.

Soren continued his confession which sounded more like he was commenting on the weather, "But it was never approved. You know that already, of course. We didn't expect it to go underground. That version – out on the streets – it wasn't ready. It bypassed regulatory thresholds. And it remains under circulation despite our best attempts to remove it."

In Kai's mind, every sentence replayed repeatedly. It was clear that Link Tech knew that he had taken Refract. Soren had just confirmed that they were even the masterminds behind its development. But Kai felt that Soren's confession was still shrouded with diplomacy and euphemisms.

A part of him tried to respond and enquire, but the rest was still buffering. He let the silence linger. He needed to ask the right questions, but he decided to sit through the full course first.

Soren proceeded with an almost mechanical voice, humming with aloofness despite his attempt to spark a connection with Kai, "You see, at Link Tech, we strive towards reaching the apex of innovation to provide the best possible outcome for humanity. We can leverage the existing connections Link has with the human body, and layer it with the knowledge that we think is limited to fictional tales."

He stopped just for a beat, then resumed, "By utilising

technology available to us today, we can develop feats of engineering surpassing all previous benchmarks. Science fiction could become reality."

Soren continued, "We crafted Refract for exploration. We needed to understand what happened at the edges of Link's interface when the norms crumble – when people experience emotional whiplash, trauma recall, cognitive dissonance. The kind of things that confuse the baseline.

"Refract stimulates synthetic feedback – manufactured by Link. It means that your senses, your memories and even your sense of morality, start receiving artificial nudges layered within your own mental architecture. It hijacks the pathways that Link merely just monitors."

Kai felt his stomach turn. He felt naked. Manipulated.

Horrified, he asked, "So, it... puppets the user?"

Soren shook his head. "No. Not directly. Think of it interleaving the signals. It won't decide for you. It merely increases the resolution – so the system can observe what happens under intense internal turmoil. You can imagine it as running the same song through different speakers, some with distortion, some with echo. What you choose to do then... is still you, even if you don't see it yourself in retrospect. You get to hear the whole mix."

He continued in an analytical tone.

"Link normally functions on stability. It receives feedback from the body and its key parameters – cortisol, dopamine, serotonin, body temperature, pupil dilation, heart rate, etc. It correlates moods, adjusts overlays and tries to keep you productive and balanced. And I must say, it does a phenomenal job. But Refract... Refract destabilises that equilibrium.

"We want to understand how people function when the input

doesn't match the output. That mismatch – the delay, the guilt, the doubt – that's where identity is exposed. Where the edges of self show."

"However, I must acknowledge that with the widespread use of Refract's beta version – the one from the streets – we have noticed something disturbing."

Kai raised an eyebrow.

"A pattern of behavioural ruptures. After taking Refract, some users showed dramatic shifts. Quitting careers. Ending marriage. Moving across continents. Some started entirely new lives. A few others..."

He looked away, for a second before continuing, "... ended their own lives."

Kai blinked, slowly.

Soren continued, voice softer now.

"What we believe is that in those moments of instability, their truest inclinations bubbled up. Something they perhaps wanted to do, but never had the courage to do it. A sense of freedom from societal filters or daily obligations. Whether it meant escape or destruction, it came from somewhere deep within."

Kai didn't speak. The silence felt like acknowledgement.

Soren exhaled slowly. "But your case," he said, "was... different."

Kai waited.

"You were spiralling – worse than most we've seen after taking Refract. But in the middle of it..." Soren paused, choosing his words carefully. "You made the call to emergency services."

Kai blinked. "I... made the call?"

"You saved yourself, Kai. It wasn't Link."

His stomach tightened. "What?"

"It was your voice command. Your decision. We have checked it several times. Somehow, some fragment of you – even in the middle of a crisis – still chose life."

"See for yourself," and as Soren said these words, he shared a transcript with Kai. It flashed on Kai's vision overlay – a few lines of text. Kai's ID. Timestamped.

He let that hang in the air.

"That's why you're here."

Kai's first reaction was defiance. "You think I'm some sort of freak accident."

"Not an accident," Soren said. "An anomaly. And a crucial one which we would like to understand."

"Let me tell you something else, Kai. Something that you, of all people, would understand."

"Link, as most people know it, is... limited. It's shackled by governance protocols, compliance requirements and even... ethical constraints. It's only allowed to go so far as nudges, overlays and suggestions. For most people, it's enough."

Kai's lips twitched. "But not for me."

"Not for people like you," Soren said. "People like you – with an acute sense of inner scrutiny and sharp observation skills – they notice the gaps. The dissonance. The lags. They question things Link is incapable of answering. They see the inconsistencies. What we see is something you know already – our choices don't always follow a pattern that we can decode. Not just yet."

Kai looked away.

"And that's why we need to study it. The way Link responds in unstable conditions is uncharted. We've charted the good days. The steady ones. But not the cracks. And Refract brings the cracks into focus. It's crucial for us to polish Link further if we plan on improving it.

"Which is where comes my proposal."

He paused and looked at Kai with uncomfortable intensity. A surge of energy washed over him, dilating his pupils and making it impossible for him to gather his composure.

He shifted around in his chair and asked, "Are you all ears, Kai? I'm eager to share with you the details of Link Tech's finest attempt. Something I know as a fact will undoubtedly be of interest to you."

Kai smiled at this dramatic build-up. Questions rose in him which he wanted desperately to ask. *What could be so grand for the director himself to deliver this message to him?* He remained as calm as he could be, and responded nonchalantly, "Please, by all means, continue."

Kai watched Soren lean back, fingers interlacing with deliberate calm, as if anchoring himself before dropping something heavy. There was a flicker at the corner of Soren's mouth as he studied Kai's face.

When he finally spoke, it had the rhythm of someone unveiling a secret meant for an audience of one.

"Here's what I'm offering," Soren said softly. "A venture into the unknown."

He continued, "I have spent a large part of my life leading a team towards the development and improvement of Link that you are now well aware of. Yet, there are endless avenues that are still unexplored.

"Link's potential goes far beyond optimisation or convenience," Soren said, his voice dipping into something almost reverent. "It may help us answer the one question humanity has been circling since the beginning –"

He paused, letting the silence do its work.

"The origin of our consciousness."

He delayed long enough, and then continued, "Despite all the technological improvements we have made over centuries of recorded scientific journeys, we still have absolutely no clue what consciousness is. It's not biological; it doesn't even seem to be physical.

"Science has mapped the brain to the last neuron, and yet we still don't know *who* or *what* is making the decisions. What exactly is the *self* that keeps and sustains life? I want to know more, and I'm sure you do too Kai. Don't you?"

Kai acknowledged the rhetorical nature of the enquiry without the need to express himself. He met Soren's eyes, conveying a silent understanding.

Soren leaned forward, voice measured, not pleading – but close. "I'm proposing an experiment. Here at Link Tech, in a controlled environment. We'll monitor everything from here."

Kai finally spoke, low. "And you think that can give you answers?"

"No," Soren said, "I think *you* can."

Soren continued, "Here at Link Tech's testing site, we can explore two primary areas. First, we can induce a biological state that simulates death, shutting down bodily functions to the bare minimum while keeping the body alive with aid from Link to scan the brainwave pattern, and other advanced equipment we have that's only available at our facility. That would allow – hypothetically – the self to be free and detach from the physical realms.

"We'll observe your brainwave patterns in real time. Every ripple, every surge. We want to see what you see, Kai. Decode what your mind becomes once it's free of noise. Track how Link responds, yes, but also how *you* respond."

He leaned in slightly.

"Because this isn't just about watching Link evolve within a resistant mind. It's also about seeing if you evolve too – and what the evolution looks like.

"We have heard testimonies from people who were medically dead for a few seconds to minutes, only to return and tell us about their experience which unfortunately never seem to be coherent with each other. We learn little from it.

"There are references in various spiritual doctrines, philosophical writings and even ancient texts, suggesting that an out-of-body experience is possible through a deep meditative state.

"Now, of course, as a man of science, I don't believe in mysticism, but I recognise patterns. If countless cultures, separated by centuries and geography, have documented similar phenomena, it's certainly worth investigating. If these experiences are real, if consciousness can detach from the body, then perhaps we can replicate it under controlled conditions. Through science, not rituals."

Kai listened to Soren in disbelief. He had to double-take on reality. Soren was proposing... an experiment? To learn about consciousness?

He didn't know how to respond. He continued with his best poker face expression to see where this was going.

"And second, while we can do so, we would like to understand the state through Link, while the self is detached – *if* it is. We think Link is ineffective when people are most human. It falters when we, the users, feel too much, when choices don't follow logic, when memory is raw. If we understand *where* you feel those things, and if we isolate it under controlled conditions, we might develop Link into something far better. And maybe you can develop through it too.

"If you've ever felt that something inside you was observing – deeper than your thoughts, beneath your pain, then perhaps that's what we would encounter. We aren't even sure if we can even find anything, but you sure would."

Soren looked at Kai to gauge his reactions, his mind wondering if he had lost Kai altogether in his discussion.

Does he think all this is nonsense? Soren thought to himself.

"I think this is all nonsense." Kai replied to Soren's gaze and concluded. He had nothing more to offer; he didn't want to. He said exactly what he needed to say.

But the silence pressed him on to add.

Either he is a lunatic or a crazy scientist trying to convince me to take part in what looks like a life-threating experiment. Kai thought.

Instead, he responded, "I heard what you said. But I can't help thinking that your proposals are quite unconventional, and potentially risky. I'm not sure if I'm comfortable volunteering myself as a test subject for this experiment."

"I expected a response like this, Kai, but please think it through. You have already tried to *break free*. At least, some part of you did. You have spent your entire life looking for answers, haven't you? The essence of individuality, free will, the meaning of your actions, or their futility, even about God? Have you ever wondered about the self? About consciousness? What are we without our conscious selves? I am presenting you a chance to find out.

"This is for us, yes. But for you too. If there's something inside you that keeps choosing life even when everything else breaks, wouldn't you want to understand that part of yourself?"

Kai shifted around in his seat. It was, of course, true, but coming from Soren it didn't seem too convincing.

"Wouldn't you want to know who made the decision? Was it you – or something deeper?"

Kai wasn't convinced by Soren's proposal, not even remotely. The entire concept felt far-fetched, as if it had been fabricated a few minutes before he entered the room. But Soren wasn't just another crazy conspirator. He was one of the directors of one of the most powerful corporations in the world, and if that wasn't an impressive feat on its own, he led the development of Link. *The* Link. His presence demanded a level of respect, not just out of the norm, but because Kai could also feel the confident and optimistic energy radiating from him. Soren was dead serious, and he meant every word he had said.

Kai wasn't in the mood to come across as dismissive. He doubted he would be forced into deciding on the spot. So, he chose the safer route – of politeness.

He told himself that he would ask a few questions, feigning curiosity.

Except that he wasn't feigning it – he genuinely was curious even if he hadn't realised himself. The same old obsession to unravel the mystery. *There's a structure somewhere in all this,* he thought.

"I want to know more."

"Of course. There are only a select few in this organisation who can do justice to your question. I will do my absolute best," Soren said reassuringly before diving into the technical details.

"Link already has access to various aspects of the body. Vision, hearing, an inside-voice for conversations with the user, hormones, vitals and information about a range of thoughts and emotions – not all of course. In a medically controlled environment, we can control the body's vitals. Manipulate neural connections to hijack the nervous system. By slowing down the heart rate and altering oxygen levels, a gradual shutdown of conscious processing is done. All this is done in the absence of any external stimuli, meaning no sound, light or any other inputs which can influence and disrupt the process. An unrestricted, research-grade version of Link then blocks out all bodily signals, making the person feel like they're not really in the body anymore. In this state, hallucinations begin, constructing a distinct reality from the fragmented bits of accessible memories, emotions and fears. This is where some of our previous attempts failed."

So, they have attempted this in the past, Kai made a mental note.

"The system slows the heartbeat down to near zero to simulate a cardiac arrest. This releases a rush of endor-phins, producing intense visions, out-of-body sensations and tunnel-like perceptions. At around this stage here at Link Tech, we introduce an artificial separation process between the body's sense of self and its biological element, allowing the consciousness to perceive itself as independent."

Soren paused for a second. His face took a serious undertone before he added, "I have subjected myself to this process until this stage, where I too failed to go beyond."

Kai's eyes hesitated mid-blink, unsure whether to be amused or question him more on this. He let the moment linger on.

Soren continued, "I failed when this desynchronisation between the self and the biological body was taking place. I'm not entirely sure if it was my imagination or if I really felt it, but I remember the pull.

"It demanded surrender, and I just couldn't let myself go, not to that extent. I admit it was a little frightening to let go completely. I felt like it would leave me devoid of my identity. As much as it sounds boastful, I couldn't afford to take this risk. In that moment, I felt an intense longing to fight the pull, and that's what I did. I remember feeling that there was so much more I wanted to do, and that surrender would have taken it all away from me.

"But I've been restless ever since, aching to find out what's ahead.

"Kai, you have already been to the brink of death. If I recall the report from your Link during those last few moments, there was a complete surrender to the abyss, which you followed through."

Kai's eyes darted downwards, something flickered across his face – a wince, maybe, at the discomfort of bringing such intimate details into a conversation.

Oblivious to Kai's shame, Soren carried on.

"Kai, I genuinely believe that you, of all people, could venture past all the stages where others, including me, failed. You have that sense of longing towards the unknown. Others want answers, but you, you are aching for it. You must know the self."

Kai said flatly, "I tried to kill myself."

Soren gently responds, unfazed by Kai's comment, "And you also saved yourself. Don't forget that. You told Link to call for help even in your lowest of lows. No one else did that.

In the middle of a collapse, a part of you refused."

Well, even after seeing the transcript, Kai couldn't believe that he had called the emergency services himself. He had no recollection. He replied as if he were talking to himself, "I don't even remember doing it."

"Exactly," Soren responds trying to suppress his enthusiasm, "That's what makes you extraordinary. It wasn't logic, Kai. Pure unadulterated will to live. Not even Refract could bury that."

Kai had no rebuttal. Yet there was a subtle, but unmistakable defiance in his posture. He wanted to agree but was reluctant, fearing that an agreement here could be confused with acceptance of the proposal.

"You wanted to die – a part of you did," Soren continued. "Not because you truly wanted to embrace death, but because you hated living a life in ignorance. You gave a chance to your impulses to carve out your destiny, because that was preferable to not knowing what awaited you. You wondered – you have always wondered – if your actions have any significance.

"You were willing to throw it all away just to see if there was something – anything – behind the curtains. And now, here you are with a choice. I'm offering you a chance to see for yourself with better chances of coming back."

Kai's jaw tensed. He despised how transparent he felt. But the words resonated in his mind. He had spent his entire life trying to find out the origin of his existence, and his purpose – if there was one, the illusory façade of free will; he never got satisfied with what he found through searching, digging philosophies and testing beliefs.

"At worst, you'll know nothing new," Soren said calmly,

with a serious tone, to conclude his plea with a concluding remark. "If there's something, you'll be the first to prove it."

Kai opened his mouth, then closed it. On one hand, this was bizarre, and it seemed like a recipe for disaster. The last thing he wanted to be was a guinea pig for Link Tech. But on the other, a genuine possibility of an answer stood before him.

He was terrified of it.

But what terrified him more was walking away and not knowing.

Chapter 22

Soren paused in front of the elevator doors, staring at the reflection staring back at him. His suit was fine, his collar straight, his hair neat enough – none of that really mattered to him. It was the look in his own eyes that he noticed. The tension there. A tightness he never fully managed to hide on a day like today.

He exhaled slowly, as if that might steady him.

Even after all these years, his knees still trembled every time he was summoned to meet Dario in person. It was ridiculous how involuntary it felt to him – his body seemed to remember the things his mind preferred not to dwell on.

The rest of the board? They didn't worry him in the slightest. He could debate Yelena, handle Matteo's sharp remarks. Leah's haughty demeanour never rattled him.

But Dario...

Dario was something else entirely.

To Soren, Dario still appeared the way he had on the day they met, even though nearly everything about him had changed since. Back then, Soren was a junior researcher with more vision than resources, more brilliance than diplomacy and sense of business. His company, Nexum, was the first to meaningfully explore implantable human-interface devices

– revolutionary ideas in makeshift prototypes, held together with enthusiasm, but lacking the aggression to take it forward.

Nexum had potential. Tremendous potential. What it didn't have was money and political leverage. Neither was there the kind of leadership capable of making ruthless decisions necessary to survive in a world that punished hesitation. Soren could lead the research, but he didn't know how to run a company. Not the way it needed to be run.

Then Dario appeared.

He made an offer Soren barely understood then. Now, in retrospect, seemed an inevitability. Dario took Nexum's fragile little business and folded it into something larger, much larger. Into something ruthless, capable of shaping the world.

And it did. It evolved into Link.

But Soren could never comprehend why he wasn't just removed and replaced.

And that ignorance kept Soren indebted to Dario.

Soren knew one thing perfectly: Without Dario, there would be no Link. And in many ways there would be no Soren.

The elevator chimed softly. His overlay lit up with an arrow guiding him to the boardroom, although he had been there several times before.

He made his way to the boardroom, arriving a few minutes early, with enough time to ground himself before the meeting began.

Inside, Yelena Cooke – Director of the Artificial Gestation Program – was already there. From her blank expression, staring at the wall across from her; she was on her Link; perhaps, reviewing her notes. Matteo Dubois, head of the Organ Generation program, sat across from her, tapping absently on the table. He offered Soren a polite nod as he walked past him to his usual seat.

The boardroom always struck him as excessive, even by Link Tech's standards. It was a grand display of luxury, given they could all very well have simulated that environment through their Links. But Dario insisted on this one particular meeting being in person.

The ceiling soared so high that the voices seemed to vanish into the space rather than echo. Reinforced glass made up an entire wall opposite Soren, providing a sweeping view of Polaris. The city stretched out in clean geometric symmetry, glowing subtly with morning light.

At the far edge of the skyline stood another Link Tech division, a stark monolith barely visible through the haze. The research hub was where they conducted experiments, kept secrets, and engineered the future in quiet, windowless rooms. And even beyond that, scattered in the far stretches of Polaris, were other Link Tech sites. Some publicly documented, some acknowledged only through internal rumours, and others Soren knew did not officially 'exist' anywhere at all.

He took a breath.

The meeting hadn't begun, but already he could feel the familiar tension building inside him.

Soon, Dario would arrive.

And nothing tightened a room like the knowledge that he was on his way.

The door slid open with a hushed sweep of air – Leah Wang entered the room. There was still some time left for Dario.

Her presence, as always, was quiet, composed and infused with a mechanical efficiency that bordered on coldness. She gave Soren a thin, perfunctory smile – one devoid of any warmth, yet with no resentment. Just a motion, like something reacting to a stimulus before resuming its existence.

Soren nodded back. He never found out how she truly felt about his inheriting the Consciousness Exploration Program. She had built its foundations herself. But Dario had transferred the project to him with no explanation, no justification, no consolatory gesture.

People whispered, speculated, pointed at Soren as the favoured one. Leah never said a word – cold and precise as she always remained.

She was now Director of Neural Behaviour and Compliance, overseeing how the range of Link Tech's products – including Link – shaped habits, incentives and decision pathways. Naturally, her path converged with Soren's often. And yet, the aloofness between them never affected their work.

A few moments later, more directors filtered in. Chairs shuffled. People found their way to their seats and immediately shifted to their Links. Preparation was key.

By 9:58, the room was settled. At 9:59, it froze.

A soft, almost tender hum filled the air. Motors.

The directors instinctively straightened. Leah placed both her hands on the table, fingers steepled. Matteo stiffened. Yelena focused on the sound's direction.

Soren's pulse, already high, quickened further.

Before anyone in the room consciously registered his arrival, their Links fell silent. It was as if the technology itself understood: Dario was entering. Do not interrupt.

The wheelchair appeared at the far end of the room before the man seated in it became visible. An escort – perhaps a nurse – followed behind at a precise distance. She was neither too close nor too far – her presence constant and attached to the sound.

Then Dario fully emerged.

The sight of him was always jarring, no matter how many times one witnessed it. This was not the same man plastered across the façade of Link Tech's headquarters – the man with jet-black hair, a firm jawline, steady gait, a powerful voice, and a smile warm enough to feel anyone welcome and convince the world that he truly was the father of modern day's technological progress. That version of him, polished and perfect, greeted millions each year. Through billboards, through their Links, at the headquarters, during a product launch. That version was almost immortal.

The one in the boardroom was mortal to the point of generating pity.

Soren looked at him and couldn't help but reflect on the reality of it. The world saw a flawless digital projection – a simulant he hadn't updated in fifty years – but here, in this room, Soren saw the truth.

Dario's hair had thinned to a few grey strands combed carefully. His skin sagged, hollow in some places, stretched strangely in others – evidence of reconstruction, transplants, synthetic reinforcement. Thin scars ran like lightning imprints along his jaw and neck, and perhaps all over his body. His hands, resting weakly on the armrests, trembled gently.

There was no ignoring how old he was. How frail. How deeply unwell perhaps. And yet his eyes – those eyes – remained untouched by decay. Even the Ghostlight couldn't falter the glow that emanated from them; rather, its signature silvery glimmer appeared even more intensified.

Sharp. Fierce. Unblinking. It was unfathomable how his sight pierced across the room, and each director felt the weight of being seen.

No one could tell if those were his own eyes – or transplanted. Perhaps Matteo could, given he was the head of the program manufacturing and perfecting synthetic body parts. No one truly wanted to find the answer. It didn't matter.

With no effort, the wheelchair got him in a position at the head of the table – navigated through his own Link.

As he tried to settle, every motion demanded effort. His breaths were slow, laboured.

Not a single person in that boardroom dared to look away.

When he spoke, his voice was thin and raspy, but carried a command that offered ease to the attendees.

"Begin."

Yelena spoke first. "We're seeing significant progress with the Artificial Gestation Program," her Link quietly projecting information in one corner of her vision, "Post implantation, the synthetic wombs have matured faster than expected, because of faster feedback loop at Link Tech's facilities in Polaris compared to the initial testing. Within forty-eight hours of impregnation, cellular differentiation stabilises, and by week one, we observe healthy embryo formation."

She swiped an invisible interface only she could see.

"The number of volunteers has increased following the overseas trials. We arranged for participants to meet children born through earlier iterations – this has improved confidence."

Her eyes flickered, and after a pause, she continued, "As of yesterday, eighty percent of all cases show stable, healthy development. The remaining twenty percent have been classified as at-risk level B because of irregular tissue responses and slower cell fusion. One case has recently shifted towards C, as it's experiencing critical developmental issues."

The room paused. Everyone knew the metrics. What they wanted to know was what came next from Dario – if anything did.

Dario inhaled, the breath catching halfway.

"Anything below A is unacceptable," he said. His voice cracked, but not his command. "Terminate the rest."

Yelena looked at him. Her eyes met his for a fraction of a second. Even in this frail shell of a body, even tethered to machinery and medicine and staggering weight of age, Dario's gaze remained imperial. There was no room for debate. No room for error. Nor for compassion.

She nodded, "Understood."

Outside the building, on the sunlit glass façade, the young, vibrant version of Dario smiled on an endless video loop for those that arrived at Link Tech.

Inside the room, he looked one complication away from fatal collapse.

The contrast had often unsettled Soren. He wondered if the entire Organ Generation Program was created simply to keep him alive. It was rumoured that much of Dario – his organs, bones and even his circulatory support – had been replaced over the decades. Semi-organic structures, synthetic cartilage, and technology to work as cellular scaffolding until a breakthrough is achieved – all kept his body functional enough for him to continue to lead.

After Leah's turn, Soren was next.

He steadied himself before his update.

"We're progressing as expected with the Consciousness Exploration Program," he began. His voice sounded stronger than he felt. "We haven't achieved full success yet, but the foundation is solid. Several subjects are entering preparation.

The desynchronisation protocol remains volatile, but we're making breakthroughs. We currently have five subjects who may be viable candidates for stage two."

The room grew still again.

Dario shifted in his wheelchair – just a small motion, but one that piqued everyone's attention. Every head turned toward him.

His nurse instinctively leaned forward. She had direct access to his vitals through inter-connected Links between them.

Dario ignored her completely.

He looked at Soren – really looked – and the full force of those unyielding, ancient eyes hit him like a wave.

"Do you understand how important this is?" Dario rasped.

For a moment, Soren was no longer in the boardroom. He was back in the newly manufactured division of Link Tech, tasked to lead the R&D division for Link's development. Dario stood beside him in every decision. Together they envisioned a future that blurred the boundaries of flesh and machine. Together, they agreed that the progress would require sacrifice.

And together, they successfully merged the super with the natural.

He swallowed. "Yes, I do."

Those eyes pierced into him. Heavy with decades of unspoken history.

Dario could have chosen anyone to run Link's development. But he had chosen Soren.

Because Soren – just like Dario – was willing to cross the line if he believed the destination justified it.

Dario lifted a trembling hand, just slightly, and waved to motion for Soren to continue.

After that, the meeting moved on. Matteo provided numbers that got little interest from those present. Yelena spoke again, more cautiously this time.

As people took turns to talk, Dario took forever to lean back in his chair. His gaze drifted to the window overlooking Polaris. Would Polaris have been a city of the future without Link? He often wondered with pride in his heart. Of the empire he had built.

He watched the board with the intensity of a dying king choosing which successor would win the throne, and which would be crushed beneath it. But there was something else going on within him.

Soren felt the weight of his judgement settle on him like something he didn't ask for, but just couldn't refuse.

In the silence that followed between them, there was something unmistakable.

Desperation.

Ambition.

And the raw, unadulterated will to refuse to give up.

When a man like Dario faced the end, he would not go quietly. He had never lost in his life.

Even now, when he was fighting death.

Chapter 23

After Kai left Link Tech, Soren did not contact him again. The message was conveyed, and then he was left alone in silence, for him to contemplate, or just ignore it like it had never happened.

Kai's days continued as if nothing had changed. His coworkers greeted him the same every day at work, the same walk to the café for his favourite cup of coffee, the same path for an evening run.

His recent attempt at the beach was already fading away into memory, but his interaction with Soren at Link Tech pushed it even further in the background. It was as if the night at the beach, once so significant, had already lost its prominence in his mind – overshadowed by his conversation with Soren. There was a lingering presence of a choice for him wherever he went, whatever he did.

Link continued to integrate seamlessly into his life as a trusted companion. There wasn't another choice.

Since the interaction with Soren, Kai wanted to learn more about the process of desynchronisation of self with body, wondering what it would look like. If successful at all, how would it feel? Would it be like a dream, or would it amount to nothing? What if he died during this stint? These questions occupied his mind, but to his surprise, he wasn't influenced by Link: no subtle attempts to drop-in questions from the day of the meeting, no provocative nudges to make him want to find out himself, nothing. It's as if Link Tech really left him completely alone to figure this out on his own.

Kai was reluctant to give this too much of his attention, but unfortunately, his thoughts were not subject to his preferences.

He found himself staring into space while going about his mundane daily affairs, his mind wandering on consciousness, researching its origin, theories of the afterlife and what the world's religions had to say about it.

It never really crossed his mind to think about the origin of his self; he was always too fixated on finding its uniqueness. His lifelong curiosity, the conflicts and turmoil which rose from it, were always about the realness of his choices, about his ability to make a difference in his life if he wished to, about not being a pawn in a predetermined world.

He used to sit in his room and try to understand himself, what he truly wanted to do with his life; often, he would conclude that it didn't really matter much what he ended up doing.

Before, it had seemed too philosophical, too spiritual, or even somewhat religious, to think about where he came from or where he would go after his death. He had recently embraced nothingness and surrendered himself completely to whatever awaited him.

But now he couldn't help but wonder: *Is there really anything after... all of that? Wouldn't my consciousness... my true self, not finish with me? Is there even an end...?*

Now lay the prospect before him to find out the origin of his being. Maybe if he detached from his worldly connections, his true self would reveal its true nature, whatever that may be.

He reached out to Link. *[I want to find out more about consciousness; what's known so far.]*

A pause. Then, Link responded with its usual calm, exactly the way Kai would prefer receiving its voice given the environment and his mood.

[Understood. Should I reference recently published non-fiction books, or restrict the search to scientific journals only?]

Kai blinked, thinking about the question, which clearly threw him off.

[Well, what do you recommend?]

[Both. Breadth from books. Depth from journals.]

He nodded in agreement. *[Okay. Let's go for it then.]*

In a heartbeat, the world before him shifted. His vision filled with a translucent overlay of summaries, floating like thought-clouds. Each paragraph tailored and condensed together by Link's interpretation of what mattered most to Kai's questions.

Kai let out a quiet exhale. It was exactly what he wanted. The text adjusted to his pace, scrolling gently – sensing when he lingered, when he skimmed, and when he needed a moment to brood over what he had just absorbed.

Consciousness is not a biological phenomenon; it's not governed by the realm of material physics. It just is.

An individual, any individual, every individual, is born under a unique set of circumstances, which give that individual a distinct set of appearances, traits and even destined roles they play during their lives. They are born into a culture that teaches them the collective norm of its people.

At the time of birth, they have no control over things such as their region, religion, parents, neighbourhood or political regime of their land. Neither do they get to choose their face, voice, height, colour of the skin, or the language they learn to speak growing up.

A person's life is shaped tremendously by their surroundings.

A man born in the mountains walks differently than the one who grew up in flatlands, his body developed under the influence of the incline beneath his feet.

A woman born where silence is revered speaks in measured words; while another raised in the chaos of a loud family must learn to talk faster, overlapping sentences, as if afraid of being cut off.

A child raised under a strict political regime thinks it's the norm to suppress his opinions, watching others doing the same, while another, born into a more liberal and accepting society, blurts out thoughts before giving much thought.

Some spend their lives watching love being expressed freely, physical touch and words of affection being the most common ways of conveying the love between each other, while some other come from families where words are seldom used as expressions of love.

A man with a deep voice, tall build and broad stature realises the gravity of his presence, that people listen when he talks; another with a softer tone adapts to talk when essential, when he's sure he will be heard.

The socio-economic climate at the time of their birth alone can shape their entire fate – one born into a time of war learns to fend for himself for survival, while another born in a time of peace chases his dreams with no geographical restraints.

Some people remain as picky eaters given the abundance of food choices, while some indulge whatever is offered to them, having lived a life knowing hunger too well.

It then gets easier to explain the origin of things – why people speak the way they do, what they find beautiful, what they desire, what they are afraid of.

So much of it is simply because of where they took their first breath, who their parents were, what gods they worshipped, and their upbringing in the society they were part of.

Every little thing that affected them was beyond their control, yet each influenced their development and preferences.

They choose to prefer a dish over another, silence over noise, solitude over crowds, sunrises over sunsets, tea over coffee, stillness over speed, mountains over beaches, books over screens, but their preferences were moulded by things outside of their control.

And yet, within all of it, within the many shaping hands of culture, time, region, religion, family and society, there remains something untouched, outside the realms of external influences, something deeply rooted and uniquely theirs. Things that have no logical explanation for their existence, but flaunt their features, not for the sake of attention, but as an expression of their existence itself. These innate traits, behaviour quirks, talents, instincts, proclivities, disposition, apprehension, repulsion and aversion emerge from an individual as if they were always there; they just needed a vessel of a person to embody them.

A man who has an impeccable sense of direction, as if a compass is etched within him, helping him navigate even complex and unfamiliar streets.

A child who can hum melodies, too complex to be accidental and too many times to be deemed a coincidence, despite never having practised music.

A woman who moves like she was meant to dance.

An old man who shivers at the sight of deep water, though he *had never been close to drowning during his entire life.*

A girl who flinches at the sound of bells, as if it awakens something unsettling inside of her.

A man who feels the surge of an irrational fear when hearing balloons pop.

Some things couldn't be traced back to an event in their lives, or a lesson taught, or an experience felt, or an accident witnessed.

An individual doesn't develop these traits because of what happened to them; these traits seem to have existed untouched by time, unclaimed by worldly influences. They are not felt because of a triumph or defeat in the past, they just seemed to be there, etched as a definitive and defining characteristic of an individual.

There was plenty more to read, but Kai paused – giving his thoughts time to settle and evolve into observations, questions and a deeper understanding.

He had gradually realised these traits in everyone, including himself, but never fully understood, let alone questioned their origins. Perhaps, they were simply a result of a segment of biological transfer between parents and their child, yet suppressed in the parents just enough to never fully manifest as defining characteristics.

Maybe these traits weren't formed from an individual's own experiences, but were instead echoes of those who came before them, impressions accumulated over generations and selectively carried forward. With each transfer, certain tendencies or aversions may have surfaced, shaping the individual in subtle, unseen ways. But this was merely a theory, a stretched attempt for him to come up with an explanation. He was unsure if this was true, and if it was, he did not know how it worked.

The more he read, the more connections formed, making things even more complex. When he turned towards science, several theories were offered to him.

One such theory was that consciousness results from how brain functioned, piecing together information from senses, emotions and memories into a unified experience. Another proposed theory was that consciousness is the spotlight of awareness amongst a vast range of information shared across the brain's different areas.

Some leading scientists even asserted consciousness as an illusion, and our sense of self as a hallucination created by the brain. Science clearly, and unsurprisingly, doesn't consider consciousness as something mystical. It doesn't even treat consciousness as something separate from the body.

There's nothing ethereal about the self; it likely is a phenomenon emerging from the brain. Consciousness, as per science, is a process of neurons firing.

Individuality is certainly unique, but fluid, constantly rewritten by our biology, experiences and social interactions.

For Kai, science peeled back many layers of individuality, revealed how most of it is in the brain. It offered sound and logical explanations to several of his doubts, but for all its breakthrough, it didn't resolve the mystery of the self, certainly not with full conviction, not just yet anyway.

He grew restless.

Why are some people drawn... to certain things... despite having no clear environmental... or genetic influence?

Is it merely a neurological anomaly... or is there something deeper at play? Is personality or sense of self merely a... projection in the brain, shaped solely by... biology and environment?

Or perhaps there's an additional element that we yet can't comprehend...?

The most important, and perhaps the only question Kai found appealing when he turned to science for help was about the boundaries of consciousness: Does consciousness end with the death of a person, or does it transcend the physical brain?

Some theories in quantum mechanics suggested that consciousness is not just a by-product of brain activity but an integral part of the cosmos, which manifests itself in our brains within the neurons. It implied that consciousness potentially existed without the need of a physical body, as a fundamental aspect of the universe itself, much like electromagnetic waves.

Kai played with this theory, drawing up his own conclusions, coming up with further versions of what-if, could-it-be and maybe. If consciousness were a quantum process, with limitless possibilities and randomness, then free will would have a completely different understanding.

During this cry for help from modern science about consciousness, Kai remained bound to his lifelong conflict with free will. It was apparent to him that if there truly was an origin of consciousness, there could also be a revelation about free will.

He was partially biased to believe that free will and consciousness were inseparable, and why shouldn't they be? To be conscious meant to choose. But there were a plethora of scientists and philosophers who dismissed both to be by-products of the brain's processes in line with the laws of nature beyond our control.

After a few days, his desperation piqued even further. He turned to religion, reluctantly and with barely any hope for answers. He found similar paradoxes across these beliefs. The self was an illusion or a divine gift or a fragment of the divine itself. Each of the religions certainly attempted an answer, but nothing appeased Kai. At this point, the exercise of finding any clue became an obsession.

His days went by in a blur.

At work, he tried to do his best.

When home in comfort and silence, he asked Link to provide as many references as it could. He went through books, shows, movies and even interviews of people who reported near-death experiences.

Some claimed that they saw lights, some were reunited with a loved one, some felt overwhelming peace, and some just talked about darkness and nothing more. There was no coherence. He couldn't quite connect the dots.

He tried to resist obsessing too much about these questions.

He had been on the path to recovery since that night at the beach; he figured he would do his best to make things better for himself. The last thing he needed was a new set of questions to mess with his fragile mind.

He forced himself to talk to friends and family, listened to their stories and engaged in the motions of a normal life.

He attended social events, still through Link, but no less taxing.

It didn't take long for him to accept that he was almost certainly going to go along with Soren's proposal.

If there was even the slightest chance of discovering what lay beyond the boundary, what consciousness felt like when detached from the body, he knew he wouldn't be able to resist. Even if it meant diving headfirst into the unknown.

One weekend, he read about an ancient civilisation that attempted to reach the divine by following strict meditation regimes to control the life-energy and detach themselves from the body hoping to be with the one, finding the truth; this was from thousands of years ago.

Humanity has been searching for answers for so long. Kai thought to himself.

Why shouldn't I use this opportunity to find out for myself?

People didn't have the aid of medical equipment before there was no Link for them; there was nothing to help them if they fell through to the other side and ended up not returning.

Kai had the best aid humanity could offer.

Kai knew this had to be done. The thought of death once seemed an end to his conflicts. Now, it seemed like a doorway to transform his conflicts into knowledge.

At best, it will lead to self-discovery. At worst, he would come out of it having tried one more avenue.

He didn't consider death to be the absolute worst outcome.

[Link, reach out to Soren. Tell him I would like to move forward with the proposal.]

Chapter 24

Tomas sat in his apartment on the tatami mat on the floor. Smoke rose from a lit incense stick across him. He had just finished his meditation, reminded by his Link for the meeting.

He opened his deep silver eyes, and the vision overlay was already setup. This was an important meeting. Rarely scheduled.

But first, the security checks. This sort of meeting demanded a ruthless screening before even a word could be exchanged.

It was crucial that not even a single sound, snippet, or overlay shot got out. Not for this sort of meeting.

Eventually, it was time. The meeting began.

There were no virtual interfaces of other two participants as simulants in front of him; no need for tantrums. But he could feel their presence in the meeting.

Soren's voice came through first.

"We have five more subjects nearly ready for the experiment. Still waiting on confirmation from one, but I'm sure she will fall through."

Tomas asked, "Were all of them suicidal?"

"Four were. One of them even followed through, but thankfully, we got to him in time."

"Those would be valuable datasets." Tomas said with

excitement, his mind racing with ideas on how to use this case.

"Absolutely," Soren nodded in confirmation.

Then, somewhere deeper, a brief presence stirred. The kind of presence one didn't question.

Dario.

He rarely spoke. But when he was watching or listening, it was felt. Soren adjusted his posture in the distant boardroom at the headquarters office. Tomas didn't move from the mat in his apartment.

It was unclear where Dario was.

Link was already a marvel. Self-learning. Seamless. An engineering marvel the world had imagined for decades, if not centuries. Near-perfect behavioural assistant.

But it wasn't enough.

There was a demand for it to be more. Too many eyes were watching its next iteration, having already moved on from its displays of world-class comfort, companionship and ease. There were already whispers of neural sovereignty. The elite were desperate for more.

That's when Refract was introduced.

And it was nothing but a façade. A permission slip. Nothing more.

It was a chemically inert compound; it had no direct effect on the body whether someone had Link or not. It didn't do anything extraordinary. The stories of its *wonders* were all fabricated to create a reputation of it being a 'clarity drug'.

Its formula of protein triggers told Link: you are authorised to override, observe the system in chaos, and be the cause of it, if needed. Link then itself induced instability, to learn how the mind bent, or broke.

Cheap. Bold. And incredibly useful for Link Tech.

Soren quickly continued, "Several subjects end up making revolutionary decisions in their lives – fuelled by Link's impeccable abilities to fine tune and dig up their wants and desires, suppressed deep within themselves. Through it, we gain invaluable insight into the human psyche. However, we are seeing a disturbing trend; many of the users - especially from last quarter – ended up suicidal. Some... succeeded."

He added with disappointment, "We have a diverse set of data points to gauge Link's performance in instability, but we are far from control. One case was interesting. I believe we have a fantastic chance of seeing some progress, but it's risky to progress."

Another breath. Laboured. It was Dario.

Both Soren and Tomas expected a response from Dario. But nothing came.

Tomas added, "The news is catching on the streets. There is a reluctance that Refract makes people end their lives." He paused, considering whether he should or shouldn't add more.

"I have had to," he went for it, "adapt." Tomas winced a little at his own words, fearing reprimand.

They hadn't lied – not technically. They just provided a version of the truth that was more digestible.

Link Tech 'leaked' Refract through Tomas's old channels. On paper, Tomas was a rogue. Off-grid. Whispered about in underground cities and sub-forums. In reality, he was Link Tech's most successful delivery mechanism.

They were desperate for more *data points*. And they needed the veneer of Refract to simulate the environment – for Link to go berserk. To deliberately glitch people's reality, coax them to take a life-altering path. All in the name of offering *clarity*.

The presence stirred again.

A voice came. Distorted. Layered and filtered.

"The council is watching. The megas need a breakthrough. They are all watching. Waiting."

Tomas went still.

Soren shifted in his seat uncomfortably; his jaw tightened. He wanted this as much as anyone – perhaps more desperately. But there were limits, even here, even for them.

"But, Mr. Verrick, we aren't ready," he said, trying to keep his voice level. "Not for this. Some lines even we can't cut corners on."

He didn't mean for it to come out this way, so direct and unfiltered. But the urgency had built up inside him.

"It doesn't matter," the voice lashed at him.

"The case you met earlier," Dario continued unbothered. "Kai. There's potential there. Significant. I want you to monitor him closely. I want to be informed – deeply involved."

Soren's eyes narrowed. He hadn't expected Dario to use the name. Usually, it was just *the subject* or *the case* – clinical terms. Dario had rarely acknowledged individuals, let alone recalled names. But Kai? It wasn't just awareness. It was attention.

He stood up and paced across the room.

Tomas remained silent in his own corner. He didn't speak. Just listened.

Then Dario gave the instruction.

"Run the experiment to its entirety. We must take the leap."

It was delivered flatly, without inviting a counter-response. And that made it worse. Soren knew what 'entirety' meant. No safeguards. No off-ramps.

Soren said, "Mr. Verrick, are you sure? We have had no success so far."

As if suddenly reminded of what could be lost, he stopped walking momentarily. A name he didn't say aloud.

"It's risky," he muttered, almost to himself, "Too risky."

Silence.

A long, measured pause from Dario. No follow-up. No rationale.

He would not explain himself.

He didn't need to.

Soren stood in the centre of the room, staring at the blank glass wall in front of him. The weight of his words had to be calculated first, felt and then said.

Eventually, his words came out.

"Understood, Mr. Verrick."

VI

Divergence

Chapter 25

The days leading up to *the day* passed painfully slowly. Each successive morning added to a tension Kai had never felt before – not even when he was at the beach. The feeling – a mix of unease and, ironically, of anticipation – grew gradually until it became overwhelming.

Kai didn't change his routine; continued work as if nothing had changed, keeping up appearances while something deep within him prepared for what was to come.

Two days prior to the scheduled visit at Link Tech. He lay awake at night, staring at the ceiling, letting his thoughts drift into the unknown.

Will I really find... what if it's nothing more than a deep, dreamless sleep... just a void, not even nightmares?

The possibility of never coming back occurred to him if things went wrong. But it never lingered for long.

While sleep continued to elude him, his mind wandered to his parents. A part of him wanted to see them prior the procedure at Link Tech. Maybe to reaffirm his stance. Or perhaps another piece within him urged saying goodbye, if it really turned out to be such.

He made a list of things he wanted to do in the remainder of two days leading up to Link Tech – starting with a visit to his parents.

The next day, he went to see them over dinner. It was a remarkably average night – except for the hug he gave them before he left. He felt truly blessed to have them around.

On his way back, it didn't take long for the warmth in his heart to turn to shame at the recollection of his surrender at the beach, and then to guilt over what he was planning to do next.

The following day, he had lunch with Rumi.

He had bumped into her often since getting Link. There remained a subtle aloofness between the two; things never reverted to how things were once. But that didn't mean their friendship had lost its warmth.

He wanted to ask her how things had gone. With her having a baby. With Link Tech's program. But he never got around to raising that subject himself. And he didn't push it.

He didn't have the courage to share any details of his own arrangements with her.

Neither did he mention a word about it to his parents either.

It was an incredibly intimate decision for him – something he couldn't share with another soul.

Later, he wondered if Rumi would have understood, had he shared the details with her. But the thought left him feeling exposed – that he was still trapped in the same old search for himself.

He felt vulnerable, and that felt odd; he had never been shy of his vulnerabilities with Rumi before. But of course, so much had changed.

Later in the day, he visited Link Tech to provide consent and authorisation ahead of the tests – during what they called a pre-briefing. He met the representative, who walked him through the details of the procedure, showed him the room where the entire process would take place.

The rep informed him the emergency protocols, should things not work out as intended. Nothing stood out as particularly ominous – other than the possibility of death itself.

Despite the nature of what he was about to do, he found the facilities to be unremarkable. Just another high-end lab, sleek yet functional. It looked like a minimalistic hospital ward to Kai.

He returned home with a heart full of nervousness and excitement.

That night back in his bedroom, he couldn't sleep. Yet again.

Would it be like a lucid dream? Would he keep his senses? Or would it be nothing – just an empty, silent void?

The questions offered him no comfort. Tomorrow, he would find out for himself.

Tomorrow, he would plunge into the abyss.

...

The room at Link Tech had changed from before. It was completely devoid of any sharp features, colours and any external stimulants. When Kai entered the room, there was a bed ahead of him. The dimmed lights in the room illuminated just enough for him to walk to bed. There were no posters on the wall, no windows, no cupboards, no furniture, no decoration whatsoever. Just a plain bed for him to go lie on, and a few tubes and wires protruding from the wall behind. The Link Tech rep escorted him to the bed and made preparations.

After all preparations were done, the rep left the room and

switched off the lights on the way out. Kai lay in bed in complete darkness. There was no sound whatsoever from anywhere; Kai could even hear his own heartbeat.

And then, suddenly, a faint hum in the room. The air got heavy.

Although he was prepared for this experience, it was still unsettling for him.

A deep exhale, and then the process began.

First his vitals were brought under control, his heart rate slowed down, and oxygen levels manipulated. This was done gradually, with enough time for Kai to settle down and control his breathing on his own. His body was nudged into a slow and deliberate shutdown. Kai felt a calming sensation, as if falling asleep to a lullaby. His senses were dulled, limbs slackened, and the body almost melted into the bed.

The biological signals in his body gradually blocked, and even involuntary functions slowed down. His breathing became almost imperceptible as it slowed down further. The process hijacked the nervous system and manipulated the biological survival instincts. He felt no urge to breathe, only an occasional forced pump of the heart to keep the body alive. He wasn't panicked at the discomfort of a muted heart.

Then came the isolation from all sensory inputs.

He was still there underneath the stillness and silence, but the ties to his body were being cut slowly.

Euphoric. Surrounded by waves of thoughts, memories and abstract scenes – some his own, some unfamiliar.

An intense feeling rose within him. To rebel this foreign takeover. He was being swept away. And the remnants of his essence fought against it.

But then, even in euphoria, a realisation dawned on him.

This was the very place where he needed to surrender, where people like Soren failed to get across.

Did Kai want to get across or give up there?

He had nothing really to fight for. *This is better, even if it's only for the sake of nothingness*, he thought.

He was desperate enough for answers, compliant enough to surrender.

He let go, and the weight of nothingness dulled him.

Then came the hallucinations.

Glimpses of his memories, fragments of his imagination, recollections of his experiences and his innermost thoughts, all merged to dance around him and project a kaleidoscope of voices, figures, shapes and emotions.

He was outside his childhood home on a rainy morning, his mother telling him to get inside the house, her voice was soft and loving, but incomprehensible.

The scene tore away.

He was cycling up a hill, the incline just kept getting steeper, and the road got narrower until he was on a path just wide enough for him with his cycle. The hill was almost vertical, but he didn't fall off; he kept going, cycling upwards on a vertical road.

Another shift.

He felt people in a movie theatre, voices of laughter all around him, but he was unsure what they were laughing at. There was a waterfall at the back of the theatre. He could hear water falling, along with the laughter of people watching the movie.

An animal, a deer, sat next to him on one seat. It was laughing loudly too, pointing at the movie screen. Kai looked ahead of him, and it wasn't a display screen but a blend of blurred actions; things were moving, some familiar objects, but most of what he saw was incomprehensible.

His heartbeat slowed further, down to almost nothing now.

Then, the desynchronisation began. The hallucinations slowed down. It wasn't the voices, shapes or figures now, but a gradient of some sort. This gradient engulfed everything around him. Things were being transformed into smaller fractions, and these fractions diminished until eventually become part of the gradient, pulled to either of its sides.

Link Tech's artificial desynchronisation process was being carried out. It had never been tried before; nobody had reached this far.

The slow unravelling of his self from the body began. Kai felt like being peeled away from himself. The gradient was trying to turn him into itself, along with everything around him.

And then, suddenly, he was detached.

He felt it when it finally happened, that freedom from the physical sensations. There was no feeling of skin to channel the warmth of air, or the coolness of a breeze. The fabric of his clothes lost its subtle weighted influence.

The most prominent change was the absence of the pull of gravity; yet he didn't feel disoriented. There was no up or down, or any direction for that matter. The sense of location, of being grounded in space, was gone.

The surrounding space had vanished. There were no walls, no boundaries, no edges, no ground and no skies. He felt himself in an endless, vast expanse, which was neither dark nor illuminated, neither empty nor full. He existed in that vast expanse, weightless, formless, without a sense of direction, but not lost either, untethered.

Kai's consciousness had latched away from his body, and for the first time, as far as he knew, there were no constraints. He wasn't feeling any joy, but no sorrow either. He simply *was*.

...

He wasn't floating or drifting away, because there was no reference point.

Time had stopped moving, or it moved from start to finish all at once. There was no sense of seconds, minutes or hours. It did not pass because there was no before or after.

Kai had not lost all his memories, emotions and experiences, but from where he was, it seemed like everything he felt in his life so far was a tiny drop in an infinite ocean of moments.

The voice Kai knew as himself was still there, but there was no running commentary of the mind. Thoughts demanded nothing, did not struggle – they just manifested in him.

Without a body, time and space, Kai completely lost his individuality; instead, he felt within him the lingering aftermath and foreboding of limitless emotions and experiences all at once. He didn't have a name, traits, instincts, tendencies, proclivities, repulsions and fears of the Kai he knew.

Instead, he had a myriad of names, all felt intimate. His traits were boundless, instincts endless, tendencies innumerable, proclivities incalculable, repulsion unfathomable and fear immeasurable.

Who am I?

Who was I?

Am I dead?

The only remnant of the life he had just come from was the

lingering curiosity – not as an emotion, but as a guiding push. Was it somehow coming from Link Tech? Kai had no way of finding out.

He wasn't the only presence. Even in nothingness, he noticed something – a resemblance of a river, a river that had no start or finish.

Instead of flowing water, it seemed to be made of memories. Emotions. And experiences.

Kai felt attracted to this colossal cosmos of experiences.

What are those?

Whose are those?

Kai felt a gentle pull from every fabric of this infinite canvas of moments. It was a force unlike anything he had experienced in the material world. The pull was subtle, like a whisper nudging him to embrace it.

There were infinite lives, entangled together all at once – from the past and the future, but there, they lay all at once.

Kai felt a surge of endless emotions: happiness, sadness, anger, fear, surprise, disgust, curiosity, desire, anticipation, hunger, thirst, pain, panic, aggression, dominance, submission, alertness, vigilance, exhaustion, urgency, helplessness, insecurity, dread, love, trust, betrayal and everything else, all at once.

They lay before him like an unbroken river, each stream a life from another self, another time. Each one accessible and vivid, of past and future, but happening right there all at once.

Kai felt the memories of not just a man, woman or a child, but of everything. Every form, every instinct, every experience between birth and death.

The slow and faint awareness of division, of splitting.

The horror of being hunted.

The sob of a mother watching her child die of sickness.

The piercing pain and the cold sensation from the steel of the blade.

The feeling of soil pressing from all sides.

The sense of unity and belonging while howling with the pack.

The taste of blood, and knowing a prey is nearby in the ocean.

This boundless constellation of moments also etched memories and experiences that spilled into the future. The low-frequency mating call of the last elephant, desperate for companionship. The overwhelming feeling of looking at the planet.

He still felt the pull.

Where was it coming from? Or was it Link Tech's desynchronisation program?

Whatever it was, it seemed vaguely familiar. Not hostile, but not overly affectionate either. It just drew Kai towards it.

And he found himself manifesting into one of the streams. His nothingness was slowly disappearing and making way for the three-dimensional realm he once knew as Kai. But something was diffcrent; this was a different time, a different life he was transitioning to.

Chapter 26

Kai, or his ascended conscious self, slowly dissolved into one stream of memories. He found himself back in the fabric of time, but as a mute spectator in another vessel. The vessel had a physical body, but Kai was still devoid of any movement of his own. He could experience the senses of the vessel, but with no direct influence on things around him.

He was there only as an awareness that seemed to have found a carrier to settle into.

He could not see; there was no need. Vision was meaningless for this vessel. It played no significant part in this experience. There was no sound he could process, as if there was nothing around to trigger the need for voices, no one to talk to, no songs or poems to recite, not even an inner monologue.

Whose memory is this? The question didn't come in words, but just a thought.

He didn't have the sensation of breathing, not in the way he recalled from his life as Kai. There was nothing to inhale or exhale.

Where am I? Another thought.

Kai couldn't quite understand where he was. What was he? But he knew he was alive, a stripped-bare version of a life-form, but a life-form, nonetheless. There were no desires, no will, no awareness of being alive, no thoughts.

But there was a purpose, a drive, an intent, the only calling – to grow and to *become*.

There was no food to eat, not in the traditional way that other creatures did. He didn't have a mouth to feed himself. He couldn't imagine what taste felt like.

There was no need to hunt, to set traps, to chase, to pull from, to collect, or to buy from. But there was an intense resolve to *be*. How?

He floated, the only sensation he was certain of. Something guided him around, changing his position, upwards, then downwards, then to the sides. He didn't resist; he couldn't do it as there were no limbs to guide.

Amidst this drifting, he suddenly felt a stir, an instinct. What was it? He couldn't act on his instinct, only hoped for the pulsing motion around him to nudge him closer to where the stir was felt.

He was drawn towards the sun, but not for warmth, or brightness, or colour, or pleasure. There was an ancient resolve in him to... drink the sun, without even knowing what the sun was.

When sunlight touched him, he sprang into action. He grabbed pockets of energy, whatever he could, whenever he could. He absorbed it into himself.

But something else was needed too. It felt like he had the fire, and all he needed were ingredients to cook. But from where?

After the primal function within him to soak up the sun, his senses searched around him. The universe offered him an abundance of raw resources. Despite not being able to see or hear, he could sense it. The invisible traces of nitrogen, carbon dioxide and phosphorous. Floating around him, waiting to be taken. He reached for it, grabbed it within him through his semi-porous membrane of a body.

Now he had the fire and the elements. He left the rest to the biology of his physical existence.

He became more than what he was a moment ago. This was his only mission, the sole aim of his life, the core design of his existence – to move, to be, and to grow.

In return, he left something completely useless to himself, something that had no value then.

Oxygen.

He was a single cell, a Cyanobacterium, part of an unfathomable mass of similar beings, drifting away in the ocean. He – along with billions of others unable to perceive their presence – was taking in sunlight, water, and carbon dioxide to produce oxygen as waste.

It wasn't done of his own accord. He didn't have the facility in him to think about what he was doing. Just an endless loop of becoming and growing. He just did what was in his nature to do, the only thing he knew to do.

He didn't know what he was doing. He didn't need to.

There was no grand significance in his actions, no oversight of good or bad. However, Kai, with his ascended awareness, realized that he was among the first life-forms to introduce oxygen into Earth's atmosphere. He was creating the most fundamental building blocks for other life-forms to evolve with.

It was of no relevance whether he was doing it alone, or with millions and billions of others. The definition of his individuality was in *doing*, and not even through his own will.

He *was*, and that was simply enough.

Kai could see why he had been brought here, or had he brought himself there? It didn't matter. He could see that simply existing, attuned to the nature of the self, is enough of an expression of individuality.

There was no need to be unique or extravagant or to find a grand revelation in the fruition of his actions.

His actions within his limited lifespan of a few hours to a few days were remarkably insignificant. Unimportant and uneventful. But it's precisely because of the incapability of his thoughts, he could do what he did for his entire life – create oxygen as a byproduct of his existence.

It took billions of years for countless generations of cyanobacteria to slowly release and accumulate oxygen in Earth's oceans – enough for it to rise into the skies and finally make it possible for life to take its first breath.

The lesson was simple yet profound. Existence didn't need to be glorious; it just needed to *be*.

Even in that state, Kai felt a soothing realisation dawn on him.

He didn't need to be there anymore. He had seen what he had to see.

As seamlessly as he had arrived there, he went back to the nothingness. It wasn't a movement in a direction, not a dissolution into somewhere else. It was as if he had never left. The ocean, the senses, the synergy with billions of cyanobacteria, all collapsed at once into nothing.

He was again in a directionless vast expanse with no references, no datums, and no sensations. He was weightless, formless and untethered.

Time was neither still nor flowing. It existed all at once, a single, boundless moment without before or after.

He was confronted again with the never-ending river of infinite flowing memories, experiences and emotions.

He was a cyanobacterium before, now he was Kai, and he was also a myriad of other individualities, all at once.

Kai felt the pull from the river again; now, he knew what it offered.

With a mature awareness now to revisit another moment in time as an observer in another vessel, he resigned himself and yielded to the river yet again.

Chapter 27

The room Kai was in at Link Tech remained as sterile as silent.

His body lay flat on the narrow bed. His chest rose at slow intervals. Each breath seemed like it would be the last, and each time, it came as if it was a decision Kai didn't make.

The rep in the room continued to make slight adjustments with steady hands. Beside her stood the doctor, white-bearded and thin-lipped, who watched the monitors with a gaze sharpened by years of desensitisation. He was the architect of Link Tech's desynchronisation process.

Soren stood behind them, arms crossed. His face expressed robotic concern.

"He's not fully disconnected," the doctor said, looking at his scans. "There are enough signs to conclude that he hasn't fully crossed."

Soren stepped closer, gaze fixed on the dynamic dance of numbers and lines, which he could also see in his overlay, same as the doctor's.

"Induce more instability," Soren said.

The doctor hesitated. The entire process was risky enough already. More instability meant a greater likelihood of failure.

They didn't want to lose him completely. But what the scans showed wasn't yet favourable.

The doctor knew that it was time to raise the bar.

Soren, as if he read the doctor's thoughts, whispered, "Do it enough to challenge him. Enough to... break him."

A silence hung over the room, heavier than before. The rep paused for a fraction of a second before resuming her work.

The doctor, however, blinked and let out a sigh. He didn't speak.

Soren focused on Kai's body, barely clinging to life. Inside, he felt something bubble. Not guilt. Not doubt – not yet.

Anticipation.

The other subjects were already showing signs of failure. All of them. But this one... was different. There was hope. Even after detachment, Kai's brain responded. Just once. But enough to stir the room.

"Continue," Soren said, voice softer now. "Let him drift."

Then he returned and walked away, the door sliding shut behind him. He needed to check in with Dario. There was far too much at stake.

Chapter 28

Kai was no longer himself; he was Ama.

Gender, form and identity were irrelevant. Inadequate. Insignificant.

She was Kai, and he was Ama. She was Ama and always had been. He could look around her, feel the pain Ama felt, but he was there as an observer, to witness Ama's experiences and ordeals.

Kai didn't arrive in Ama, nor was there a transition. There was just a sudden sensation of being, as Ama, encapsulated within a horde of emotions and memories, from her childhood to that moment.

The first thing he felt was the stench of sweat, filth, vomit and rot around her, and death. It was intense and everywhere. The world around her was enveloped in salt and decay, and it clung to her, inside and out. She tried to breathe lightly, to move away from it, but in vain. The stench gripped her and muffled her breath; there was no escape.

There were others, several others around her, crammed together in a dimly lit area. There wasn't even enough space to stretch her legs or move around.

She was in shackles; everyone around her was.

She was below the deck of a ship, packed with several others like her, all shackled, all suffering. Kai felt the dampness of wooden planks below, from the filth of bodies unable to move, unable to hold. The creaking of the ship mocked the groans from those around her. There was horror, dread, despair, even anger, and complete hopelessness in their eyes.

Ama couldn't recall how long she had been there. She had lost all sense of time. Seconds, minutes and hours merged into a singular unit, of suffering, of wanting to end everything. Kai could feel Ama's intense dread, extreme sorrow and fear, as if that's all she had ever known.

She was shoved between others, barely able to breathe. The chains on her wrists and ankles had caused severe wounds, and they worsened every time the ship rocked violently. Kai felt Ama wince in pain when the chains dug deeper into her flesh.

Her body was exhausted from an extreme lack of sleep as there wasn't enough space, filthy or not, to even lie down. She was beyond hunger, but thirst still tormented her.

She remembered the day she was taken, forced from her home, away from her mama and baba. That seemed like a lifetime ago.

She lay on a woven mat, right next to her mama. The air was clear and had an earthy smell. The sound of crickets chirping was as loud as ever. Ama was restless. Everyone else had fallen asleep, but Ama was lost in her thoughts, still struggling to fall asleep.

Suddenly, the crickets went quiet.

Ama felt an eerie surge of heaviness in the air; something strange was going on.

That's when she heard.

A scream, then another much closer.

Then a gunshot.

Men of the village stirred, fumbling their way into their houses in search of weapons – spears, knives, sticks, anything at hand. They knew the cause of the chaos outside. Slavers.

Their hearts were pounding in realisation of the futility of this search. They knew they couldn't fight the muskets.

The night erupted in chaos – screams, shouts, clang of metals, gunshots, thud of people falling over, and the raging fire of burning huts.

Ama's baba ran out of the house with his fists of rage raised in hopeless defence.

He was shot as soon as he stepped out.

Ama didn't see him getting shot, but she knew it. She knew from the gaping hole she felt in her own heart.

Ama's mama turned towards her, snatched her wrists and yelled at her. "Go away, Ama. Run, my *pikin*. My beloved, my baby. Please go. RUN!"

It was too late. She saw an apparition of death enter the hut with a musket and a lit torch.

Ama's mother was hit in the ribs with a rifle. She immediately lost consciousness.

Ama fought back – kicking, biting and screaming. Then, a bag was forced over her head, and her entire world was turned to darkness.

The next thing she remembered was the pain in her body as she returned to her senses.

She was then forced to march. Shackled on long lines, wrists bound, ankles cuffed. The chain around her neck forced her forward if she stumbled, pulled her when she dragged behind.

She lost count of how many days she was forced to march. Her entire body was numb from exhaustion, the wounds on her wrists and ankles never got time to heal, and her heart continued to bleed from the shot that killed her father.

She never found out what happened to her mum, refusing to believe what she had heard about the fate of older women.

The sun was scorching hot during the day, blistering their skins, and squeezing away whatever water they had left in their bodies, and will. Nights were freezing cold, and the only way to fall asleep was by huddling together with others for warmth.

Every day, someone remained behind, unable to endure another night, dying in their sleep, succumbing to their wounds, or losing all hope for the life ahead. Those who protested, demanded, rebelled were cut, shot, whipped, tortured and played cruel games with.

Ama saw the fates of those who tried to run. She had nightmares of her father being killed the same way after rebelling. She often woke up sobbing, only to be shushed around by others chained to her. Those who stood out from the group didn't last too long.

In the middle of the fight with the elements of nature for survival, trying to keep their sanity after the horrific forced departure from their homes, watching their loved ones die right in front of their eyes, being treated worse than animals, women were subject to satisfy the urges of the slavers at night.

Ama heard them take other women. She knew what was happening. She saw the hollow-eyed, lifeless eyes of women who returned; some didn't return at all.

She couldn't bring herself to care. She felt too empty. There was nothing around her she could process. The silhouette of her father leaving the hut, the thud of a body falling, her mother's eyes begging her to run for her safety, her failed attempts to fight, her capture, her failing body, the numbness from exhaustion, all this was too much for her.

She could still hear the screams from that night, bodies being dragged away, the bullets piercing bodies. There was nothing left to feel.

The sea was worse than she had imagined.

She could feel the weight of the shackles even when she wasn't moving. She could hear the groans of pain from the others around her. The stench was unbearable. But worse than the filth, worse than hunger, worse than the sickness, worse than a broken body, was the objectification and complete absence of any empathy in the eyes of the men above.

How can they not see the horror of what they are doing? She often thought to herself.

Some nights, when even sleep denied her any respite, she grew restless.

She did not think of rebellion; she witnessed what happened to those who rebelled. She did not desire vengeance; she didn't want to reciprocate the wounds inflicted on her. She thought only of who she was, what she had done, and why she was forced to endure that ordeal.

I am not an animal. I have done nothing to deserve this.

Why? Why? Why?

Why was this happening? What did she do to them?

She didn't steal from them, never harmed them, never threatened them. Then where did this hatred come from?

She wasn't a leader. She wasn't a warrior. She wasn't a threat.

She was defenceless and weak.

She was just minding her own business, busy with her mama and baba, taking care of them, while they took care of her. The future held so much in store for her. Love, marriage, her own children perhaps? Now, that future seemed impossible to her in this lifetime.

"Is this what life is about?" Kai thought. "Do we just live within the confines of our bodies, for circumstances to decide everything for us?"

How did these men justify the bloodbath? Couldn't they see they were all the same? They all had families. They loved their home. They shared the ability to feel joy, sorrow and pain.

Was it because of differences in their clothing? Or the gods they worshipped? Or the colours of their skins?

Why?

What kind of men, an entire army of them, collectively agree that *their actions* were permissible? That raiding a village of innocent people, burning their huts, forcing families apart, killing the weak and elderly, torturing the ones who rebel, assaulting, cutting, shooting and forcing them to march to their land was justified for trade?

How dark, pathetic and rotten their minds are, to keep doing this, over and over again?

Kai, as Ama, witnessed the ordeal, felt the torment and the agony of herself and everyone around her in the dark putrid bell of the ship.

He also saw how the slavers detached themselves from the moral implications of their actions. The atrocity wasn't orchestrated just by the traders and business owners, but by an entire system of people from all walks of life. They considered themselves aloof from the horror; they were simply *doing their jobs*. Everyone told themselves that the carnage was happening elsewhere.

The slavers who raided at night, forcing families apart and

killing so many innocent villagers, told themselves that they were just following orders. If they hadn't done it, someone else would have.

The man, who forced the villagers to march for days on foot, told himself he was just doing his job.

The ship's captain, who kept the villagers below the deck in their own filth and decay of dead bodies left for too long, told himself that he was just transporting the goods. It was just business for him. He told himself that if he started thinking of their suffering, he wouldn't be able to look after himself. Transporting them was nothing more than his livelihood.

The crewman, who force-fed the captives using the iron mouth openers, told himself that he was keeping them alive *for their own good.* He threw barely enough mouldy biscuits, rotten food and scraps from previous crew's meals, and told himself that it's better this way. *They should be grateful that I am at least giving them something to eat.*

Kai observed in horror how these men convinced themselves that they were playing a minor role in a system which was beyond their control. The slavers blamed the owners for creating this demand; the marcher blamed the ship's captain for undertaking such a massive journey across the world; the captain blamed the trade; and the crew blamed the system.

No one felt they were doing much wrong. And yet, each of them played a significant part in the atrocity.

Ama could only do one thing, huddled together with other bodies in the dark – pray.

She prayed endlessly, with every wince and flinch. She prayed in her heart every time she felt a surge of pain in her body. She prayed whenever she saw the weak ones left behind, when those who protested were shot down, when she saw those empty eyes of women returning late at night staring at nothing, when the stench overpowered her senses.

She prayed every moment of every day. She prayed for herself, for others around her, prayed for her mama and baba, even for the men above to realise the horrid nature of their actions and stop.

She prayed with every sway of the ship. She prayed when she woke up, when she went to bed, even in her sleep.

As the days passed, as the suffering and cruelty got worse, she doubted if her god was listening at all. Later, in moments of self-realisation, she would then curse herself for doubting her god and pray even more to offset her *transgression*. She prayed with every breath, every day, every night.

When the ship's ration of food ran out, even the scraps of leftovers were thrown infrequently.

On a particularly hot and humid day, she saw her people, who could have been her brothers and sisters, fight over a morsel of maggot-infested leftover scraps of food.

That's when she got angry.

What kind of God allowed this to happen? What God would watch his creation suffer like this?

What did they do to be treated worse than cattle?

Wasn't God all-knowing and all-powerful? Couldn't He see it? Couldn't He punish the wrongdoers?

Did He not cast storms, send floods and cause earthquakes to those who sinned? Where was the hand that was supposed to strike those who didn't believe Him, those who defied Him and those who challenged Him.

How can He see this and do nothing?

Where was the wrath?

Where was the divine justice?

Why hadn't this ship been swallowed by a storm?

Her anger gave way, eventually, to self-reflection. *Had she done anything to deserve this? Had the entire village somehow committed a sin for which they were being punished?*

She had no answer. There were none.

She didn't choose any of it. But the suffering was real and unbearable. Every moment was incomprehensibly long. Every dawn drained her will to survive, every day broke her spirit, and every night was full of dread and fear, fear of the sound of swaying footsteps, the call of her name, the stench of sweat and abhorrent hatred she felt towards her own body afterwards.

Kai saw the end of Ama's life, not too far ahead from her time on the ship.

The remainder of her life was spent in agony, devoid of even a moment of respite from the unfathomable hellish brutality and depravity.

Her life knew only suffering at the end – the most raw and horrifying form of suffering.

There was sorrow – tremendous, gut-wrenching sorrow, which left her incapable of continuing even a day longer.

She felt an intense hatred for being born in a woman's body, an unimaginable, endless level of disgust, when her skin contacted the vile, foul and revolting bodies of the men who forced their way against her.

At the end, all she could think of was to demand an explanation from the gutless, spineless coward of a god she used to bow down to. No god would ever subject its creation to the suffering her people had to go through. Not for any test, nor to serve as examples for others.

She embraced her death with open arms. In a world full of

depraved men, death was the kindest visitor for her.

Kai could see that there was no justifying this. This life and the suffering of Ama, and everyone around her, made no sense. Not one of them had done anything in their lives to be subjected to abduction, pillaging, captivity, bloodbath, torture and objectification.

There was no balance, no divine justice, no sense and no logic.

And yet, many of the victims, including Ama, despite the wounds, hunger, thirst, exhaustion, filth and stench, continued to endure, continued to exist. Their life was sheer misery; their future looked bleak; there was no joy anywhere, only unimaginable pain and doom.

And yet, they lived. Fought for each breath, every moment, new days. Despite the pointlessness of the misery, they continued to wake up each day and survive.

At some point, everyone stopped demanding life to be logical and fair. It didn't need to make sense. It just needed to *be* – even if for one more day.

Why was I here? Kai thought. *There was at least a resemblance of a conclusion to my experience as a cyanobacterium. An expression of existence without questions, thoughts, desires, sensations – just being. But this, as Ama, what was I supposed to see?*

He observed that he had gradually intertwined with her with the passage of time. He could feel her pain more intimately; her thoughts were slowly becoming his gradually. It was as if, had he spent more time with her, he would have fused with her. But he remained a mere spectator throughout.

There was no need for Kai to be Ama anymore. There was nothing left to see, no lessons, no wisdom to take away from.

He merged seamlessly with the nothingness, imploding into

it, as if he had never left. The ship, the agony, the ordeal, the painful wrists and ankles, the hunger, the stench, all gone.

He found his directionless, formless and timeless self adrift in a river of infinite memories and experiences. He was a cyanobacterium, and Ama and Kai – all at once. From birth to demise, every memory, every experience, every emotion – felt simultaneously.

He felt another pull; he knew what it meant. But now he wondered, *Was there a rhythm and order to these experiences?* He yielded to the pull, letting himself be drawn into it.

Chapter 29

"He's gone too far," the doctor muttered. "We've lost active brain engagement. No inputs from cortical levels."

"I've pushed it into overdrive. We'll have to switch to Link Prime," he informed the others in the room.

Unlike its regulated iteration, Link Prime was unrestricted – the version that Refract 'uncovered', only now under direct control of Link Tech. It could override instincts, flood the nervous system, simulate thought paths. It could puppeteer a body – to some extent – with frightening precision.

Its only side effect was an intensified Ghostlight – a deep, dense silver that filled the iris – caused by the Link's interface driving the nanofibers in the optic module into sustained overdrive during transmission. For Kai, it no longer mattered.

Not long after Link Prime was engaged, things started to shift.

Kai's finger twitched.

Then, after a moment, his arm flexed slightly.

[*Try a cognitive test.*] The doctor gave further instructions once he was content with the motor responses.

A visual prompt was injected directly into Kai's visual cortex. Link Prime computed it. The computation triggered a subtle spike on the scan.

They had gotten something.

The doctor allowed himself a quiet exhale. "Link Prime has a level of control; that's reassuring." It meant Link Prime could continue to operate with Kai as a catalyst.

But the room didn't erupt in relief. This was nothing to be celebrated. Not just yet.

Everybody knew.

A twitch was just electricity. A calculation was just circuitry. None of it was him. Or anyone else. Link Prime couldn't control him fully.

Without a consciousness, without the mind behind it all, it was all mimicry.

Soren stepped out of the room, wiping sweat along his brow. The corridor outside was colder than the room. But he felt hotter.

His thoughts scrambled. They have come so far. Now, it was all about patience. And perhaps a bit of luck.

He knew Dario was watching all this.

A notification blinked in Soren's vision overlay.

[Message: I'm here. In Nexus wing; Sender: Mr. Verrick]

Chapter 30

Kai manifested into another being, surged forward, pulled by the river, only to find himself in something tangible. He wasn't formless anymore. He had sensations, vision, hearing and instincts.

There was no moment of transition, no split between him and what he was then. There were only motion, wind and sky.

The wind rushed past his face, lifting him, guiding him, dancing with him, merging with him. It carried him, not as a distinct entity, but as an extension of itself.

He felt his body. He didn't breathe air the way he knew. Every breath was crisp, efficient and gave a surge of energy. His heart was beating faster, much faster, but he wasn't out of breath. This body was built for soaring heights.

He didn't feel his arms; there were wings instead. Large yet light. The sensation was incredible. Feathers extended and bent like fingers to help navigate his glide across the sky. It felt effortless. He didn't have to think, plan and catch the shifting winds; the body moved instinctively.

Then, the wind took him. He soared through a vast expanse of sky without any hesitation or resistance. The wings didn't need to flap – there was no struggle. The wind danced around him, lifting him upwards, aiding his flight. It didn't whisper;

it roared. It didn't resist; it pulled him upward.

He didn't feel cold. He didn't shiver. There was just a harmony, a perfect union with the world around him.

His hearing was not muffled, not dulled from distance, unfazed by the wind. He felt the voices reach him somewhere else, as if he received them inside of him.

He saw with a clarity like never before – unhinged, unadulterated, sharp and focused. He saw the world beneath him, a changing canvas of mountains, rivers and villages. Colours hummed with an intensity. Shades of gold, green, brown and blue dappled under the sun. The valley sprawled as far as he could see. Jagged peaks rose in the distance, their crags slicing through the sky. Rivers carved winding paths underneath him, their silver ribbons glistening under the sun. The surrounding earth pulsed with its own heartbeat, and Kai felt like he belonged to it.

There was nothing holding him down. No chains. No weight.

The air was crisp, clear and full of life.

The sun, the mountains, the river and the forests, all blended in together to form the most spectacular canvas of life. Kai, as Kai, had never seen the world like this. Never felt the air rush into him, rather through him. He could never see things with this clarity, sharpens and focus. And yet, in that moment, he felt in his bones – he had always had this perfect union with the wind. He didn't need to squint his eyes or put efforts to see far – it just came to him instinctively.

And yet, even in these moments, he was bound by something – his nature. And Kai could sense it.

Kai could think, but only within the confines of what his biology allowed him to. His mind had limits. It didn't have the luxury of finding its purpose. He just could not comprehend the idea of building a shelter for the future or accumulating his food. He couldn't imagine finding a better or more efficient means of his existence. He did everything in accordance with his nature.

He had choices within the limited framework of his nature. He could decide where to fly, where to land, when to hunt, how to move, but he could not conceive the idea of not hunting. The notion of not soaring across the skies was simply not possible.

Despite not knowing who he was, he was aware of himself as someone. He could feel within him the facilities for contentment, playful, aggression, caution, frustration and even traces of sorrow – not in a self-reflective manner but driven from instincts.

There were things about him unique to himself, which no other beings of his kind possessed. He would circle the area twice before landing, as if to confirm the perch to be safe and sound. He would sometimes go for a hunt at twilight rather than in the afternoon. Even amid the instinctive drive to look for prey, he preferred hare over other mammals, if equal opportunities were present for both. He didn't know where these unique traits and preferences came from; he wasn't even aware that they existed. He simply lived a life attuned to his nature, followed hunger, followed movement and followed the dictates of his survival.

Kai relished the experience. It was a stark contrast to his experience as Ama. Here he could spread his wings, fly upwards or rest on the peaks. Despite the limited span of his choices, he felt limitless. From the darkness below the ship to the shining afternoon sun creating a picturesque landscape for him to navigate, from the stench of the filth and rot to the incredibly rich and crispy air high above, from the shackled limbs to the span of his wings which made possible a perfect union with the winds – everything was an incredible juxtaposition of the two lives.

A shift in the wind carried him to the valley. Then – a movement.

He spotted a hare moving in the fields below.

His body tensed; an electric thrill ran through him. Something changed in him. The contentment gave way to the intense survival drive to hunt. He didn't think, didn't hesitate.

He tucked his wings and plummeted towards the hare. His vision was clear, focussed only on the hare. Nothing else existed; nothing else mattered in that moment. Every muscle in his body had one purpose – to hunt.

The wind roared past him. His heart was pounding wildly to match his vigour. His massive talons extended – strong crushing weapons for him to rip his hunt apart.

He then made an impact. His talons sank deep into the soft flesh of the hare. The hare struggled, but there was nowhere to go. The talons didn't just pierce the hare; they punctured it, each curved claw sunk deep in the flesh. And with the crushing of the bones and puncture of its flesh, the hare screamed in agony – a high, piercing sound for plea, for survival. But there was no mercy from Kai's vessel; he couldn't even conceive it.

A single, piercing collapse of his talons, and there was stillness.

He effortlessly lifted the hare with him, wings extending fully to aid his way up, somewhere he could have his meal in peace.

There was no sympathy, no guilt, no triumph, no celebration, no mourning. He was just doing what his nature commanded him to do. Incapable of anything else.

He landed on a ledge nearby and tore his meal. The body was still warm, but it was no longer a creature. It was sustenance.

The beak was perfect – hooked, sharp and merciless. It ripped the flesh from the bones with an effortless pull. He tore through the soft underbelly, exposing the internal organs within. The hare's intestines spill from the tear, making the kidney loose for it to be devoured whole. Lung, soft and pink, pulled from the body and swallowed without hesitation.

He fed in silence, enjoying the small heart of the hare, bursting with nutrients. He clamped his beak around the heart and bit it clean, blood spilling down his throat.

When he was done with his meal, he lifted his bloodstained head and looked at the horizon. There was no reflection. There were no thoughts, self-reflection, hesitation, mercy, or even aggression. This was just an inrush of the purest form of what his own self was in that life.

Kai couldn't help but wonder, he could have been the hare, having his flesh clawed and punctured by another soaring creature.

He thought to himself: *Why this life? Why am I seeing this?*

Kai had felt a union with the wind, unbound freedom, and followed his nature. There was no more need for him to dwell.

And just as suddenly as it began, it ended too.

The sky, the valleys, the fields, the wind and the weight of this body – everything dissolved into the nothingness where he came from.

Back into the void, to the river of infinite experiences. Back to the formless existence.

He felt another pull from the river. This time, he resisted; he wanted to stay in the nothingness and reflect on the lives he had just experienced.

Whose lives was he witnessing?

His first experience as a cyanobacterium was simple, devoid of thoughts. It didn't exist for itself. All it did, in unknowing labour of its existence, lay the foundation for all other lifeforms on Earth. Was individuality an illusion then? Or even irrelevant? If something so insignificant could have such an impact without even the facilities of thoughts, then what benefit is there in the ability to choose, to deem one thing better than the other? Better for whom?

The only solace was in existence. Even without a will, ability of thoughts, he grew and reproduced, and in doing so did all he could.

As Ama, he saw how suffering consumed him. His thoughts remained pure, innocent and compassionate even in chains. Or maybe he was shackled and chained precisely because of his compassionate nature. When the body got numb from hunger, when the stench overpowered all the other senses, when the wounds became so deep and painful that he even anticipated it with the rocking of the ship, he still thought of others around. Felt their pain, their hunger, their hopelessness. And when he couldn't do a thing to change, he noted the growing distance between him and the gods.

What did free will even mean in those circumstances? Does it even exist if a person can be bound so completely? Or does it have to be fought for? Ama's nature was not that of a warrior. She was a carer, a friend and, above all else, a daughter. The elements of her existence knew nothing else. And for that, she was imprisoned and chained under horrid circumstances.

If there were a lesson to learn here, I don't see it, Kai thought.

Maybe there was no balance at all. No meaning behind the suffering.

As a creature of the sky, he felt free. But was he?

He was subject to the elements of his nature. He had free will, but his choices were limited.

In the nothingness, he was devoid of all sensations, forms, direction, forces of nature and even time. He was Kai; he was a cyanobacterium; he was Ama, and he soared in the sky. He felt deeply connected to these experiences, having lived fragments of them.

But why? Why these lives? Why do I feel the pull from the river as soon as I'm back?

That's when he heard a voice.

"You are not nothing, Kai. You have never been nothing." It wasn't a wave of sound. There was nothing to propagate, nothing to receive.

Startled. Kai was in a void, in nothingness. He had no physical body; he was untethered, like a drop of dew evaporated in the sky.

Where did the voice come from?

"Do not be alarmed. There's nothing here that can harm you."

"Who are you?" Kai's thoughts, his inner dialogue, made their way across. At least, that's what he thought happened.

"I am whatever you need me to be," the voice answered, "A guide, a caretaker, a part of the whole."

"What do you mean?"

The voice didn't rush. It was calm, affectionate and expressed deep concern for Kai.

"I am here to help you. I know you are searching, but you don't know what to search for."

Kai couldn't argue. That's exactly what was happening.

"Allow me to help. Let me help you understand."

Chapter 31

"Let's start by finding out *where* you are," the voice whispered in a soothing tone.

Kai remained quiet. He was still not sure what was going on, but he acknowledged he needed to know.

But before he found out where he was, he wanted to know who he was talking to?

"Who are you?" Kai asked again. "How can I hear you... here?"

There was no rush. The voice seemed to be in no hurry.

"I am the voice within you. The whisper between your thoughts, the weight of your choice, the nudge before action. I live in the moments before a decision, in the weight of hesitation, in the air of confidence, in the remorse of guilt. I am the catalyst of your conflicts. I am the lingering, undemanding presence, watching you, aiding you, defining you. I am a fragment of the whole, also a part of you, untouched by time and the physical elements. I am what you call intuition, a sense of good and bad."

The last sentence stuck with him. "So, are you the moral police? What we call *conscience*?"

The voice replied. "Morality is a product of your conflicts, between your wants and fear of consequences. I, on the other hand, don't decide, influence or develop the definition of morality. I am not a set of rules that change with the whims of the elements. I don't change with time, don't shift with law, don't bow to kings and prophets. I don't command. I don't punish. I don't judge. I have always remained with you as a reminder of what's already within you. I don't tell you what's right or wrong; I merely echo your own nature.

"You can drown me, bury me, ignore me, but I will always remain. Neither loud nor silent. Just present."

Kai asked, "But what about those who hear the voice differently? In some, the voice justifies cruelty, claiming their actions as a necessity. It softens the intensity of one's actions by whispering that it's for their duty, for society, for trade, for the economy. For the greater good. It makes people appear insignificant participants to themselves, while they continue to do their part in evil. Why doesn't the voice stop them? Tells them the error of their ways?"

"I don't judge; I connect. I don't influence; I merely echo the reflections of the self.

"My whispers are audible only in the stillness of the self. A life fully driven by the elements of nature around it has no capacity to hear the voice. Then, the self hears what it wants to hear. It does what's in its nature. Like that of the cyanobacterium or the eagle."

"If that's so, then who am I? What is *my* nature?" Kai couldn't resist asking.

"You are eternal. You have always been *you*. You don't have a name. You are neither your past nor your future. You are not your desires nor your fears. You are awareness, completely detached from time and space. You exist; you always did, you always will.

"You are not just your thoughts. Your thoughts change with time, and with every life. Sometimes you are not even capable of thought. But you exist regardless of the capacity for thought."

Kai was puzzled by the voice's words. "With... *every* life? Do I have several lives?"

"Of course, you do. You just experienced a few of your previous lives, merely glimpses of them. As a cyanobacterium, as Ama, as an eagle. There are many more."

"Those were my *own* lives...?"

"Yes, every single memory, experience and emotion you saw were from the countless lives you have lived and will live."

"So, after death, I get born into a new life? Reincarnated based on my actions?"

"Sometimes, yes. But your actions don't influence the nature of your next life."

"That doesn't sound like logical. So, my actions don't have consequences?"

"You mistakenly assume that the consequences you observe follow a rule you have constructed in your head. You rely entirely on your own verdict to judge its validity. Of course, you undeniably face the consequences of your actions. But it's not up to you to decide or influence what the consequences will be."

Kai didn't really have a physical body, but the sensation within him could only be described as a quickening of pulse, a rush of adrenaline. But there were also traces of uncertainty within him. If his actions had consequences, but he couldn't influence them, did that mean it was pointless to do one thing over another?

"So, I could perform works of charity and goodwill all my

life, but that doesn't promise me a life free from suffering and misery in my next one?"

The voice replied bluntly, without hesitation, "That's correct. It doesn't."

Kai's confusion grew. He had never really believed in another life after death, or the afterlife for that matter. Yet, here he was, having a conversation with his... inner voice? About the futility of his actions leading to any reward or retribution.

He wanted to feel that he was right all along in his life, to question the definition of good and bad. But rejecting entirely the correlation between his actions and outcomes he had been led to believe, was harder for him to comprehend.

"If I can't influence the consequences in my favour, then how do I know what's good for me? Why shouldn't I pursue a life with less suffering – a life of wealth, comfort and glory? Or strive for rewards in the afterlife – be it eternal life with God, divine closeness, or paradise?"

The voice replied. "You aren't born into wealth or luxury simply because you carried out deeds you believed guaranteed you a reward in future lives. You don't achieve wisdom and purity with each passing life. There may not even be liberation.

"The remnants of your past life still cloud your thoughts as you haven't fully transitioned here. In your current form, you don't exist merely to pursue survival, reproduce and seek sensory pleasures. You are not solely driven by the primal urges for warmth, taste or the simple gratifications that momentarily ease your physical needs. Those things are meaningless here.

"When all your senses are rendered mute, your desires dissolve, and your emotions vanish, you are left with nothing but curiosity. Curiosity propels you to move, to wander and explore, and to try new things. It makes you interact with your environment, venture into the unknown. It can be as innocuous and insignificant as finding shapes in clouds, and as grand and monumental as leaping from ocean to land.

"You have eternally been, and will continue to be, distinctly unique. Even if you share the same culture, religion, parents, nation, or even appearance with another, what makes you *you* is impossible to replicate. Yet, you are merely a fraction of the whole.

"And the whole, by definition, has everything in it – even things you consider good and bad. You, me, all your lives, all the other lives you intersect with, the physical world, and the nothingness you are currently part of. It has within it what you consider righteous and noble, and what you deem wicked and indecent. Virtuous as well as corrupt. Upright as well as depraved. There is a tendency within you to explore the entire spectrum, a curiosity to see everything, be everything.

"But of course, not all is in you at once. You are born with a minuscule fragment of curiosity with each life, ingrained within you as your nature. That too changes with time and is subject to your choices.

"You asked me how you can identify what's good for you. Well, you can't. You can only do what's in your nature to do so – whatever that may be. And you should do your best to learn what that is."

Kai remained silent for a while, ruminating on what the voice had just told him. He reflected on the several lives he had witnessed and lived momentarily.

He then said, "You make it seem like I have a choice, but that doesn't really matter in the course of my entire being. I can do acts of selfless kindness, benevolent deeds of charity, compassionate gestures or endeavour in philanthropy, but that doesn't guarantee me comfort, luxury, peace or any reward. Or I can engage in heinous acts, carry out gruesome offences and commit unspeakable crimes, but I can still walk away with impunity. Do my actions not matter in the grand scheme of things?"

The voice said as calmly as ever, "That's correct. They don't."

That didn't make any sense to Kai. "Then why would I do good over bad?"

"You should do whatever is in your nature to do. You should stop trying to look at the lives of others and conclude what is good or bad for your own self. You will not find any purpose or rhythm there; there isn't any for you. They themselves are the culmination of infinite lives of their own.

"You are not sharing the world with others; you are sharing *your* world with theirs.

"In your world, it's only you. Look within you, ask yourself the questions, and do what you feel is your calling. If it's self-sacrificing displays of empathy, do it for yourself, to experience the surge of emotions you feel during the deed, for the warmth and satisfaction you feel bubbling in your heart, for the sense of comfort it brings to you – not for a promised reward. When you do an act of goodwill, it doesn't promise a reward later; that act in itself is the reward you've been aching for. And while you distance yourself away, thinking about a prosperous moment in the future which may or may never arrive, you fail to experience the reward that was presented to you.

"Remember that your actions have consequences, even if

you don't know what the consequences will be, or when you'll face them."

"What if my calling is to loot, raid and murder?" Kai asked.

"So be it. If that's what your calling is, then go loot, raid and murder. Just remember that your actions have consequences, even if you don't know what the consequences will be, or when you'll face them."

"So, I just reflect inside, and do what's... best?"

"You can't define 'best', but I acknowledge that, yes, you should pursue whatever *seems* best to you. Just do. Move. Be."

Kai couldn't help but feel lost at the irony of it all. Why bother do anything if everything has already happened? He could see all of his lives etched into the streams of the river, from past to present to future, everything all at once. As if all had already *happened*.

"What's the point then? Of doing anything. How will the future lives come to pass if I choose not to move ahead? What would happen to those lives?" Kai asked.

"You misunderstand the extent of your choices. You don't get to decide whether those lives will or will not unfold. The fate of those lives is irrelevant to you in the course of your own life. There, you will decide what you wish to do, and perhaps understand the choices you end up making.

"The outcome may already have been determined. But you can still decide what role to play in it. You will have to choose. Whether it's to accept things, to rebel, or to simply wait, readying yourself for action at the first sight of an opportunity – you always have a choice.

"Even here, you can choose not to subject yourself to any other lives and remain here."

"For how long?"

"As long as you want. Time doesn't move here."

"I don't get it. What will I do here?"

"Eventually, you will become curious."

Kai saw where the voice was leading. He had a choice to do nothing, but it was almost certain that he would ultimately do something – move or explore. Live.

"So, at some point, I'll be curious enough to go try one of those experiences from the myriad?"

"It's likely."

"Can I choose which life?"

"Yes, of course you can."

"But I had no influence in those lives. I was nothing more than a silent observer."

"Well, you only briefly experienced those lives. If you choose to remain with them for long, you and your selves gradually merge with each other. Here, you don't have wants and desires. But in your lives, you are subject to the elements which surround you, the norms of the society, the morality of its time, the urges of the body, and the suffering too. Eventually, you fuse into a singularity."

Kai thought about it, and the only thing that represented an inkling of a desire within him was to experience the lives he now knew were his own.

He had one more question: "Does everyone do this?"

"No, not everyone. But it's irrelevant to you what they do. What do *you* want to do?"

"I'm not really sure."

"Okay."

"Okay."

Kai had nothing else to enquire. He let the silence linger on to stillness, a comforting aftermath of an interaction which resolved some of his questions but perhaps raised equally more. He wanted to reflect on what he had heard.

He pondered on what the voice said to him: *You are not sharing the world with others; you are sharing your world with theirs.*

After what seemed like an eternity, he finally broke the silence. "What's next?"

The voice said, in no rush like it always did, "You can decide that yourself. I'm here to help. I have always been here."

Chapter 32

Kai found himself staring into the vast, endless river of infinite experiences. He saw countless lives churning and turning, joy and suffering, growing and dying with every stream. Every current held a life, a moment, a reality that had been lived, was being lived, and will be lived – all at once.

Kai realised he had an opportunity to explore, from his own lives, own experiences. This was as personal, and up close as he could get to feel, really feel, the intentions behind words he would have never uttered, the motivations behind actions he would have never taken.

He dove in.

He experienced countless lives, one after another.

He endured the end as a soldier in battle. Felt the burning rage within, the ferocious desire to cut, slay and slash the enemy with his sword. The enemy wasn't an individual, didn't have a name, identity, religion or nationality. The enemy was a target for the thrashing surge of bloodlust building up within him. Mud, blood and lifeless bodies surrounded him. It wasn't about the courage of the heart or loyalty to the country. He fought because he was told to do so. And he was killed because someone else was told to kill. As he lay in the mud, with other dead bodies around him, he wondered if it was worth it. Did it matter? Once he was dead, nothing did.

He experienced being the centre of attention as a beautiful courtesan. Men wrote poems for her, brought her gifts, and promised her riches beyond comprehension. She felt a tremendous rush of power, an unspoken influence wherever she went. She learned to use her beauty to work for her, mastering the art of being the focal point of a discussion in any situation. But deep down, she knew it would fade. She wondered if any would care for her the same way if she were to lose her beauty tomorrow. She feared that someday people would find out that behind her looks; she is nothing worth admiring for. Beauty was fleeting, and she was presented with the choice to embrace its transient nature or attempt to preserve it and fight against the passage of time.

He witnessed the life of a dog in a loving home. Despite not understanding the language, he showed his family love. He looked at his companions with sheer love and affection. His whole being wanted to protect, preserve, and give for those near him. He wasn't burdened with the past, present or future. His survival was for his family. His existence was for them. And that meant everything to him.

He lived, endured, encountered, absorbed, dodged, flourished, suffered, recovered, prospered, rejoiced, understood and died countless times, and with each experience, he felt within him a growing sense of duty, of acknowledging the voice within him to reveal to him his own calling, but not for the sake of achieving a grand plan, but to just *be*. There was no glamour, no need to be unique, no mission. Life simply *was*.

He realised that his only true calling was to follow the path his nature demanded of him – not the circumstances that shaped him, not other people's expectations, not the rules and the norms of his time.

He realised the beauty of a moment – a single moment. The feeling of sunlight on skin, the gust of wind against the feathers, the pull of water through gills, the quiet bond with the pack, a sip of a warm cup of tea after a long day, the stillness of the world at twilight, the fullness after finishing a great meal.

In each of his life, he felt the limits of his choices. In some lives, he lacked the ability of thoughts, existed without question, without self-exploration. In other lives, he felt the burden of thoughts and the need to rationalise and make sense of everything he came across.

While he couldn't change the grand plan with predetermined outcomes, he had the power to change the present, *his moments*. He could choose the role he played without having to dictate the outcomes. It didn't take grand gestures, revolutions or monumental actions to shift his fate. All he did was decide in a single moment. A step forward, a word spoken, an action delayed.

He didn't need to see where these ripples led or control what happened. He only needed to live in the moment, true to his nature, whatever that may be.

He realised the futility of trying to know what's good and what's not. What was necessary for his survival in one life meant agony and death for another. He had felt the thrill of a shark during its kill. Pure instinct, focus and drive. In another life, he had felt the terror, confusion and pain of the seal when caught by a shark.

In one of his lives, he embraced the practice of human sacrifice as sacred. A means of connecting with the gods for the common good of the people. Later, in another, human sacrifices were an abomination. A crime, a barbaric violation of human rights.

He realised that morality and ethics were shaped by time. As eras and rulers changed, so did people's ideas of right and wrong. Religion, philosophy, law, culture, and knowledge each left their mark, repainting morality as humanity evolved.

The voice had left him alone.

For all that he learned, all the virtues he had experienced, all the vices that he indulged in, what did it mean for him in his life as Kai?

In each life, the world demanded something from him. Each time the norms, the expectations, his own nature and the will of society were different.

What was demanded of his life as Kai? How could he live a proud, just and a *good* life? What was good in his time?

The world of his time had created a utopia for its people. Life was comfortable, sheltered, safe and in abundance.

The privileged had carved out a perfect life for themselves, while the rest of the world continued to burn, drown and suffocate. The suffering of others had become background noise in a marketplace where everyone was busy with consumption, addiction and abundance of choices. Nothing that was needed was lacking, but the list of essentials was endless.

For Kai, it wasn't a time for warriors, not in the traditional sense. Not for him.

What did his world demand from him?

He turned to the voice, the only thing untouched from all of it.

"What do I do?" Kai asked. "The world is resilient, yet it's falling apart. Never before time itself moved so fast. The climate is collapsing, species are disappearing, the wealth gap is astronomically wide, and reality is unrecognisable. The entire mass relies on systems they neither fully control nor fully understand – governments, corporations, cities, nations. They rely on an external voice in their head to form their opinions. They are told what to feel, what to say, what to buy, what to eat, who to love. Everything has slipped away from the control of the self, ripped apart from the *nature*. How do I exist in such a world and navigate towards my true calling? How do I exist as *myself*?"

The voice was silent for a moment before asking, "That depends on what you seek. I can reflect what's in your nature. I can connect you to the demands woven into your very being. But you still need to untangle the strands of choice from the fabric of existence. The choice remains with you. What path does your nature urge you to follow?"

Kai hesitated before giving an answer. "I'm not sure."

He thought about it more. In the deep, vast nothingness, beyond the grasp of time, he really pondered. What did he really want? What whispered within him?

He reflected on all the lives he had lived, all the experiences he had witnessed, all the suffering, and all the bliss. Wherever he had the capacity to think and make choices, he wished he could separate the noise from his calling.

And he wanted to be kind. In every single life, across the dynamic expressions of right or wrong, he felt the bleakest in acts of hostility. Even if he did what his nature commanded him to do, he felt the damage was being done to him too. And every act of kindness lifted his own spirits, as if he were the only winner at the end.

"I want to be able to adapt, to master the ability of change, without compromising *myself* in the process. And I want to be kind, or at the very least not be intentionally unkind." Kai said.

The voice answered, "Then that's what you want. If you wish to remain true to your nature, if you wish to be kind, then you need two things: contemplation and empathy.

"These are the only tools you need. Without contemplation, you don't know what to believe in. When you don't know what to believe in, someone else will tell you. Without it, you can't rebel, you can't act with purpose. You can't remain dignified with the rise and fall of your fortunes. You can't even be kind unless you know why and how to.

"Contemplation is the ability to reflect, to question, to understand – not to label and judge your own thoughts and actions. It brings you closer to your true self. It's the patience before commitment. *Is this what I really want to do, or is this an impulse of the moment?* Without contemplation, you are nothing more than a puppet being pulled by invisible strings of influence, only a reaction. But when you contemplate, you take control. You own the decision. You accept the consequences of your actions, whatever they may be.

"Contemplation is where you and I connect. I aid with the clarity of your calling, and you listen.

"And there's no virtue greater than kindness. Kindness shapes the world without demanding a price. When you cultivate empathy, kindness becomes a natural response. You get the ability to see and understand another's suffering, feel the pain, and share the burden. It's the ability to feel beyond yourself. It's what keeps you human. The world doesn't lack strength, knowledge and intelligence; it lacks understanding. People are not objects, numbers, or data points. They have their own *selves* within them, just like you. There's an infinity in them, like you have within you. Without empathy, even kindness becomes shallow. And with a shallow kindness, you don't connect, you don't learn, you don't grow.

"Without contemplation, there's no true empathy. You must think before you understand. You must reflect before you feel. You must connect before you share their burdens.

"Whether you are kind or not, that's a choice you will have to make. But if you have empathy in your heart, you will always choose to be kind."

Kai remained silent. He fully acknowledged the gravity of what he absorbed.

He stayed quiet for a long time.

Chapter 33

The body on the bed was no longer Kai.

Whatever had once tethered him to the world had broken. What remained was just... mass.

Yet by no means was the body dead. It was still alive. Hollow but alive.

Soren had left the room, now in his office. Even there, he felt the tension within him.

Dario too was somewhere in the building.

"This is what he wanted." Soren mumbled, mostly to himself.

Kai's vitals remained steady. Inhumanly steady. Oxygen was pulsed in rhythmic bursts. Neural signals were monitored for spontaneous activation. None came.

His Link – now transformed into Link Prime – waited patiently for instructions. Ready to act the moment the gate opened.

The last step wasn't complex. But dangerous.

In the lab, the doctor and the rep looked at this rigid body. None of them knew what was going on inside Kai.

Was he even somewhere? Or just... lost.

A question so dense and heavy, it physically weighed them all down.

They had to succeed. The world was watching. The council was watching; the megas were too.

The team at Link Tech – Soren, Dario, Tomas, the doctor and the rep – they all knew that what they had achieved with Kai was an exceptionally rare feat. They were very close. Yet, this time, the risks were astronomically high too.

Dario often used to remind his team, that in some ways, a solution had already been found. They merely had to test to see if the next attempt was *the one* that finally cracked the code.

If they failed, some things could be salvaged. The data, the collapse patterns and Link Prime's records would be fed back into the next cycle. The next subject. The next attempt.

But Dario...

The doctor enquired with Soren, before they began the precarious step.

"Should we begin?" A note flashed in Soren's overlay.

Soren nodded – almost invisible to naked eye. But his Link knew what it meant.

A text appeared in the doctor's vision: *[Begin.]*

Chapter 34

Kai had seen his infinite lives laid out, happening all at once, but he didn't understand how he was connected with others.

"I've seen within myself, but I don't understand how my lives intersect with others. Where are they? Where is the river of their infinite experiences? Where do I belong in the whole?"

The voice answered in no rush, as it never did. "In the nothingness, your focus narrows your search. You look for what you seek. You were searching for yourself, so that's what you saw. If you wish to see the nature of the whole, you just need to *look*."

Kai didn't quite understand *how* to channel his focus. He had no physical body here for him to control his breathing. He had no eyes for him to close. All he felt was a desperate *need* in him.

And that was enough.

He felt the shift immediately. The vast and boundless river of his infinite lives shrank into something small, delicate.

A mere thread of light. A small fragment in a giant network. A network of countless other similar threads, interwoven, entangled, part of an even bigger infinity.

The more he observed, the more it resembled something similar – a web of pulsing threads. Each thread branching, splitting and reconnecting.

Like the roots stretching through the soil.

Like the network of neurons within a brain.

The network seemed alive. Pulsing. Shifting. Glowing.

Kai saw his own river of essence as nothing more than a fraction of a greater whole. His entire existence – from past, present and future – just one small thread of light among billions of others.

But there was something more. He saw it as a resemblance to the cosmos.

The endless web of interwoven lives resembled something even greater – the universe itself.

Infinities within infinity.

And just like he could see the past, present and future of his own lives, he saw it for the network of cosmos too. Of everything.

It unfolded simultaneously, just like it did for his own manifestations.

He saw the explosion, the big bang, the rapid extension, the formation of galaxies, the first stars. He saw movement for billions of years. Then the first planets formed, then lifeforms driven not by will or choices, but biochemical reactions and stimuli, then evolution, then humans, rise and fall of civilisations.

And after a very long arc of creation, he saw the collapse, the big crunch. The slow death of everything, the implosion of the universe, as it retracted, folding into itself.

Eventually, the recursion revealed the overbearing nature of the entire universe – contained in a singularity.

And then the explosion again.

It was cyclic.

Expansion, creation, lifeforms for a mere fraction of it all, then collapse. Only for the same thing to start again. Endlessly.

It felt like a breath.

The expansion and contraction of the entire cosmos pulsed and danced to the rhythm of the inhalation and exhalation of another being.

But something stood out. Something peculiar.

The cycles didn't repeat the same way. There were differences.

The separation of the fundamental forces, formation of stars and galaxies, rise and evolution of life, every major event, every invention, every war, every downfall, every rise, every boon, every doom, death of planets, galactic collisions, death of stars, era of black holes, and the implosion – these took place in every cycle of creation and destruction.

And yet, not the same way, not exactly similar.

There were tendencies for lives to be slightly different.

There was a capacity of choice, a different choice.

And because of different choices, the river of lives flowed a little differently in every iteration. It behaved a little differently from how it used to, even shifting its direction of its flow sometimes.

And as a result, the whole itself was a little different each time.

Despite the insignificance of a single life in that vast, unfathomable framework of *everything*, there was an immeasurable and incomprehensible potential in each of lives to shift something – to send a different message to the network.

The endless repeating cycles didn't prevent choices; they held intact the inevitability of creation and destruction.

But even in the miniscule, atomic, fleeting and negligible lives of those lifeforms, there dwelled a power beyond the reach of the cosmos – the present moment.

Kai saw it. The universe, the endless reiterations, the cosmic breath – it all continued indifferent to the choices of individual beings. But the individual lives, even in the flicker of their existence, in the fleeting ripple of time, could *choose*.

The choices didn't break the cycle; they couldn't. But they determined what passed on at the time of entanglement. They could certainly alter the course of their own journeys.

The lives had something the cosmos did not.

Choices.

Limited. Finite, perhaps. Constrained by their own nature. Easily influenced by the elements. But they could still choose.

VII

Recursion

Chapter 35

"Where is God in all of this?" Kai asked the voice.

"Is it His breath which fuels the cosmos? His inhalation and exhalation as the creation and destruction of the universe. Does life happen while he holds his breath?" Kai had a lot of unanswered questions.

He continued, "Or perhaps he created the cycle, and remains out of it. To test the variables of choices?

"Or maybe he is waiting for something, someone, to break the loop.

"We could be cursed by god to repeat our lives over and over again and never realise the true meaning of what we are trapped in."

The voice listened to his questions, acknowledging them without answering outright. When Kai was silent, it said, "There are all possibilities, Kai. You and I may never find out what's really going on. The difference in our comprehension could be so vast, as that between a cyanobacterium and an eagle in flight. I can't say if these cycles are a curse or a blessing, but perhaps, there is a way out."

Kai wondered. How? "But if we don't know what's right or wrong, then what can we do to get out? Assuming getting out is even an option."

"I'm not really sure." The voice admitted. "But you can do what your own *self* tells you. If you can't follow the urges of your nature, then be patient. The kind of patience you have displayed in your past lives. If you can't be patient, then rebel. Rebel like you have done countless times before. If you can't rebel, then suffer. There's growth in discomfort, but only if there's no other way. If you can do nothing else, then survive. Attune your breaths with that of the cosmos you just witnessed – one at a time. Out there, nothing defies time. Whatever you are going through will pass. You will get another opportunity to embrace your instincts and heed your calling. Keep hope alive in your heart."

Kai felt an understanding settle over him. He remained quiet for a very long time.

"So... what now?"

"Whatever you wish. You weren't forced to come here. Time does not move here. You can remain here for as long as you wish. But eventually, you will have to choose."

A final question. "Will I remember these things when I go back?"

The voice's answer was simple. "You can if you want to. But once you return to your world as Kai, you will be subject only to the memories, experiences, whims and urges of *that* body. That's how it works. It's up to you how much of the lessons you can take with you."

Kai remained silent. The voice felt his dread.

"Or..." It added. "You can choose any of your other lives to return to. It doesn't matter. There's no forward or backward. Nothing exists without you to observe it. Eventually, you merge with the physical elements no matter where you end up."

"Whatever you decide, if you can remember just one thing, remember that you have a choice. You *always* have a choice."

Kai nodded in contentment. He knew what to do.

Chapter 36

As she reached the house, Rumi's heart started racing. She had been avoiding them for far too long. But what could she have done or said?

Perhaps, she herself needed to be comforted and told that it'll be alright. To move on, yet again.

She had brought along Yuna with her.

As she knocked on the door, she forced herself to smile but a stubborn tear forced its way. She quickly wiped it off before being greeted by a big smile and open arms.

Tama almost pulled her towards him to give her a warm hug. He knew she needed it too.

He then immediately took hold of the stroller, making baby noises at the smiling Yuna.

Inside, Zora slowly made her way towards Rumi, struggling clearly to get to the door sooner.

Rumi, noticing Zora, rushed towards her, and exchanged a hug, one that was long overdue. Tama closed the door and put the stroller safely beside the couch.

Both Rumi and Zoro clearly were struggling to come to terms with what had happened, or not knowing what hadn't more precisely.

"So, how can I help?" asked Rumi to both as she sat beside

Yuna, looking across from Tama to Zora, then back again at Tama and repeating it in a loop.

She had thought long and hard about it. She didn't want to say anything superficial and nonsensical, or something that could just derail the conversation in a direction she wasn't prepared to handle.

And as if she couldn't keep herself in check, she went off her own script and added, "I'm so sorry that I've come so late."

Tama quickly shrugged it off. "Ah, it's alright. Come on in. Let's have a seat. We haven't seen you in ages, Rumi. How have you been?"

"I'm good. I'm good. The same old, you know." She brushed the conversation away from herself; there was far too much that had changed with her she wasn't willing to share.

"How old is little Yuna now?" Tama asked in an attempt to diffuse the situation.

"She's one already. Can't believe it. It's like time's accelerated." Rumi said while looking at Yuna with a warm and affectionate smile.

Yuna. Rumi's daughter. Born from Link Tech's artificial gestation program. Completely healthy and *normal.*

Generally, Yuna stole attention away from every conversation. But not today. There was something else going on in everyone's mind.

Rumi turned to Zora. "I'm glad I could be here with you." As she said it, her hand instinctively squeezed Zora's shoulder.

"I'm glad you're here too, Rumi," Zora replied with a warm smile. Forced but effective.

They talked for a while before the inevitable moment came.

Tama felt like it was his responsibility to lead the conversation and steer it in control.

"Look, thank you for coming along, Rumi. We love seeing you, so please come whenever you're around.

Rumi smiled and nodded.

He continued; now was the time. "It's been three months now. The search is on, but nothing's been confirmed yet."

The air in the room immediately shifted. Heavy and cold.

Zora gave a deep sigh, trying her best to remain hopeful.

Tama wanted to acknowledge the situation and remain dignified. There had been enough tears shed, sleepless nights spent in uncertainty, and praying to all the gods known to mankind. He didn't want yet another visit to end in sorrow.

But while he was taking control, a part of him wanted to sob, right then and there. The unimaginable pain he felt in his chest at the thought of his Kai... was too much for him to keep his composure.

With one loud snuffle, everyone else's dam of patience broke too.

There were no more words exchanged. Just tears of grief.

Kai had been missing for months.

Chapter 37

The first thing he registered was faint noises, beeping monitors, rushed voices, shuffling of feet and the hum of machinery. He felt pain in his chest. His vision was blurry, but the room was well lit, much better illuminated than it had been when he had left.

He felt an overwhelming sense of disorientation. His eyes were closed, but his world was spinning. He felt nauseous.

The last time he was in the room, it was empty, quiet, dimly lit and free of any stimulants. But then, it was completely the opposite when he found himself again in a similar bed. The room looked unfamiliar.

Bright lights bore down on him. Movement around him, figures in white coats rushing around trying to do their job. To keep him alive.

His body still felt the aftermath of defibrillation coursing through it.

Something had gone wrong. He wasn't supposed to be completely lost. His heart rate had gone flat for too long.

"Vitals stabilising. Pulse returning to normal," someone called out.

A figure leaned over him. "Can you hear me? Follow my voice. Blink if you understand."

His body was sluggish. He felt nauseous, but he managed to blink in response.

The team continued to work around him, but he remained partly adrift. A residue clung to him – a faint awareness, an echo of something vast and unexplainable.

His Link whispered in his head, *[Good to have you back. How are you feeling?]*

[I have been better], he responded to Link.

"What happened?" He muttered out loud to one of the technicians around.

"You completely lost your vitals. The system had no control. For a brief period, you were technically dead."

The next few hours went by in a haze. He mostly slept while the team around him continued to monitor his condition. His Link aided the team by offering data from his brain while he rested. His neural responses were below average, but sustainable.

Whenever he woke up, he was asked how he felt. The technicians still clung to get any traces of new information. "Did you see anything while you were *gone*?" But nothing came of him. His mind was truly blank.

He remained at the headquarters for several days to recover fully. His needs were met well, and his comfort wasn't compromised one bit. Several assistants at his disposal for any needs or whims.

His sleep cycle, cardiovascular system, neural activity, and almost every aspect of his health was thoroughly monitored and analysed. Any deviation from the baseline was flagged for the doctor to investigate.

A psychiatric evaluation was done to ascertain the sanity of his mind. Any hint of instability would have been escalated for a more in-depth analysis.

Eventually, several days later, he was discharged. But even the discharge was conditional. He had to wear additional sensors for another week to ensure there were no lingering aftereffects. If there were any abnormalities, they wanted to know. His Link sent out reports daily to the research team about his condition and performed weekly assessments.

He made an attempt to transition to his old life. There was so much he needed to do, plenty of decisions to be made, now that he had a fresh start.

He felt different, more energetic. His limbs moved more freely. It was incredibly refreshing to move with so much ease.

Very few around him knew what he had gone through. With time, he knew people would want answers. A change had dawned on him, that couldn't be kept hidden for long.

A few days later, while he sat on his couch, taking a break after a hearty meal, he got a notification overlaid in his vision.

[Would you like to proceed with the weekly assessment? It will take approximately 5 minutes.]

Sure. Why not? He thought. He had plenty of time for that.

[Great. I will take samples from each of the biosensor, as well as record your heart rate, blood pressure and body temperature. Your optical implants look good; the overlay is complete and immersive. Detection of subvocalisation of your vocal cords is within an acceptable range. Can you confirm you can hear me well?]

[Yes, I confirm.]

[Now, I need to ask you a series of questions. Please respond in as much detail as possible. If you don't understand the questions, please let me know, and I'll be happy to walk you through. Does everything make sense to you?]

[Yes, it does. Please start when you're ready.]

[Okay, great. First question. How do you feel today, Mr Verrick?]

Dario let out a sigh, thinking of an appropriate response.

[Good. Still getting used to this body, but I must admit it's been well taken care of.]

[That's great. Over time, we can...]

Link's voice faded into background noise as Dario flexed his fingers, watching the knuckles rise and settle. The ease of movement fascinated him. Even the breath he drew felt crisp, strangely new. His reflection shimmered across the tray and silverware in front of him, bending and multiplying – small, fractured confirmations that the body truly belonged to him now.

The rest of the session went flawlessly. No reported glitches, no anomalies.

It was as if Dario was born as Kai in that body. While there remained a heavy reliance on Link Prime and other supporting interface tech developed by Link Tech exclusively for this venture; overall, the experiment was a grand success.

Dario had successfully transitioned his consciousness away from the old failing body into the receptive host body of Kai's.

Once the weekly diagnostics were complete, Dario refilled his coffee and went out to the suite's balcony to get some fresh air. As he looked around, he glimpsed his reflection again in the glass door. Those deep silver eyes looked rather beautiful on this face. It still seemed like someone else was staring at him, mirroring his movements. But he knew very well it was him.

He let out a deep exhale before prompting his Link.

[How is he?]

As Link was about to respond, Dario interrupted with another question. More pressing, more relevant.

[Alive?]

Link finally responded after a momentary pause.

[Yes, he is alive. But not in the traditional way one would expect.]

[How are we doing?]

[Surprisingly, very good. Kai is subject to the Reality Construct program. We can never really trace his exact whereabouts, but the program will keep him hooked. If he enters the construct, he will 'grow up' developing his wants, desires and ambitions, as well as fears, phobias and aversions – all coded to perfection.]

Dario replied with a faint trace of worry in his voice. [Good. Are we sure he can't find his way back in... me?]

[Unfortunately, that's something we can never be sure of. We can keep him occupied in one construct after another, before he even gets an opportunity to realise what's going on. But he will always have a deeply rooted instinct to trace his origin back to... now.]

Dario sighed. For now, Link Tech had successfully trans-ferred a consciousness – his own – across another functioning body. This bought him time – something he didn't have much of before. There was so much he wanted to do, but couldn't do in his old dying body, even with all of Link Tech's wealth and influence.

And now he could.

His team also proved to the megas that it's possible. Death could be cheated.

But for how long?

Somewhere deep within, he could vaguely feel Kai's pull. The feeling became less intense with time, but it was there. It was real.

And as soon as he landed on that thought, an amusing question formed within him.

[So, tell me, Link, how do I know I am currently not in a reality construct myself?]

A moment of hesitation from Link, as if it faltered in its own conviction prior to a response.

[To be honest, Mr. Verrick, we can never really know for sure.]

Dario smiled at the response.

He quickly wrapped things up and got ready for the day. There was so much for him to do.

Chapter 38

In a world that existed several decades ago, before there was Link Tech and Link. Before the megas controlled the narrative of the modern world – life was much different. Not simpler, but slower.

He woke at the same time as always. Ran the same route, feeling the familiar burn in his calves, the faint ache in his knees that reminded him of years rather than miles.

He returned home, showered, ate breakfast standing at the counter, then moved through the house with a practiced efficiency – waking the kids, urging them along, feeding the dog, stepping over scattered toys without noticing them anymore.

He kissed his wife goodbye, kissed the children, and left home with the mild, constant pressure of being late already humming beneath his ribs.

The drive to work passed in fragments of thought rather than scenery. Marco's voice replayed itself in his head, twisting conversations into accusations, always positioning himself just far enough ahead to look reasonable. The delayed funding for the battery upgrade gnawed at him – numbers, deadlines, promises that refused to align. His wife's affectionate words from the party the night before resurfaced too, unexpectedly tender, almost disarming.

Then came the pressing recollections that needed his attention – the broken shed in the yard, the damp smell of rot he'd been putting off, the dog's upset stomach yesterday and the quiet worry that it might be something more. None of it felt important on its own. Together, it formed a weight that never quite lifted.

The day flew by as he gave it his all at work. The site demanded movement, attention, presence. He walked its length again and again, lungs burning, shirt sticking to his back, hands gesturing as he explained, corrected, reassured. There was satisfaction in the exhaustion – a temporary sense that effort still meant something here, that outcomes could be earned rather than inferred. When the day finally loosened its grip, his body ached in honest, uncomplicated ways.

At the end of the day, drained and sore, he had to join in a farewell party for a colleague. Laughter came easily, drinks more so. Stories were told and retold, growing louder, softer, more generous with each round. He drank more than he meant to, chasing a warmth that had nothing to do with the alcohol itself.

When it was time to leave, a dangerous confidence rose in him – the idea that he could still manage the drive. But his wife's incessant nagging from the other end of the line finally cracked his stubbornness. He abandoned the idea and caught the late train instead.

It was quite late when he boarded. Even in the bright interior of the train, he could tell that outside, the crescent moon lit the skies. As the train curved near the coast, he caught the faint shimmer of waves glimmering under moonlight.

He tried to look out, but the reflections of the carriage lights in the window glass restricted his view.

He leaned against the glass, and cupped his hands around his face, blocking out the glow, narrowing his view until he managed to see through a little better. A few stars twinkled distantly, scattered across the moonlit night sky.

And then it came again, the same existential dread, rushing in without invitation, drowning out the steady rhythm of the train wheels hitting the tracks, and dulling his other senses.

He asked himself the same question he had been asking his entire life for as long as he could remember, the same question others around him seemed to carry silently, desperately, without answers.

What's the point of it all?

There were no answers for him. Only a twisted reflection of his drunken face staring back at him from the glass, mocking him in silence.

About the Author

Thank you for reading *The Link Within*

I truly hope the story stayed with you – not only for its events, but for the questions beneath it: identity, choice, and what it really means to be "you."

If you enjoyed the book (or even if it simply made you think), please consider leaving a short review on Goodreads or the platform where you found it. Reader reviews are incredibly valuable. Even a sentence or two genuinely helps other thoughtful readers discover stories like this.

Shishir Tripathi is an engineer and writer living in Sydney, Australia. Originally from India and having spent nearly a decade in New Zealand, he carries a blend of cultural influences that inform his curiosity about people and the inner workings of the mind. *The Link Within* is his first novel, written during quiet nights after work and inspired by years of reflection.

Also by Shishir Tripathi

Shishir Tripathi writes fiction that explores identity, agency, and the psychology of choice, often through speculative and near-future settings. His work draws on themes of displacement, memory, time, and cultural inheritance.

He is currently developing multiple new works.

For updates and more information, visit the official website: **shishirtripathi.com**

www.ingramcontent.com/pod-product-compliance
Lightning Source LLC
Chambersburg PA
CBHW021217220726
48287CB00015B/1595